THE SERPENT

DAN COETZEE

Published by

MELROSE BOOKS

An Imprint of Melrose Press Limited
St Thomas Place, Ely
Cambridgeshire
CB7 4GG, UK
www.melrosebooks.com

FIRST EDITION

Cover designed by Catherine McIntyre

ISBN 978 1 907040 51 1

Printed and bound in Great Britain by:
CPI Antony Rowe. Chippenham, Wiltshire

FSC
www.fsc.org
MIX
Paper from
responsible sources
FSC® C013604

For Becky

Germania in 9CE

(Showing modern borders, coastlines and river courses)

Landmarks
Tribes

Settlements

1. Castra Drusus
2. Oberaden
3. Castra Octa
4. Vetera
5. Neuss
6. Colonia Agrippina
7. Moguntiacum
8. Capital of the Semnones

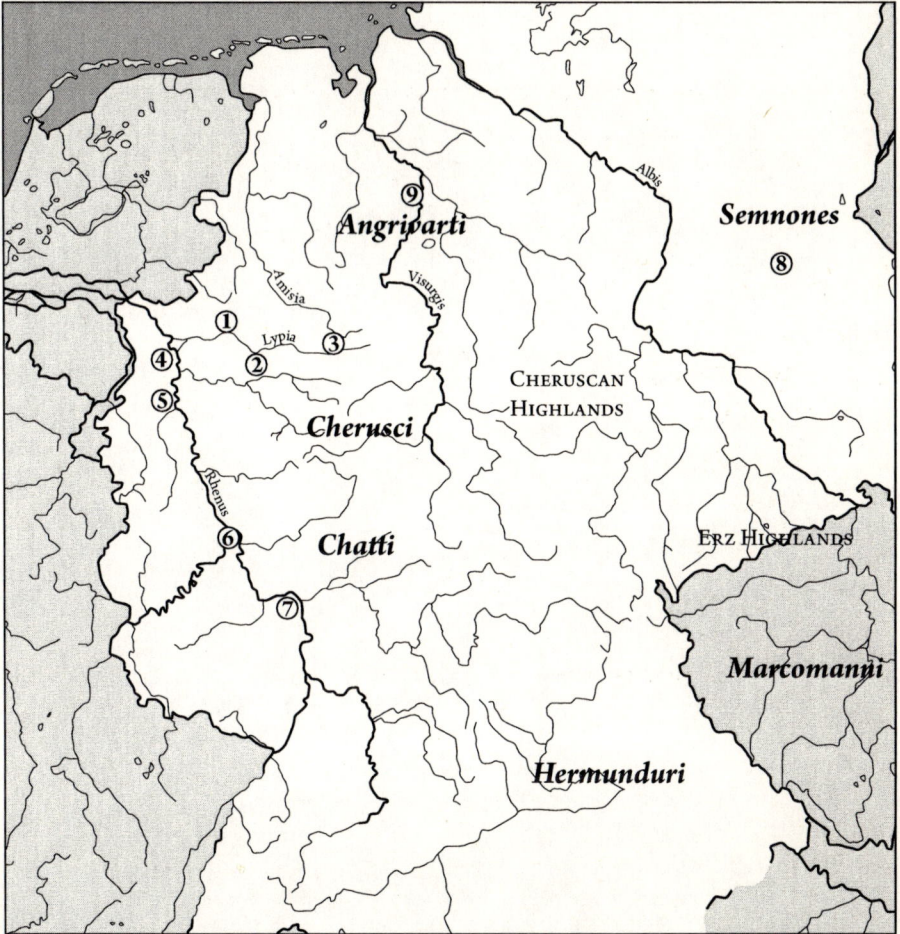

Angrivarti

Semnones

⑧

⑨

Albis

Amisia

Visurgis

① Lypia

④ ② ③

⑤

Cherusci

CHERUSCAN
HIGHLANDS

Rhenus

⑥ Chatti

ERZ HIGHLANDS

⑦

Marcomanni

Hermunduri

Contents

LIST OF CHARACTERS

Arminius/Armin: a Roman cavalry commander; son of Sigimer of the Cherusci

The Barbarians

CHERUSCI

BOAR CLAN

Sigimer: chief of the Cherusci Boar clan

Flavus/Frimunt: brother of Arminius; son of Sigimer

Inguiomer: brother of Sigimer; nobleman of the Cherusci Boar clan

Imma: second wife of Sigimer

Lamar: son of Imma and Sigimer

Amala: daughter of Imma and Sigimer

Caglem: elder of Cherusci Boar clan; advisor to Sigimer

Hlutheir: elder of Cherusci Boar clan and father of Imma; advisor to Sigimer

Andred: wife of Inguiomer

Berinhard (deceased): father of Sigimer; conqueror of
    Boar clan territory from the Valich

WOLF CLAN

Cegestes: chief of the Cherusci Wolf clan

Thusnelda/Tiberia: daughter of Cegestes

Berhilda: past nanny and servant to Thusnelda

Segimund: son of Cegestes

BEAR CLAN

Kuonraet: chief of the Cherusci Bear clan; father of Bannruod

Bannruod: son of Kuonraet; warrior of the Cherusci Bear clan

Carnoth: Bannruod's blood brother

Fruwin: a sage

MARCOMANNI

Maroboduus: king of the Marcomanni tribe

SEMNONES

Hildreth: first wife of Sigimer and mother of Arminius and Flavus

Eysle: mother of Hildreth and former high priestess of the Semnones

CHATTI

Adgandes: chieftain of the Chatti; uncle of Vegates

Vegates: warrior and nephew of Adgandes

OTHERS

Hiru: tracker to the Roman army

Aba: wife of Hiru

Bjec: brother of Hiru

Obed: a member of Arminius's *comitatus*; a Kushite, sold to
    the Romans as a child

Arbex: a trooper in Arminius's *ala*

Brunald: a barbarian prisoner

THE ROMANS

CIVILIANS

Publius Quinctilius Varus (Varus): Commander-in-Chief
    and Governor in Germania; husband of Emperor Augustus's great-niece

Orontes: major civilian contractor in Germania;
    old business partner and creditor of Varus

Sextus: Roman civilian contractor, Germania

MILITARY[1]

Aius Caecina Severus (Caecina): General and Commander-in-Chief, Pannonia Theatre

Sentius Saturninus (Saturninus): General and Commander-in-Chief, Germania Theatre

Lucius Nonius Asprenas (Asprenus): General, Rhenus Command; Varus's cousin

Gaius Apronius (Apronius): Legate commanding 19th Legion, Germania

Marcus Vinicius (Vinicius): Legate commanding 18th Legion, Germania

Lucius Corvinus (Corvinus): Legate commanding 17th Legion, Germania

Numonius Vala (Vala): Legate, Commander of Cavalry in Germania in charge of army intelligence and counter-intelligence operations

Lucius Caedicius (Caedicius): Prefect of Castra

Octa: attached to 18th Legion

Silius: friend of Vala

Petilius: centurion in charge of Hermunduri road

Tertius: a centurion on the Hermunduri road

Neno: a legionary in Pannonia

Banno: keeper of the archives in Castra Drusus

IMPERIAL FAMILY

Augustus: Emperor of the Romans

Tiberius: stepson of Emperor Augustus

Drusus (deceased): younger brother of Prince Tiberius and stepson of Emperor Augustus: led initial Roman invasion of Germania circa 12 BCE

HOUSEHOLD OF STATILIUS TAURUS, ROME

Statilius Taurus: Arminius's host and patron in Rome; architect to the imperial family

Quintus: the steward

Cleon: Greek slave; tutor to Arminius and Flavus

OTHERS

Gracchus: Arminius's son in Rome

Caecilia: Arminius's wife in Rome

Licinius: a boy at school with Arminius

---

[1]   Names in order of rank, with most widely used portion of name between brackets

CHAPTER 1

9 BCE (SPRING)

A GLADE NEAR THE RIVER LUPIA

BLOOD OOZED FROM THE BOAR tattoo on the familiar freckled flesh.

'Are you ready?'

Armin took his father's hand. 'Yes, Father.' He grinned at the battle-worn face. His father did not turn to Frimunt, who was only four years old. Armin was seven.

Sigimer wore the topknot of a great warrior, but the war was over. He walked away from the glade and the keening – the forest's new birdsong. The tribe watched: bloodied men propped up on the laps of their wives; women with dresses marked crimson by their kin. Widows pressed their foreheads against the ground and dug their fingers into Nerthus.

Armin struggled to keep up with his father's great stride, but he was elated to be with him. He had been made to hide in the forest from the battle. He was old enough to cheer on the warriors behind the lines with the women and the old men, but this fight had been different, so they had to make him hide. His father had led the clan to war. He had heard chants and bellows, women's ululating, and war trumpets. Howls had cleaved the undergrowth. Iron had hammered wood and flesh.

His father had returned, stained.

They ascended a hill. The trees soaked up the people's sounds. Birdsong trickled back. His brother began to moan. This irritated Armin. *His* legs were not aching; he could keep up with his father's pace. He wanted to snap at Frimunt.

A sight at the apex of the hill snatched his thoughts. It was a man on horseback. He possessed acorn-coloured skin and sooty hair. The horse was large. It had a smoother hide than his father's big-bellied ponies. The man wore a coat of mail, a chief's armour and a helmet of metal. He wore a scarlet skirt. His shield was red, and so was his horse's saddlecloth. He carried javelins and a sword. Even his horse's chest was covered in a chain mail apron. The mail jangled as the apparition twisted the animal away and disappeared down the far side of the hill.

A Roman.

Armin's heart beat faster.

'Is he a chief?' Armin asked. He received no reply, so he could only imagine. Lying among the furs of his mother's bed, he had listened to arguments raging in his father's hall. The Romans were different: that he knew. This morning, the invaders' blow had finally struck the Cherusci.

They reached the crest. Armin was startled. As far as he could see, there were Romans. The man they had spotted was now lost among a group of thirty others. They were all equipped in the same way. Armoured footmen stood atop a rampart beyond the cavalry. They were a lake of metal; an army of chiefs. The sunlight struggled through the canopy onto chain mail, iron sheets, bronze masks on horses and men. Swords were everywhere.

Armin looked up at his father. Sigimer's eyes had sunk since he had left his hall to marshal the clan. The familiar boar-painted flesh and piled hair, the torque of bronze that encircled his father's muscular neck – all things of which Armin had always boasted about to his friends. Now the iron army mocked them.

'Never forget this,' his father said, and he led his children into the dell.

CHAPTER 2

NENO COWERED BENEATH HIS SHIELD. He pressed his back deeper against the tree roots and swore as he pulled his legs against his body. Rain poured. The wind tore through the wooded valley, but the cries of the wounded and the barbarians' howls could not be drowned.

We are all dead, he thought.

He had signed up for the legions six months ago, long before the rebellion. He had confidently expected boring garrison service in some cowed land. Now, he was surrounded by the screams of legionaries being butchered by a barbarian horde that had descended upon their column as it snaked through the confined valley.

Neno gritted his teeth. A javelin or arrow could skewer him at any moment. The front of the column was a pile of corpses. The rear was pinned down miles away from camp. Night would fall…

'Get up!' a voice roared. Neno knew only that it was Latin, and had authority. He got into a crouch, keeping his shield up.

He received a kick and a torrent of curses. Someone grabbed him by the neck and yanked him onto his feet. He saw an iron cuirass and an officer's purple as he was dragged across the mud. The man seemed unaware of his armoured weight. He bellowed invectives. Neno scrambled as he was held nearly horizontally, his sword dragging on the forest floor, his knees bashing against stones.

The officer yelled at the legionaries that he would kill them himself unless they fought. He swung Neno ahead of him for emphasis. Neno smashed into the ground and temporarily lost his shield. An arrow sliced into the earth a few feet ahead of him, and he scrambled to find the shield again. He came to his feet just as a horse careened past, its rider dismounting at speed a few yards ahead.

The officer was kicking another prone legionary. He was a tall man with broad shoulders and the narrow waist of a champion athlete. He strutted as if death were a delusion. The crimson horsehair crest on his helmet rippled as he advanced up the hill, sword drawn, chest pushed out like a cockerel, shouting 'Move or die!' in a bark such as Neno had not heard since training camp.

Neno raised his shield. His legs had recovered their strength. Cavalrymen were dismounting in ever-greater numbers around him. They had the green oval shields of auxiliaries. A blond-bearded, grinning, half-savage mercenary flashed him a broken-toothed smile. The auxiliary mocked him in his foreign tongue before darting ahead, as impervious to the corpse-lined scene as his commander.

'Move!' the prefect of cavalry bellowed as he yanked another Roman from a hiding place. More men were heading up the incline from where the rebels were shooting. Rain exploded on armour. Neno stumbled. The officer spat more oaths in his direction.

Neno pushed ahead. He swallowed hard as he passed a near-dead legionary mewling through a smashed face. Blood bubbled from the wounded man's nose and lips. He clasped his chest, where some wound was sucking away his life.

The officer bounded ahead of the line of legionaries, at long-haired Pannonians stripping the dead, and crashed into the first barbarian. His sword wheeled ferociously, lifting a savage off his feet. The impact sent the officer sliding in the muddy soil. For a moment, Neno feared that he, too, would become a victim in the quagmire to the nimble enemy. The officer, who was down on one knee, thrust at another goatskin-cloaked savage. The man turned tail.

The officer shouted at his men not to pursue, and ordered them to form a line. He spoke like a Roman nobleman, but his light-brown hair and heavy cheekbones were barbarian. His half-civilised men wore amulets or tattoos under their uniforms. The barbarian officer repeated the orders in their own guttural tongue. He formed the centre of the new line.

The officer called for Neno, who ambled to the shield wall. Neno's mouth went dry at the man's fierce glare. The officer demanded to know what had happened.

'The column was cut in half. Nobody made it out from the front end, and we were being—'

The officer had heard enough. He pointed his sword brusquely. 'Join in. We're going forward.'

Neno hesitated, paralysed at the thought of re-entering the slaughterhouse. The officer, amazingly, smiled. 'What is your name?'

'Neno.'

'Stand by me, Neno,' the officer said softly, as if he were speaking to a child. He moved aside so that a space opened up to his immediate left. 'You can fight behind my shield.'

Neno obeyed, open-mouthed. Downhill, a second, larger echelon of Roman cavalry hurtled into the forest, riding down the rebels.

'That is my brother, Neno,' the officer said solemnly. 'He is driving up the valley to save your comrades.' The officer studied the forest. He now had about ten men on either side of him. 'Will you join us, Neno?' he said calmly, like a man in Rome on a market day.

'Yes, Sir.'

'Then let us take that hill.'

The officer barked an order, and the line strode forward in unison.

CHAPTER 3

A POISONED FOREST OF CROSSES.

Arminius's eyes glided over the dead and dying Pannonians. A year before, the province had been at peace: the lowlands settled by Rome, the highlands yielding to civilisation. Then wild men from the hills had incited their lowland cousins against Roman settlements. The Pannonians' grandfathers had been conquered by Rome. They were tired of taxes and land-grabs. The torrent had slammed into the forts guarding the Hellas road. Thousands of Romans had died. Hundreds of miles away, Rome slowly rose from slumber and stretched its iron muscles. First two legions, and then four, had entered the province, only to be mauled. Rome had awoken to the scale of the threat: a mob of two hundred thousand fighters. Even savages from the deep interior were involved. Now, ten legions – eighty thousand men – concentrated to exterminate the rebels.

'What a disaster!' Arminius mused. He passed more old corpses in the summer sun. His *ala* initially performed scouting and raids, but as the rebels had overwhelmed the infantry sent inland, his mercenaries had been used to bail out withdrawing legionaries. His unit strength was down by a third. He had replaced four hundred horses.

Massive Castra Carnuntum loomed ahead. Around it, Rome's military might arrayed to extinguish the Pannonians.

His *ala* thundered past, their equipment clattering. Their kit was worn, and their faces sunken with stress and lack of food. Yet every man saluted him. He had promised to bring them back to Carnuntum. Arminius returned their greeting, calling after individuals by name. The men had fought well and as a unit, even though they came from a dozen tribes. They spoke barely any Latin, yet they followed his orders. They had proved their worth in the ravines of Pannonia.

One rider drew up.

'The rebels nearly succeeded,' Flavus said. They surveyed the crosses. As always, he used Latin. Flavus took off his helmet, and his curly blond hair spilled over his ears. Like Armin, he sported a week-old beard.

'Yes, nearly,' Arminius replied gruffly, glowering at the crosses.

'Do you think that they will try again?' Flavus studied his brother. Arminius had been moody for days now. Their last mission had taken them deep into broken country, where traps had continually threatened catastrophe. In the end, even Arminius's energy had worn thin. Since the campaign had started, he had personally lit the funeral pyres of over sixty of his men.

'They will, for as long as the Marcomanni remain free beyond the Ister.'

Over the past four years, there had been ominous rumblings of a new leader uniting the tribes north of the river.

The sinewy muscles on Arminius's bronzed forearms flexed as he tugged at the reins.

'Well, we will not be going after the Marcomanni for at least another year,' Flavus said phlegmatically. He felt a nervous tic start in the corner of his left eye, and raised his finger to hide it. The act was pointless: he knew that his elder brother had spotted the twitch long before, though he had remained tactfully silent. Flavus wondered whether Arminius was as haunted as he was by the savagery of the past months. In many a valley in Pannonia, there was now only death and ruins. Rome offered one choice only: submission or extinction.

Arminius gazed at his brother. It was a moment before his brown eyes softened. 'We will leave that for next year.'

Flavus smiled, even though the thought of another campaign depressed him.

They continued into the stone citadel. The camp dominated the landscape. It seemed to have been on the plain for centuries, rather than a few months.

Flavus fell in slightly behind Arminius as they passed through the gate. Riding among the barracks, he again felt at ease. Soldiers hailed and cheered his brother – word of the *ala*'s exploits had been spreading. They could certainly expect hospitality tonight.

General Aius Caecina Severus had summoned them from the hills three days before. His quarters, at the centre of the camp, resembled a governor's palace, bustling with scribes and aides.

A servant told them that the general was busy, and they had to wait. Arminius maintained his composure while asking how long the wait would be. The scribe was evasive.

'In that case, you will have to excuse my brother,' Arminius said. 'He will have to go and see that our soldiers are properly taken care of.' He told Flavus to make sure that the men received good quarters.

It took most of the afternoon before the general's doors opened. Arminius had met the old soldier before at the Imperial Court. Caecina was a conscientious and able administrator in an army where too many senior officers were promoted because of family connections. His office showed no ostentation. Three large tables dominated the great room. Maps and scrolls were neatly stacked or displayed, and managed by two middle-aged clerks. They frowned at the tall auxiliary officer as he entered.

Caecina turned around from one of the piles at the sound of Arminius's hobnailed boots. 'Ah, finally,' the commander said pleasantly. He wore a cuirass and uniform, even though he was far behind the lines. His fingers were stained with black ink.

Arminius saluted, while Caecina continued writing a letter. The general joked that he could only offer him water to drink. Arminius refused politely.

Caecina's heavy features and thick brow made him a caricature of a peasant, but his stubby fingers nimbly jotted down a final note.

'I have heard excellent reports about you.'

'Thank you, Sir.'

'They say that you saved an entire column of infantry, at great risk to yourself.' He finished the letter and pushed the quill into a pot. 'Is that true?'

Arminius admitted that his column had come to the aid of a cohort of the Eleventh Legion.

'You rallied them.'

'The cohort had lost over half its strength, Sir. So we can hardly call it a success.'

'You are too humble. Every report I have heard about you has been positive. Your unit fights hard. You are daring in your initiative and faultless in your execution. You are a credit to Rome.'

'Thank you, Sir.'

Caecina nodded silently, regarding the muscular cavalry officer. 'Let me see what I remember. You are the son of a German chief, adopted into Roman life?'

'I am, Sir.'

Caecina leaned back against his desk, folding his arms across his barrel chest, and studied Arminius. 'How long have you been from home?'

'I have not seen Rome for three years, Sir.'

A smile flickered across Caecina's features. 'No, I mean Germania.'

'I left there when I was seven, Sir. So it is nearly sixteen years.'

'You still speak the tongue of your tribe?'

'I know Suebic just haltingly, Sir. I was not encouraged to retain it in Rome.'

'Well, what you remember will do,' Caecina told him. He paused. 'We have decided that it is time for you to return to Germania.' He did not allow Arminius any time to respond. 'As you can appreciate, the intended move into Trans-Istria to conquer the Marcomanni will not happen this year. This barbarian king…'

'Maroboduus,' Arminius supplied, when the general halted.

'Yes, Maroboduus – what names these people have!' The general laughed. 'He will have to wait a year or two. Several of the legions in Germania will now be diverted here.' He sighed. 'And that means that my colleague Saturninus in Germania might need some help.'

'I thought that Germania was quiet.'

Caecina nodded pensively. 'It is, but it may not remain that way.' He crossed his arms. 'Have you been communicating with your father?'

'My father cannot write, Sir. I have had messages from him, and I have sent gifts, but he has never been invited to Rome, so we have not spoken.'

Caecina shrugged. 'An oversight – your father is one of our most loyal supporters. Unfortunately, all is not going well with him. Your father survived an attempt on his life about four months ago.' He raised his hand. 'Fear not – he survived. We suspect that this chief Maroboduus used agents within your tribe to make the attempt. Nonetheless,' he continued, strolling forward to the young officer, 'we are worried that your father is getting too old.' He touched Arminius upon his shoulder. 'We are, therefore, sending you back to Germania to help the authorities there.'

'I am honoured, Sir, but I would not want to usurp my father.'

'You are but there to stiffen the sinews, young man. Your father's position is safe, but he has asked for you, and we have agreed to send you. We have every confidence in you.'

'Then I do so gladly, Sir.'

Caecina smiled and guided him to one of the maps. 'The new Governor of Germania, Publius Quinctilius Varus, is a civilian. He has extensive experience in Syria and Africa, and is the husband of the Emperor's great-niece.' The map showed most of Germania north of the Alps, from Gaul through to the plains of Scythia and the kidney-shaped Pontus Euxinus. Most of the interior of Germania was blank. 'The Governor will continue building an infrastructure: bathhouses and villas, market towns and courts. We are making progress. We are confident that we can establish a border on the Albis, and civilise Germania.' He ran his finger up the major river from an ill-mapped coastline in the north, until he reached a hilly zone identified as the Marcomanni kingdom. 'We only need to keep Maroboduus from causing problems from his enclave.' Caecina pursed his lips meditatively. 'Do you accept the assignment?'

'I accept, Sir.'

'Good! You will travel north tomorrow. You will meet up with a man called Numonius Vala, Commander of the Cavalry in Germania, in the lands of the Hermunduri. He is our intelligence chief there and he will brief you. See your father as quickly as possible, and root out traitors. Germania is almost won for Rome. We hope that all of your people will follow your example.'

'I trust that they will, Sir.'

'Your brother can command your contingent in your absence.'

'Will Flavus not be joining me, Sir?'

'We will see.'

'And my men, Sir, will they be following me? If I am to succeed, I shall need men I can trust. I know hardly anybody in my tribe…'

'You know that we do not send auxiliary forces back to their lands of origin. We make an exception with you personally.'

'I understand, Sir, but, if I am to be of any use to you, I shall need at least a hundred trustworthy men.'

Caecina raised his hands. 'I do not want to appear uncharitable, Arminius, but I have already been asked to surrender you, one of my best junior officers. A hundred men on top of that will make things far harder for me.'

'I ask for ten then, Sir.'

Caecina studied the bronzed features of the officer, and sensed his easy charm. The young man was an exceedingly good soldier. The general cursed the order. Had it not come from Tiberius, the Emperor's son himself, he would have swatted it away.

Moreover, Caecina felt uneasy about sending Arminius back to his homeland. Had he been given the choice, he would have sent him to the Upper Nilus.

Perhaps he was simply *too* talented to let run loose.

'Very well; I shall send a few men of your choice with you.'

'I am much obliged, Sir.'

'Yes, yes,' Caecina grumbled. 'Now go. I have Pannonia to reconquer.'

CHAPTER 4

FRIMUNT SOBBED, SHUDDERING AS HE burrowed into Armin's arms. It was four days since the strangers took them. Since then, the four-year-old, who had never strayed far from his mother's hearth, had gone from hysterical wails to occasional anguished moans. Exhaustion had now blunted Frimunt's senses. He seemed barely conscious.

Armin was alert. His tears flowed quietly and in darkness. He wanted no one, not even his brother, to see his terror.

Sigimer had kissed them farewell. Armin had fought panic. Even when the bloodied chieftain stepped back and one of the armoured foreigners took hold of them, he remained silent and did not resist. He had searched his father's eyes while Frimunt screamed. Sigimer had not been able to hide his shame, but Armin had required no explanation. That, the battlefield had offered, even to his untutored eyes: the bank of Cheruscan bodies in the clearing; the Roman infantry under their bright-red standards; the majesty of the Roman chief, enthroned before the smouldering tribal hall.

He had snapped at his brother to remain silent, forcing himself not to cry. His words had done little to lessen Frimunt's fear, but he had seen pride in Sigimer's eyes. That was the last thing that he remembered of his father.

They were herded onto a barge with twenty other children. By the time they had finally exited the Lupia, the stream on whose banks he had grown up, and entered a far bigger river, there were a hundred child hostages from all the tribes: Cherusci and Chatti, Bructeri and Tencteri, Chasuarii and Dulgubinii. The oldest children were perhaps ten; the youngest, two. The Romans were vicious and vigilant. None of the children even attempted to escape, even when their ropes were cut.

Now they were in a wagon, travelling on a stone road snaking ever further from home. Darkness covered them. Occasionally, the invaders would growl in their gibberish language. Sometimes they beat on the wagon if a child cried too loudly for its mother.

Armin winced. The thought of his mother was like a stab of light. He had to blink and turn away.

He hugged his brother, his eyes on the wagon's rear door.

'Now, now, Frimunt, do not worry. Do not worry.'

* * *

7 CE (MIDSUMMER)

HERMUNDURI TERRITORY

Arminius touched the giant hornbeam that cast its branch across the road crawling north. The tree stood the height of eight men, its smooth, grey bark fissured with antiquity. He allowed the horse to halt, and rubbed the serrated leaf between his fingers. He could see for no more than ten yards in any direction before the oak, hornbeam, and beech closed in. The oaks, especially, were unlike any he had ever seen, rising straight and branchless from the steaming earth to a canopy a hundred and eighty feet above.

There were eleven of them. They had rarely seen the sky during the last week, since re-entering the tree line on the northern slope of the Alps. The vegetable world just tantalised them with glimmers of sunlight. The summer rains poured directly from the leaves. Downpours were followed by mists, breathed by the soil into an atmosphere humid enough to assail the lungs. Bands of frogs occasionally leapt across the path, and mobs of red squirrels careened between branches. The creatures treated the path, the main thoroughfare in Hermunduri lands, with disdain. Rivulets and bogs mocked corduroy roads constructed by hubristic Roman engineers. The place was rank, dank and primeval, rent by the shrieking of bird and beast.

The route had petered out to a mere footpath once across the Alps, mysteriously branching off every few miles, its main trunk indicated only by white Roman milestones besieged by moss. At day intervals they would reach a settlement. Most frequently it was only a small Roman fort, containing a half-century of auxiliaries, and surrounded by barbarian lean-tos. Twice, they had exchanged their horses at cohort stations. Commanding centurions regarded them with pity.

Ahead sounded a whistle – the scout's signal – and Arminius dug his heels into his horse's flanks, eliciting new life from an animal sapped by the humidity and gloom. He met the rider as he came cantering down the path. The man, called Arbex, was Tencteri, a tribe famed for its horsemen, and which lived on the upper right bank of the Rhenus. Like most barbarian auxiliaries hired by the Roman army, he had been cleaned up: his furs and simple homespun clothes changed for Roman military uniform, and his face shaved. However, as always with auxiliaries, signs remained of his recent barbarian origins: a copper amulet of a horse's head, his people's deity; a thick moustache in the Valich style; and a horsehair lance pennant.

Arbex spoke with Arminius in a thickly-accented Suebic. There were Hermunduri ahead.

The group of warriors became visible as Arminius's column rounded a bend. They came upon a steep incline.

The Hermunduri carried large oval Roman shields with thick central spines. These were army surplus: the Romans had phased out this shield pattern thirty years before. The shields' new barbarian owners had dappled them with green paint. Some wore Roman-style armour, two even sporting mail shirts, but all were dressed in rags. Their hair was short, again in imitation of legionaries, but the majority had used white lime to style their hair into bristles, to resemble angry beasts. The Hermunduri had formed a substantial proportion of recruits for his *ala*. However, to be surprised by these natives in the suffocating woods raised phantoms of Pannonian ambushes.

Arminius raised his hand, but allowed Arbex to communicate with the tribesmen in a pidgin of Suebic and dog Latin – a mishmash common in the training camps, where barbarian youths were deposited to train in Roman ways.

Arminius eyed the surrounding forest with unease. Superficially, he was stone calm.

The Hermunduri told them that Numonius Vala was half a mile up the road. They were here to track Marcomanni raiders. The Hermunduri wasted little time in informing the newcomers that the Marcomanni were their ancient enemies. Arminius responded sympathetically.

They found the Commander of Cavalry easily. He stood astride an enormous spruce felled by some forgotten storm that had ripped the canopy open. Moss, as thick as a thumb and dotted with myriad fungi, carpeted the dead bark.

Vala was about thirty-five and taller than most Romans. His swarthy skin spoke of his Iberian ancestry. Despite being of legate rank and commanding thousands of men, he wore a simple cuirass and travel cloak. He was filthy. The thick, black beard that hugged his jaw showed that he had been travelling for days. His frame was stripped of fat, and his muscles were taut with energy.

As the column approached the tree, Vala threw a clod of earth in the opposite direction. Arminius realised that they stood on a ridge that gave way to the north to undergrowth torn by landslides.

Soldiers and auxiliaries filled the area. Nearly sixty were Hermunduri, their equipment ranging from antiquated legionary mail armour to loincloths. Only a dozen actual Roman troops were visible, but there were other Iberians like Vala: his guard.

Vala faced the newcomers without dismounting from the stump. He rested his weight casually on one leg and surveyed the men below him like a monarch.

'What are you doing here?' the cavalry commander grumbled, half-interested, when Arminius dismounted and identified himself. Listening to the explanation, he muttered an obscenity. 'Oh yes, I received a message about you.' He studied the newcomer more closely. 'You are to be stationed with me?'

'I am, Sir.'

'Well, *excellent*,' Vala said dourly. 'From what they told me, you are very good at hunting down savages.' He glared at a group of Hermunduri, who appeared nervous. Vala flicked some dirt from his fingers, his eyes narrowing. He had scars on his forearms and legs. A cut, ivory with age, disfigured his left cheek.

'Come and see what you make of this.'

Arminius joined him on the tree.

Before them, bedewed by summer rains, lay a slaughter pit. Dozens of rotten corpses, scraps of clothing, snapped spears and broken shields lay scattered. The death stench had disappeared, but the terror lingered. Some of the men had been tortured, and bodies had been defiled, nailed to the trees, stakes driven through now blackened flesh. Heads swung forlornly from branches.

'They caught them on the march three weeks ago,' Vala said. His Latin was accented with the olive groves of Hispania. 'There was a half century of Romans and a hundred Hermunduri.'

'It was the Marcomanni?'

'Yes,' Vala said, glowering impotently at the remains. 'They always torture the wounded and dismember the bodies. The Hermunduri say that they take survivors with them for sacrifice.'

'I heard that too.' Arminius knew of the great fear that accompanied any Roman fighting in the northern wastes. Everybody mistreated captives. All defeated could expect slavery at the very least. However, these barbarians lived according to laws that were more brutal. 'It is disgusting.'

Vala studied the auxiliary officer's chiselled features. 'They told me that you are Cherusci.'

Arminius nodded.

'Good tribe,' Vala said, pensively running his finger over his forearm. 'Your father is Sigimer?'

'He is.'

Vala's features flexed sympathetically. 'Pity about what happened to him. He is a good man. He has been of great use to me.'

They took in the devastation. The corpses had been stripped of metal. Arminius noted that the victors had even detached the iron spear-points.

'The Marcomanni raided all summer, but this is the first Roman vexillation they got. They probably ambushed them in the thickets and then chased them up here. A few survived a while – we found a rampart that our men built as a last stand. They were wiped out. The bastards even killed the mules.'

Vala jumped from the log and began to order his men to burial duty.

Left alone, Arminius noticed a figure that appeared different from the others. The man was squatting before an immense larch. He had, incongruously, started a small fire, and was gentling the lazy smoke over his skin. He was bony, with long, tangled black hair and a matted beard. Whorls of blue pigment covered his body. He wore only a small animal skin loincloth, and had a bow and a primitive hardwood club. Only his iron knife betokened civilisation. He was swaying on his haunches.

'Not much point having him here,' Vala said, as he followed Arminius's gaze. His men were sorting the Roman dead from the Hermunduri, who would presumably receive their own funeral customs. 'The dead could not have been displayed more openly if the gods had blasted the forest with fire.'

'Who is he?'

'The tracker – his name is Hiru. He does not belong to any of the tribes we know. The others treat him with superstition. He can smell like a dog, they say. I tend to agree! I use him to hunt people.' Vala spat at the dirt. He added under his breath, 'This time the Marcomanni are long gone, but the Hermunduri are still shitting themselves.'

Arminius gave the creature a final look. The man had begun to place mud on his forearms. He was muttering some prayer.

Vala broke the silence. 'So, with you here, I suppose that the orders are final,' Vala continued quietly, his black eyes flickering with frustration. 'There will be no move against the Marcomanni from the west?'

'None: all available troops are being sucked into Pannonia.'

'Our esteemed allies will not be happy,' Vala remarked, looking at the nearest Hermunduri with disdain. 'They were counting on us to wipe out their old foes.'

'Is it that bad?' Arminius wiped sweat from his skin. Even here, on the ridge, the damp, hot air barely circulated.

Vala sighed sharply, his eyes searching the horizon across the verdant basin. 'Up north, we have few problems – the majority of the tribes are as meek as lambs. Most of the fighting occurs in summer, to the east, when we attack the Semnones on the Albis.'

Arminius recalled the map he had seen in General Caecina's office. The Albis formed the eastern border of Roman Germania. The Semnones, relatives of his own Cherusci, were still free.

'Here, however, things are different,' Vala told him, shaking his head. 'I killed thirty-four Marcomanni last week, as they came back from a raid. I do that almost every week. But they keep returning.'

They stood on the lip, peering down at the burials. One man was vomiting. Clouds of flies swirled.

'We can kill them,' Vala noted, 'but we cannot kill them all. And the forest has no end.' His tongue rolled against the inside of his cheek. His eyes wandered over the rolling foliage again. The trees covered the land in every direction – a viridescent cloak, hiding any human civilisation.

Arminius nodded. 'How are your men?'

Vala pointed at men lounging in the rare sun. 'Just drying out is a luxury to them! I suppose that is why you are here. You are more suited to this climate. And you can *think* like them.'

'I hope so, Sir.'

CHAPTER 5

'**H**OW MUCH DO YOU REMEMBER of this place?'

Vala and Arminius were riding near the head of a column twisting through the forested highlands of the Hermunduri.

'I was but seven when I left. I can speak the language, but I remember very little.'

'Your Latin accent is better than mine!' Vala guffawed as the auxiliary officer shrugged in mock apology. 'You have been well educated.'

'I was placed with the family of Statilius Taurus.'

Vala did not appear to recognise the name, and Arminius did not care to enlighten him. He was certain that the man would remember to make enquiries.

'They gave me a good education.'

'Well, let us hope that it hasn't robbed you of your ability to navigate this wasteland.' Vala gazed across the canopy swathing the eastern valleys. 'I have been fighting here for eight years, and the place still awes me.'

'It is different where you come from,' Arminius noted, his brown eyes dancing with humour.

'Quite,' Vala replied. 'And my tours in Africa and Numidia certainly did not prepare me. There the savannah and desert might seem endless, but at least you can see where you are!'

Arminius laughed with him.

They reached an outcrop, and allowed their horses to bask in the clear-skied midsummer's morning. Away from the steaming dales it was pleasant.

'Out there,' Vala said, looking east, 'beyond those far hills, Maroboduus waits. They say he has at least fifty thousand men and four thousand cavalry, many trained in Roman ways of war. He had been one of our auxiliaries.'

17

'That just proves how careful we have to be about whom we take on in service.'

'Indeed.' Vala leaned forward in his saddle. 'He promises his hordes a free Germania. It is all nonsense, but the Semnones seem interested. Even some people in your tribe are siding with him.'

'That is why I am here.'

'And what are you going to do?'

'Kill them.'

By nightfall, the column was in a fort at the northern edge of Hermunduri territory. African auxiliaries from the city of Leptis Magna garrisoned it. Unlike the smaller forts to the south, this gateway to Germania possessed proper ramparts, built from turf and logs and reinforced by wooden towers.

Vala and Arminius shared supper with the commander, a grizzled campaigner who had been part of the original invasion by Prince Drusus eighteen years before.

'What is the worst thing about this place?' the commander echoed, when Arminius asked him the question. 'There are so many! When it is not wet, it is freezing cold, with snow up to here.' He indicated his hips. 'The food is dull, mail is non-existent, and as for time off duty… the barbarians have problems with whores, and besides, what civilised woman is going to set up stall here?'

They laughed at the old soldier's gripes, and as the barbarian *beor* continued to flow, they swapped war stories. Arminius described the Pannonian revolt. The sight disturbed Vala: the young barbarian, whose shining eyes, swiftly moving hands, and engaging manner drew the fort's officers to him like moths.

The conversation turned to the war with Maroboduus.

'The Marcomanni are not stupid,' the fort commander told them. 'They avoid the fort. They have wiped out half a dozen Hermunduri villages to the east, and we catch some on the way back, but we cannot stop them.'

Indeed, the fort's brig contained seven prisoners, whom Arminius was allowed to inspect. His torch lit the cage to reveal sullen warriors: massive creatures with long, loose blond or light-brown hair and pallid, tattooed skin. They closely resembled the Cherusci warriors that he had seen as a child.

'The Hermunduri used to keep them as slaves, but now they just torture them if we let them,' the commander told them. He had traded the prisoners for goods. They would now sell them to passing traders for profit.

'If it were not for the Africans, this whole area would go to the dogs,' Vala said the next morning. 'The Hermunduri were losing the war before we got here.'

The area seemed to be under siege. The Hermunduri villages of thatched-roofed, mud-walled hovels were all fortified, and appeared impoverished. Huge, black, bristle-haired swine rooted in the rubbish around the huts, along with mangy bantam chickens and a few ducks. Lupine hounds basked in spots of sunlight, and rarely bothered to inspect the passers-by.

The people also paid little attention to the militia, except if one of their numbers were among the auxiliaries. The barbarian women were dressed in simple ankle-length smocks of roughly woven cloth, usually of a dull brown or grey woollen colour, with the odd dash of dirty green. Many men wore nothing more than loincloths, and the children were naked. Footwear was rare. There was an intriguing mixture of jewellery, ranging from polished wood, bone or stone balls pierced to fit on a string, to the occasional watered-down versions of Roman copper adornments. Arminius even saw coins worn as ornaments.

'What do you think of them?' Vala enquired as they rode out of yet another hovel.

'Barbarians are the same everywhere.'

'Things are a little better further north, but not much.'

The amount of cultivated land gradually grew as they moved away from the frontier with the Marcomanni. At first, they were mere patches scratched with wooden hoes, but eventually there appeared a Roman-style plough – drawn by sweating men instead of oxen. The livestock consisted of shaggy cows, stunted by Roman standards, and ubiquitous pigs had the run of the place. There were no horses not belonging to the military.

Barbarians travelling down the road invariably stepped aside as the Roman column approached. On numerous occasions, small groups would be standing by the side of the road, sullen, staring.

'One problem we have,' Vala said, 'is that this territory is infested by the Marcomanni, and by other Suebi – the army insists on calling them "Germans!", but I dislike the term. Do you know the name?'

Arminius nodded.

Vala continued, 'They all look alike, and they all speak Suebic. There are tribal markings, but it is easy to fake those. A Marcomanni or wild Suebi can easily be walking around here, and we cannot tell them apart. And then there is this blasted landscape.' He ended with a sigh, his hand expansively indicating the forest. 'I would cut down every tree if I could.'

Vala glanced again at the young officer, whose pleasant manner had drawn him briefly to reveal his feelings of helplessness. I have been in the woods too long, he told himself. On the other hand, perhaps it was just the man's easy charm. Most of the soldiers seemed to like him instinctively.

A few days further north, they came upon a contingent of Roman legionaries accompanying Roman settlers.

'Straight from Cisalpine Gaul and Latium itself,' declared the centurion, Petilius, who was in charge of the trek. He was very happy to see Vala's men, even though the trip north across the Alps had been uneventful.

The settlers included every type of tradesman and artisan, small traders and even some civil servants. Arminius asked to be introduced to some of the settlers, and the Prefect found one of their supervisors. The man, called Sextus, had the squat shape, hairy arms, and jovial manner that Arminius associated with Greeks. The master builder traced his receding hairline with his stubby fingers as they spoke. He had brought a hundred and eighty-three people with him, including his family. 'The pay is excellent, and we are to have more land than we can use. The army has equipped us with every tool we have asked for, and has promised us all the contracts we can deal with.'

'What kind of buildings?' Arminius asked. They were seated on stumps around a fireplace, surrounded by a small crowd.

Sextus grinned like a boy. 'We have been asked to build a governor's residence at Castra Drusus. I am also to send men to Castra Octa. Even the barbarians are enthusiastic: we already have a deposit on a new hall for the king of the Cherusci.'

'Then we will meet again,' Arminius said warmly, explaining that he was the son of the Cherusci chief.

Sextus produced a waterproof container holding precious engineering drawings. Arminius commended him on his skill as they pored over the project intended for his father. It was, Sextus explained, a variation on a Roman villa. 'You will be able to fit a hundred guests in that, in true Roman style.'

'I look forward to seeing it,' Arminius said, his eyes softening.

'Well the problem is… and please forgive me if I say this, Sir,' Sextus began uncertainly, 'that these people are so *primitive*.' He was reassured by a nod from Arminius. 'They have almost no stonework! They have almost no metal tools! We have to find our own quarries, and construct our own workshops, as well as our own timber yards!' He sighed in exasperation. 'Even so, we must be among the first professional builders to come here. They will marvel at whatever we erect!'

'I am sure they will. Do come and search for me when you come to Castra Octa. I shall make sure we build a proper bit of Rome up here.' He tousled the hair of one of Sextus's band of dirty-cheeked children as he departed.

They entered the upper reaches of the north-flowing Visurgis a day later. At night, wolves howled in the wilds. The sound drove the settlers to distraction. There were wolves in the Apennines, and of course, in the Alps, but here the beasts ruled the dark.

'My wife is becoming increasingly angry with me, the further north we go,' Sextus admitted ruefully.

The continuing threat from Marcomanni did not help. At night, the column still built defences. Once, they came upon the charred remains of a village, its inhabitants utterly erased – even the bodies were missing. The sight, and ensuing panic from the settlers, caused Petilius to start ranting against his posting. He halted, though, when Vala came within earshot.

'It is *his* job to keep this road safe!' Petilius hissed conspiratorially at Arminius. 'And look at it.'

Despite the settlers' pleas, Vala's men left the column one morning to patrol to the east. The Hermunduri had reached the edge of their territory, and he wanted to avoid friction with the Chatti, who controlled the route further north. 'I shall see you soon,' he told Arminius. 'I am glad we met.'

The telltale whitewashed hair and oval shields of the Hermunduri disappeared, but after a day of seeing no barbarians at all, they spotted a party of men among the trees. These wore bright chequered trousers in reds and blues, and smaller oval shields with the tops chopped off. Arminius recognised them as Chatti.

'They just want us to know that they are there,' Petilius said. 'There is still a lot of fighting here. As long as they don't bother us, I don't care.'

About four days later, around midday, the landscape changed radically, for Arminius at least, with a casual phrase from Petilius. They were riding up to a ridge, the land around them thickly bristled with pine, when the centurion pointed at an object placed by the road at the summit of the hill.

'We are in Cherusci land now.'

It was a crudely carved post about the height of a man, the top resembling a roaring human head surmounted by a mass of knotted hair, the rest a twisting mass of animals: boars, wolves and bears contorted in combat. 'There used to be a bigger one,' Petilius told him, 'but we had them cut it down. The old one, of course, had a real head on it.'

Arminius barely heard. His eyes were drawn towards the horizon. Innumerable phalanxes of beech, spruce and oak, ash and lime covered the undulating land. Such country had dominated his vision for many days, but now it seemed to pulse and hum, as if the beasts that called it home had one, synchronised life. In the distance, birds wheeled above the treetops – he guessed that they were ravens – eyes of a green world in which men were of passing consequence.

He had not expected the first sight of his old tribe's lands to touch him this deeply.

He wanted to lie down and kiss the earth.

Instead, he sent three of his men ahead to find his father and tell him that Armin had returned.

Chapter 6

THE TREK REACHED A RIVER in the late afternoon, and Arminius was told that it was the Amisia, which wound through the centre of Cherusci lands. The stream was barely an arrow-shot wide. The water was clear enough for him to study the weaving water plants as he guided his mount through the ford. Sunlight dappled its surface.

On the far bank sat an old man. He leaned on a walking stick. His long hair, once russet, now grey and scraggly, was twisted into the ubiquitous topknot. Some wisps escaped around the side of his mottled face. His body was all time-eaten muscle and saggy, weatherbeaten skin. Ancient scars were visible on his arms and chest. His tattoos still played on the deteriorated canvas. He regarded the Romans rheumily.

Arminius passed him, and then halted up the path and looked back. Hundreds of Roman settlers got through the ford and passed the ancient. Every now and then one would try to speak to him. The man remained silent even when Roman children attempted to tease him. Finally, one boy poked the old man with a stick. Arminius turned his horse away. He followed the Amisia north-west.

The column halted in a field that had once held a legionary marching camp. It was close to the river and to a sizeable Cherusci settlement, whose women came to trade. The settlers produced trinkets and bartered.

Arminius rode out to the settlement. A palisade and a ditch, filled with water and rubbish, surrounded it. It swarmed with flies. Inside the ramparts were a dozen longhouses of wattle and daub. The steep roofs were thatched with a thick layer of reeds. Low fences of oak stakes and woven hazel saplings held chickens, pigs, and sheep. Other fences bounded small gardens of flax, herbs, leeks, and beans.

The barbarians were at their daily tasks. *Beor* was brewing, and bread was being prepared. Gaggles of small blonde girls played with rag dolls. They stared at Arminius with alarm. A few feet away, two boys, who had been excitedly moving clay animal figurines through the dirt, were openly hostile, if quiet. A woman appeared in a doorway. She nudged grimy hair from her face and glowered at him. A mangy dog appeared by her feet and sniffed the air.

Arminius rode on, ignoring the barbarians' resentment. Near the centre of the village was a great decorated pole, the Heaven Tree. It dominated the central square. He stopped under it, glancing at the ribbons and flowers placed against it.

Then he noticed a puny smithy. It was presided over by a muscular brute whose blue eyes bore into Arminius. Unperturbed, he studied the workshop. It contained only basic metal tools: enough to produce axe heads, kitchen knives and scythes, and perhaps the occasional spear-point. There were no swords. Armour was utterly beyond the smith's capacity. An array of farming tools stood in the one corner. They were made entirely from wood and bone.

Arminius finally made eye contact with the smith, and held the man's gaze until the artisan grumbled and turned back to his work.

This petty victory gave Arminius a chance to survey the village. It contained only rutted, muddy paths between the huts, and it reeked of human and animal waste. The hovels served simultaneously as homes for beasts and the filthy people. Men, idly sitting in front of the houses, regarded him with either muted hatred or bovine apathy.

The place seemed little different from the Hermunduri hovels. The males wore loincloths or breeches, with no shoes. The barefoot women wore sleeveless shift dresses. Only their hairstyles clearly identified them as Cherusci. Every class of person had their hair styled in some fashion. He only dimly recalled the significance of the different patterns. He was familiar with the topknots of the adult men. The young girls wore their tresses long and flowing, or tied into a simple braid. The older women had their hair carefully plaited – they reminded him of his mother's auburn cascade.

Arminius turned his horse back towards the village gate. On a post above the roof of the biggest longhouse, the owner had mounted the skull of a bear. It was the clan totem. His father's village would have a boar watching over it.

He had not been prepared for the squalor of his people. He was dismayed.

Chapter 7

'Come, Little One, it is not that bad,' the woman told Armin.

She resembled someone from his tribe. She had hay-coloured hair and pale skin dusted with freckles. However, her thick accent made her difficult to understand. She was clothed in a dress made of two mantles. When she squatted, her fleshy waist and thighs bulged out of the slits in the clothes.

'Do it now,' she said, more firmly, wiping perspiration from her face with a thick arm. She grabbed him by the wrist.

Armin stood in a courtyard amid other dejected children. They had been stripped of their clothes and doused in water. A Roman slave had held him down while another had sheared his hair, first cutting off his topknot, and then scraping the hair until his bald scalp bled into his eyes.

He was shivering, but determined not to show his humiliation, even as the woman tugged at his penis with a cloth.

'There, you are clean now,' the woman finally told him, laughing. 'You have *cultus.*'

They travelled for weeks. The distance from home became so great that the children were no longer locked into the wagons at night. They journeyed through mountains and then into valleys where the sun burned differently and the trees took unaccustomed shapes. Gone were familiar breeze-borne scents. But they were still in the forest, and that gave them some comfort.

People's way of life also changed. In the northern towns, closest to home, the inhabitants still looked normal. Their houses were of wood, thatch, and hard-baked mud. But one day they saw a stone house. It turned out to be a hovel. Eventually, whole towns were made of stone, and finally, even the road. Roofs turned from thatch to baked clay slabs.

The forest began to thin.

In the first great town south of the mountains, they saw an entire man carved from rock.

Gradually the people changed. First, their clothes altered. The cloth became finer and there were no furs and skins. As they descended the mountains, even the people's skins and hair darkened. Armin gaped at a man who looked like he had been rubbed with soot. The man looked at him disdainfully.

They crossed a great river, the Po. The banks were dense with settlements. The forest died. It was swallowed by enormous fields upon which toiled crowds of people. Armin looked in vain for signs of deer, and for familiar birds. Frimunt cried again.

Everything became bigger: oxen were sturdier, horses longer-legged. Wheatlands grew into sun-coloured meres.

They had a Valich slave with them now. He knew some Suebi and the Roman language. 'You are to be put in Roman homes,' he assured them. 'They are far better than anything in your shitty Germania.'

At first, Armin had thought that "Germania" was the name the Romans had given to the Cherusci's lands, but the interpreter explained that it meant the lands of all the tribes.

By the time they entered the Romans' heartland, the children were allowed to walk beside the wagons. The air burned. Sometimes the horizon trembled.

'Tomorrow you see Rome, the greatest city in the world,' the interpreter warned them one day, as they crossed a sun-baked plain. 'All that you have seen before will seem like nothing.'

'Even the forest?'

The man laughed. 'A forest is just trees!'

The roads of stone became ever broader. Hundreds of people travelled the road with their bullocks and carts, horses and small, long-eared ponies.

The city rose like a mountain, serrated upon the horizon beneath a pall of smoke. It stood on several hills. A river snaked through it. Towards it ran very high bridges, higher than ten men, yet too narrow to walk on. The interpreter said that these were rivers that the Romans had built. There were thousands of roofs made of red tiles.

He pitied his father for having fought these people. The walls made Sigimer's arm seem like a sparrow's fragile wing.

The children entered through massive gates. They walked up streets where the world traded and lived. The streets were covered in slabs that had been scored with ruts by wagons. The slabs were strewn with rubbish and, like the adjoining walls, were caked with excrement. The buildings were enormous, with three, four or five levels that teetered over the thoroughfares. There were hundreds of clothes-lines between them, upon which the rags of multitudes flapped in the oven-like breeze. The walls were plastered with beige mud, or consisted of bare stone, but everywhere there were drawings of people and animals, and small alcoves for innumerable demons. People had scribbled lines on empty surfaces. Armin spotted someone scratching these shapes on a house. The interpreter said that the Romans used them to talk without actually speaking.

The guards pushed through the main road. It was choked with traffic: peddlers selling food, pots, and services. There were many animals, and he saw men carrying boxes within which, behind curtains, lay people. There were bursts of music: horns, pipes, and drums, clanging metal, foreign voices. The city drowned in colour. The people were like flowers, their loose clothes dipped in reds and yellows, decorated in deep blues and greens. The throng of strangers seemed to wash together. Scents, pungent and sweet, invested his nostrils. Some were the familiar earthy smells of shit and sweat. Others from the stalls pricked his senses.

The world grew ever larger.

They headed up a hill. The buildings became lower, the streets broadened, and the crowds thinned. The Valich interpreter explained that they were going to where the chiefs of the Romans lived. Here, the children would be sent to their new homes. This caused dismay. The children had been told what would happen in Rome, but the immediate prospect of being split up proved too much. Armin clutched Frimunt to him as the little boy, who had been enjoying the sights open-mouthed, began to whimper.

'Don't be scared,' he repeated, although his own courage was waning. 'I won't let them separate us.'

The houses became more impressive, and were hidden behind grim walls. Singly or in pairs, the young hostages were diverted to the gates, where stern porters received them. Behind the walls, the interpreter said they would become Roman – or Roman slaves if they resisted.

Armin watched the ground carefully, and when they stopped at one point, quietly picked up a potsherd discarded in the road. Then he surreptitiously tore the hem of his tunic and began to tie his wrist to Frimunt's. The other boy continued to moan softly.

The dwindling group halted, and one of the soldiers came over to them. He spotted the potsherd and their adjoined wrists almost immediately. The guard

27

snorted and produced a knife. Armin snarled and prepared to strike. Frimunt was bawling.

The guard grabbed Armin's arm. Growling, Armin lunged at him with the shard, raking his skin. The guard swore and drew back. His companions laughed at him. With a string of oaths, he advanced upon the boy.

'Stop!'

The man emerging from the gate was obeyed as if the guards were trained dogs. A long white cloth was draped around his bony shoulders and waist, and drawn over his left arm. His lean features were topped by iron-grey hair. He moved without hurry, with his chin raised haughtily. The soldier stepped back obsequiously.

The newcomer regarded Armin and Frimunt. Then he called for the interpreter, who approached him with bent-backed humility. The man in the white cloth spoke sharply.

The interpreter turned to Armin. 'He asks whether you are brothers.'

'Yes,' Armin replied, his throat thick with fear. The interpreter relayed his reply.

The man spoke at length to the interpreter, who nodded at regular intervals. Then the Valich turned to the boys. 'His name is Quintus. He runs this house for his lord. He says – and I tell you exactly what he told me – that he can see that you are nobles. His master respects nobility, and is a great lord himself. You are to be his guests.' The interpreter paused to make sure that Armin understood. The boy studied the grey-haired Roman. The man had delicate hands and squinted.

The interpreter was gentle. 'If you are polite, you will be treated like Roman princes. If you are rude, you will be beaten. He asks whether you agree to this.'

Armin met the gaze of the steward. 'We agree.'

The interpreter relayed his answer.

'Then, he says, you are welcome to the house of Statilius Taurus.'

CHAPTER 8

7 CE (AUGUST)

BANK OF THE LUPIA, GERMANIA

THE PLACE WHERE ARMINIUS'S FATHER arranged to meet him was a ruined Valich fort. Arminius arrived there first. Two of his men accompanied him. The ramparts were overgrown with weeds and were partially washed into the old ditch. The fort commanded a formidable hill overlooking the upper reaches of the Lupia. It had no doubt been the seat of a major chief. Now it was the domain of trees a half-century old.

Arminius sat down on the rampart and stared out over the land. The river was tan hued and nearly obscured by trees. Pine and yew dominated the hill, and alder, willow and stunted birches fought for space by the water. He imagined the old village and the moorings for canoes, now surrendered back to the sweltering vegetation.

Arminius's scouts easily spotted Sigimer and his dozen warriors. The old man, alone among his party, wore a toga. He retained signs of the old culture – a thin gold torque around his throat and the old tattoo of the boar on his arm – but his hair was shorn in the Roman style and his beard shaved. There was grey at his temples. He carried fat beneath his chin. The skin beneath his eyes sagged. His face contained many new lines. There was an odd shape to Sigimer's toga. Arminius realised that he wore a mail cuirass.

Sigimer smiled brokenly when he saw Arminius. He struggled to dismount – a bodyguard had to help him. Arminius rose, but he did not walk down the rampart. Sigimer paused. Then he walked forward. He limped. He suddenly looked even older. After a few feet he stopped, and sought the eyes of the young stranger. 'What, will you let me walk to you all the way?' He used the Cheruscan dialect of Suebic.

A smile drifted across Arminius's features. 'No, Father, I come to you.' He descended the mound to the chieftain. There, he paused. He was uncertain which

29

etiquette to follow. He pressed his hand against his breastbone and bowed his head, as barbarians did to show respect. 'Father,' he said, in Latin.

His father asked in heavily accented Latin: 'How I know… it is you?'

'It is I, Father. Arminius. Your last words to me were "Never forget this" as you led me to the Roman general to be enslaved.'

'Slave?' Sigimer burst out, again using Latin, and then abandoning it for Suebic. His hand trembled as he touched Arminius's face. 'Look at you! You are a man, and a…' He wanted to use the word 'officer', but Suebic did not have that word. 'You are a leader.' He waved his hand, his lip quivering. 'I have heard great things about you!' He waved his hands about, the very gestures that the toga was supposed to prevent. 'How can you call yourself a slave?' He brushed past him and started up the slope. 'How is Frimunt?'

'He is called Flavus now,' Arminius replied, sure that his father would know this already. 'He is a good Roman, like me.' He followed Sigimer.

'They are very happy with you. The Romans told me. Your mother, Eysle, will be proud of you.'

'My mother's name is Hildreth. And there is no need to test me further.'

Sigimer shrugged. 'One can never be too sure.'

They reached the centre of the fortress, where formerly the chief's great hall had stood. It had been burned to its foundations. The benches and tables were long turned to ashes. The mead sacks had been torn and lost to time, the cups shattered. No harp had played here for decades, no stories sung.

Sigimer caught his breath as he gazed wistfully at the ruin. His upper body still appeared fit, his arms sinewy from sword practice.

'Your grandfather, Berinhard, burned this place down. He came here in the year that Gaul fell to the Roman, Caesar.' He smacked his lips. 'The Valich were in a mess. Half their warriors had gone to help their brothers in the great revolt under Vercingetorix. Many never returned. We swept into their lands.' He faced his son, his eyes warming. 'Your grandfather was a great chief. This place here was their last great fortress on the river. The Chatti asked for terms.' He paused, his eyes caressing the trees. 'Your grandfather agreed to spare the people, on condition that their chief gave him his daughter. On that day our Boar clan was born. This river is ours.'

'You told me this story when I was a child,' Arminius said, switching to Suebic for the first time. He felt a secret joy as the words crossed his lips – he nearly touched his mouth.

'I know,' Sigimer said absently. The wind swept up from the river and tugged at his toga. 'That was fifty-three years ago, and in that time, the Romans came. I always wonder, Armin, whether my father would have stopped them had he not been murdered.'

'Who knows?' Arminius replied, but he was certain that the old man would also have failed.

'We brought you here as a baby, to where his funeral pyre had been lit. Your grandmother had wanted his head to be preserved in oil to honour him, in the manner of her people, but we disposed of him according to the old ways. His ashes were scattered over the earth here. When you were small, the ground was still black where he had burned.' He searched the land for the spot. 'I rubbed your face with that blackened soil.'

'I do not remember.'

Sigimer shook his head sadly. 'Of course not,' he said, glancing back at their men. 'We are all good Romans now.' He smiled. 'And the years have been kinder to you than to me!' He again raised his hands, in a way that no Roman gentleman would do, and then let them drop. 'It is true that you guarded the Emperor? I could not believe it when they told me.'

'The Emperor is guarded by German troops,' Arminius said, slipping back to Latin, as if the topic was not suitable for Suebic.

'I was so proud! They told me when you commanded five hundred men in war. Your grandfather would be proud of you. All has not been lost.'

'We are part of something great now.' A gust stung Arminius's face.

'Yes, we are.' Sigimer looked at the sky. He did not speak for a while.

'Who was it that tried to kill you?' Arminius asked eventually.

'Kill me?' Sigimer looked down at his leg. 'Yes, they tried. I think that it was Cegestes, but I can prove nothing. They got away.'

'Who is Cegestes?'

'Of course, you would not know him. He is the leader of the Wolf clan. He is jealous of my rule over the tribe, and my friendship with the Romans. He wants to be paramount chief over the three clans.' He studied his son. 'You remember about the three clans?'

'Boar, Wolf and Bear.'

Sigimer smiled. 'I have been chief of the tribe since the war. To take it from me, they would have to kill me.'

'…Or have the Romans kill you.'

'Oh no, they would not do that! They know that they can trust me. I have proven it; and so have you. Did Cegestes have a son who would guard the Emperor? No, his boy is a shitty little priest at the Romans' temple in Colonia Agrippina!'

'And who rules the third clan, the Bear?'

'Kuonraet!' Sigimer spat. 'And he would have the Romans driven out tomorrow if he could.'

'*Could* the Romans be thrown out?'

'They still have three legions here, and that is after sending several south. That is thirty thousand men, permanently at arms, and armed very well.' He sighed. 'Moreover, we need the Romans now. Without them, your mother's people would swallow us.'

'How is my mother?'

'I have a new wife. Your mother is gone seventeen years. She never forgave me for giving you to the Romans. They tell me that she is a high priestess now to the Semnones, true to her mother's ancient line.' The chief cursed. 'I have to calm down the Roman generals every time her savages raid the province. She simply cannot understand! The Romans punish us all for what she does!'

'They do.'

'And what choice do we have, but to cooperate with them?'

'None. It is the best way.'

'Look at what they can offer us! You have seen Rome. I did the right thing to make peace with them!'

'You did, Father.'

Sigimer clenched his fists and glowered at the earth. 'We must be their friends.'

Arminius nodded. He said in Suebic, 'But the Romans will never be ours.'

CHAPTER 9

7 CE

Near Castra Octa, Germania

T HE COLUMN RODE ALONG A new Roman stone road into the valley of Castra Octa. The late-summer evening swarmed with insects. They reached the tree line as the sun dipped.

Before them, on the Amisia, Arminius saw good-sized fields of wheat and barley for the first time in Germania.

'It has been a struggle,' Sigimer reflected. 'As you might remember, our people traditionally do not plant much. The last ten years have seen the first great fields like these. But we cannot find workers for them – our people want their own patches. So we use slaves.'

They soon saw a file of near-naked, emaciated men shuffling towards the road. They were chained together by the neck, and bore the scars of old battles and abuse from the mounted Cheruscan guards.

'Slaves are cheap,' Sigimer said. 'We use Valich from Gaul. If they try to flee, they just end up prey for some itchy warrior band between here and the Rhenus.'

'Are there many of those left?' Arminius asked, paying little attention to the hollow-eyed field hands.

'Too many,' Sigimer sighed. 'Of course, nobody attacks the Romans around here, but I have to preside over some feud every week. We hope that the new governor will sort it out.'

Arminius noted the good quality of the road. It compared to some of the better provincial highways south of the Alps. 'What do you know about him?'

'He is a relative of the Emperor. He is to build law courts all over the province. Hopefully, the people will then obey Roman law rather than tribal law.' He shook his head. 'It is a struggle to make them see sense.'

Castra Octa lay to the south of the river, at a fork where streams from the hills to the east and south combined to form the Amisia. The Romans had erected a permanent fort, large enough to hold an entire legion, and supplied from the river by flat-bottomed boats – some of which were currently moored at the jetty nearby. The fort possessed double-turf and wood ramparts. The guard towers were mounted with ballistae that could hit any force trying to cross the nearby ford. From the walls, legionaries kept a wary eye. Within the fort, Arminius knew, were smithies, bathhouses, and offices, arranged in the same pattern employed all over the Empire.

The Cherusci hamlet to the west of the fort had no palisade. It consisted of about eighty haphazardly arranged longhouses. They looked like upturned ship's hulls, thatched with reeds and sod and with wattle-and-daub walls. Diagonal wooden struts supported the weight of the roofs. Smaller outbuildings surrounded the longhouses. The community bustled in the evening light.

The settlement comprised nearly two thousand inhabitants, Sigimer told him proudly. 'We are starting to convince the people to stop wandering. This is the furthest upriver that the Roman boats can come from the sea, so there is a lot of trade. And the Romans are establishing plantations along the river. Food is plentiful.'

They began to ford the river. A herd of the shaggy German cattle was watering a few hundred yards downstream. They were guarded by youths dressed in loincloths and carrying staves. The boys did not have their hair twisted in the traditional knot, as warriors did, but wore it loose and long. Tall, fleshy Cheruscan women gathered water nearby, and from a copse, others carried wood balanced on their heads. Smoke permeated the air. Scruffy dogs loitered with naked, long-limbed, blonde children delighting in the last, orange hues of day. Arminius doubted whether they had ever seen writing, or art, or heard of science.

Yet for all its filth, the forest's writ no longer ran here. For about a mile in every direction from the fort, there were almost no trees. The jungle had been sliced back by Roman iron, and the alluvial soil tilled with Roman tools. Four Roman-style warehouses serviced two big wooden jetties. He spotted some dark-skinned Roman traders in tunics, directing ruddy, blonde natives.

'It was built from nothing. They set up the fort and told us to come here. The Marser complained,' Sigimer chuckled, 'but they knew there was nothing to be done. Now they ply the river for the Romans.'

Arminius recognised the name. The Marser were a small tribe, whittled down during earlier conflicts to the point where the remnants survived only by managing trade between the Cherusci and their great enemies, the Chatti. When he was a boy, naughty children had been warned that they could end up bundled into one of the great flat-bottomed Marser canoes, to end up slaves to the Valich. There was a knot of them by the warehouses, shaven-haired, bearded brutes, their arms heavily tattooed up to the shoulders in blue and black – homage to their goddess Tanfana.

'Even the Marser are growing wealthy,' Sigimer noted. 'We are getting more people to settle along the river, and in towns. Too many still want to live in their holes in the sticks, but those that do come – we have the beginnings of a province here and all along the rivers to the west.'

Sigimer nodded as a Cheruscan male of about forty saluted him from the side of the road. The man did it in the native manner: pressing his fist in his palm and bringing his hands to his forehead. Other Cheruscans by the road also acknowledged their chief, but Sigimer did not slow down to speak to them.

Sigimer's grand hall was twice as long as the other longhouses. It stood within a palisade. Unlike the other buildings, the roof was neatly covered in baked tiles. The building's façade was a monstrosity: an imitation of a Roman villa, constructed from wood and stone. Arminius barely hid a smile at the ungainly homage. He could only imagine the Romans sniggering at the sight, as they would at his father's cheap toga.

Sigimer had sent warning of his approach. The courtyard was torch-lit. Upon the steps leading to a carved double door, a small party waited, dominated by a striking woman of about twenty years.

The woman was dressed in Roman style. A blue linen *stola* draped from her shoulders to her ankles. The dress was green, and she wore a gold chain necklace. Gold pins penetrated her long hair, done up in a semblance of the Roman mode. By her side were two children: a boy of five and a girl of three. They were also dressed like proper little Romans, in a blue tunic and red dress respectively, but were incongruously blonde. Arminius guessed their identity even before his father belatedly announced, 'This is my new wife, Imma.'

Arminius dismounted before her disdainful stare. While the girl sought the cover of her mother's dress and closed one eye shyly, the boy remained stiff lipped, until he saw one of Arminius's bodyguards. The child had never seen a black man before. Arminius smiled inwardly as the Kushite's smile made the child's stern exterior melt to amazement.

'Imma, this is my eldest son, Arminius,' Sigimer announced in Suebic. 'He is our guest.'

Arminius met the woman's icy stare.

'Welcome to this hall, Armin,' she said in a reedy tone, using primitive and halting Latin. The language stuck in her throat.

'Lady Imma,' Arminius began, switching to Suebic, 'I am pleased to meet the wife of my father.'

She did not reply and nor did his father speak. Servants waited around the edges. The scene appeared frozen. At its centre, the young woman remained imperious and unyielding.

Sigimer swore under his breath

'Lady,' Arminius, smiling softly, said in Suebic, 'I am eager to render you the respect that you deserve. I do not know the proper manners, though. If it is Roman ways you seek, I shall of course oblige, but of Cherusci manners I am ignorant.'

'I understand.'

He continued, 'I do know, however, that it is the custom here to ask the lady's permission to enter her home?'

'It is,' she replied.

He turned to his saddlebag, and produced a gift wrapped in calfskin. It was a very expensive brooch, done in the Roman way. He handed it over to her, bowing. 'May I have your hospitality, Lady Imma?'

She glanced at the wrapping, and then handed it to a servant next to her. 'You may.'

He thanked her, knelt down, and spoke briefly with the children. The girl remained skittish, refusing to reply even though softly prompted by her mother. The boy, though, was a simple matter. He had not taken his eyes off Obed, and Arminius took the child's hand and asked the Kushite soldier to dismount. The warrior lumbered over, his armour jangling, and then squatted before the child, who gaped as he touched the man's rich, dark skin. Obed rumbled a laugh. The boy giggled.

'Your brother has travelled the world,' Sigimer said. 'He no doubt has many strange tales to tell!'

Arminius raised the boy and tossed him into the air, winking at Obed. 'And I shall, I promise.'

For the first time, Imma smiled.

* * *

The interior of Sigimer's great hall was, by barbarian standards, impressive. The supporting beams were gargantuan and carved into intricate animal shapes. The floors were of smooth planks.

By the standards of Roman nobility, it was a hut.

The main chamber consisted of a sunken central pit, with open stone hearths. Smoke billowed through the room and, eventually, exited through holes cut in the roof. Around the pit were benches and tables instead of couches, enough to seat about a hundred people. The place stank of refuse. The walls had the odd touch of Rome – wall hangings purchased at great expense, but of laughable workmanship. Two cheap statues, one of Mercury and the other of Diana, stood on either side of a great, Roman-style wooden chair.

Alongside these Roman objects was a vast clutter: antlers, horns, and skulls of stags, aurochs and bison bulls, bears, and wolves. Piles of furs stank in alcoves behind the benches, waiting to receive guests glutted with wine and beer.

Arminius had seen such halls before on every fringe of the Empire.

'What do you think?' Sigimer asked. He had given up completely on Latin. His Suebic was dark like the forest soil.

'The Romans have been kind to you.'

'It is but a start,' Sigimer said, waving his hand expansively.

'The new building will impress.'

His father set him down on one of the benches closest to the throne-like chair, and barked for liquor. It was delivered in Roman-style glass goblets – though of exaggerated size to suit barbarian tastes. The servant girl bringing the liquor wore a tunic, as if she were part of a Roman household.

Lady Imma remained by the door, still uncertain. Her children moved halfway up the hall to stare at their half-brother. Sigimer quaffed the first goblet of wine without pause. The girl dutifully refilled it, even as Arminius took his first careful sip.

'What, don't you drink in the Roman army?' Wine flecked Sigimer's shaven chin.

'We do, and I hope we do tonight,' Arminius grinned, emptying his own glass. Frontier life had accustomed him to plonk.

His father promised that a feast would be held that night to celebrate his arrival. 'Did you hear that?' he shouted down the hall at his wife. 'Bring his men in, and let Inguiomer and the others know!' He slammed the table with his fist when she paused, then guffawed as she turned and stalked out. 'Silly wench. I adore her.'

The boy was creeping ever closer to them along the benches. His sister still held back.

'Come over here, Lamar,' Sigimer said after another gulp of wine. 'Come and meet your brother.' As the child came bounding up to his father's embrace, still warily glancing at Arminius, Sigimer laughed. 'You will join the men tonight. It is a night for us all to celebrate.' He let the boy have a bit of his wine. The child was revelling in the attention.

'Good to meet you,' Arminius said slowly.

The child giggled and buried his face in Sigimer's shoulder.

'No need to be shy!' Arminius assured him, as the boy whispered into his father's ear.

Sigimer roared with laughter. 'This one takes his mother's side. He says you speak our language like a baby!' Sigimer ruffled Lamar's hair. 'Perhaps you should teach your big brother to speak properly, then!'

Arminius's men were brought into the hall. Sigimer had them made comfortable. The servant girl came back to stoke the fire, which seemed to burn perpetually.

Then the mood changed. A warrior strode in, and it seemed as if the sky had darkened.

'Inguiomer,' Sigimer said.

Unlike Sigimer, this man had neither shaved his beard, nor shaved his hair, which he wore very long and piled up over his skull. He wore mail armour, but he donned a barbarian-style tunic and trousers. He carried his great sword, sheathed, in his left hand. Two similarly dressed brutes followed behind him.

Inguiomer halted a few feet away and studied Arminius. He had massive shoulders. His arms were enormous from wielding the great sword. He wore a necklace of boars' tusks.

'So *this* is little Armin, here to save us all from the Hairies?' He spat out the last word, using the army's derogative for barbarians in its original Latin.

'They're behind you,' Arminius quipped, not rising to his feet.

Inguiomer glared back.

Sigimer swore. Lamar scampered off a short distance and then paused to watch the confrontation unfold.

'This is my son.'

'War hero; killer of savages; guard to the Emperor. My, my, and now you are here.'

'Uncle,' Arminius began in Suebic.

'Still able to speak the old language?' Inguiomer snorted. He strutted around Arminius's back until he was standing on the other side of Sigimer.

'Do not do this,' Sigimer bit. 'You are being no better than Imma.'

Inguiomer growled, 'Ah, but she's pissing herself. I am just bemused.'

Arminius stared back. He had softened his gaze.

Inguiomer walked over to the great chair and leaned over its back.

'This is no way to welcome my son.'

Inguiomer did not even acknowledge his words. He was just glaring at Arminius. After an uncomfortable silence he said, 'Look at this chair.'

Arminius decided to play along.

'This *Roman* chair – it is very expensive.' Inguiomer slapped the armrest. 'It is a throne by comparison to the benches around it. Coming in here, who would you guess sits in such a chair?'

'A king,' Arminius replied nonchalantly.

'The Cherusci do not have kings. This is a Cherusci hall. So who sits in the chair?'

'The chief.'

'Do you remember your father sitting in such a chair?'

'There was no throne. The men sat in a great circle, on benches.'

Inguiomer smiled. 'You have a good memory. Yes, there was no throne, because the Cherusci have no men who sit on thrones.' He paused. 'Why then did you Romans give us this expensive thing, to place at the head of our hall? Who is to sit in it?'

'Who sits upon it now?'

'No one. When the Romans send an officer, he has it, but otherwise it stands empty. No Cheruscan will sit in it. Not even your father. Not even I, a great warrior.'

Sigimer glared into his goblet.

'Am I not a great warrior, brother?' Inguiomer continued.

'You are.'

'Yes, I have saved my brother's life, and defended his name eighteen times in single combat. My brother has grown fat. I kill still. My name is known as far north as the sea, and as far south as the mountains.' His voice thundered. 'I am Inguiomer *su eb* Berinhard *eb* Thunald *eb* Wulfan *eb* Hildmaden *ev* Bornslech, Slayer of Valich. My line is warriors and priestesses, back through the Frost Time, back to Mannus and the flame of Tuisto, God-hero, born by the Heaven Tree. Who are *you*?'

'Inguiomer!' Sigimer snapped, slamming his hand onto the table.

'Are you here to be my king?'

'No. I am not.'

'Rome sent you.'

'It did.'

'To sit on that throne?'

'No. I am here to crush the enemies of my people.'

'And who are they?'

'All those who oppose my clan's prosperity, *Uncle*. Those who offend the *Pax Romana*.'

Inguiomer pressed the tip of his sword into a nearby bench, and leaned upon the blade. He nodded, 'Well, young Armin, do not be fooled by shaven hair, nor trinkets and imported wine, or Roman boats upon the stream, or the slave-worked fields. The forest is a big, big place.' Inguiomer's eyes shifted to Sigimer again. 'Let's feast tonight. This boy is a stranger. We might as well make him welcome.' He raised his sword onto his left shoulder, and stared at Arminius. 'Remember: no kings.'

'I understand.' Arminius used Suebic. He ordered the serving girl over, and poured wine into his own goblet. Then he walked over to Inguiomer, and, taking a sip from it himself, offered the old warrior the cup.

Inguiomer's eyes narrowed, but he took the goblet and drained it. 'Now,' he said, as he returned the cup, 'Tell me of Rome.'

* * *

Other men filed into the hall. Some were hulking warriors; others old men, whose hair-knots were smaller and collected at their temples. They came for the venison, the suckling pigs and birds on wooden plates. Most of all, they came for the vast amounts of *beor* and imported wine. They approached Sigimer, and pressed their palms to their foreheads in greeting. He took their hands and shook them between his. For Arminius, they had little to say. They nodded to him, as they would to a Roman, keeping their hands by their sides. They arrayed themselves on the benches, and the serving girls brought them drink. A *scop* appeared, to sing of ancient battles and long-dead heroes, strumming a harp as he recited his poetry.

Arminius gave himself over to drink, guarded by Arbex and Obed, whom he had secretly ordered to remain sober. The fire, lit along the length of the central pit, blasted heat. Men would get up from the benches – sometimes standing on them – and urinate into the hearth. The fire also received the bones picked clean of flesh.

The men – there were no women, except for the slave girls – drank, bursting into communal songs. Once or twice, men grappled violently amid cheers. As the night drew late, some collapsed over the tables, and others withdrew into the alcoves. Eventually, a few simply slid onto the floor amid the piss and vomit, where hounds growled for scraps.

Throughout, the throne remained empty.

One moment stood out for Arminius. His father leaned over to him, his speech slurred. 'When I was a young man,' Sigimer said, 'I visited Gaul. The Romans had torn through it thirty years before. The Valich said that before the Romans came, their warriors had iron swords and spears, and armour. Timber and stone had surrounded their great towns. Their chiefs used writing and coining, and had traded with the world. To them, we were poor and backward. Yet the Romans had conquered them in *four years*. Four years. I realised that Rome is to those towns as the forest is to a copse. And when our time came, I knew that we could not defeat them.' Anguish filled his drunken gaze. 'I made the right decision?' He was drooling liquor. 'I did?'

'Yes. You made the very best.'

CHAPTER 10

7 CE (AUGUST)
CASTRA OCTA

ARMINIUS AWOKE DRAPED OVER A table and surrounded by the detritus of the feast. He had a ferocious headache. Around him, almost a hundred men were sprawled. The smell was foul. He rose, fighting nausea. The wine that the barbarians bought from the Romans was poor, and they did not bother to water it down.

The morning light was almost blinding as he staggered out, looking for a washhouse. There was none. He found a pit in one corner of the compound. It had a wooden railing, over which a barbarian woman was already squatting for a shit. She barely blinked when she saw him, finished her business, and drew her skirt down without cleaning her arse. He shat, wishing that a sponge, or an old piece of cloth, was available. It was one thing to rough it in the field, but quite another to walk around filthy in one's own house. He did not hold out any hope for a bathhouse. He would use of the local fort's amenities when he went to greet the commander.

Sigimer's compound seemed like an open sewer. Not that they would understand what a "sewer" even was, he thought.

The household was already alive with servants. They greeted him – his identity was by now generally known. He wondered how many of these people had played with him as a child.

Imma awaited him on the stairs to the hall entrance. He slowed his pace to give himself time to study her. Her skin was freckled, and she had blue eyes. Her hair was carefully combed. She still affected Roman dress. Her hair was coiffured to reflect her marital and social status. By the standards of her people, she was a great beauty. Compared to Rome's ideal of petite, fine-featured, coal-eyed beauties she was too tall, too heavy-boned – the kind of woman you would use to breed field slaves.

42

And, despite her beauty, she was no queen. His mother had been a queen.

Imma still looked wary of him. A young girl accompanied her. She held a clay ewer and a wooden charger, on which lay an oblong bread loaf. The girl's blonde hair was tied into two pigtails, united into one behind her back. A design resembling a sun, or wavy-petal flower, had been tattooed in blue upon her bare left shoulder. She kept her eyes averted.

'Arminius,' Imma said in Latin, before continuing in Suebic, 'I hope that you enjoyed the feast.'

'I did, thank you. Your house is most generous, Lady.' He placed his right arm on his heart.

Her mouth twitched. 'It is *customary*,' she said, 'for the lady of the house to offer milk and bread to a guest on his first morning in her home.' Imma paused, smiling politely. 'I tell you this because you are unfamiliar with our ways.'

'I shall learn, Lady.'

'It is considered an honour for the lady to serve the guest herself.'

'I am most honoured.'

She took the pitcher. 'It is customary to drain the cup.'

He took the pitcher from her, careful not to let his hand touch hers, and brought it to his lips. No doubt, he thought, it was also to test the ability of the guest to stand the previous night's drinking.

The milk was still warm. Some of it dribbled down the side of his mouth. Breaking wind, as was the barbarian custom, he handed the pitcher back and thanked her.

The lady waited, and then sighed. 'I look forward to the day when you know our ways properly.' Later, he would learn that he was supposed to have commented on the fertility of the land at this point.

She broke the bread, and passed him a piece. It was delicious.

'You should offer the host some of the bread. But I do understand that you have been away long.'

'Thank you for being so patient.'

She smiled.

'You must forgive me, though, if I cannot treat you as my mother.'

'I understand.' Worry crept back into her eyes.

'I can only guess, but if you are concerned for yourself and your children, let me reassure you.'

She nodded. 'I am not sure what becomes of them now that you have returned.'

'They are my father's children, my siblings.' He smiled kindly, and then changed the subject. 'Did you know my mother?'

'I was very young when she left for her people, though others have spoken of her frequently.'

'Has she communicated with you?'

'She sent me a wedding gift, and gifts upon the birth of my daughter.' Imma looked bashful. 'Hildreth *ev* Eysle is a formidable woman. She could have hated me for taking her place in your father's bed. I think that she does not care.'

'They broke badly?'

'They have not spoken in seventeen years. She fights Rome, and he does not.'

'Then my mother is my enemy. What do you think of Rome?'

'I stand by my husband's side.'

He thanked her again for the food. She left. He waited outside the hall, enjoying the sunlight.

His father exited the hall eventually, stinking but remarkably cheerful. 'You drink well,' he said, his face wrinkled in a smile.

'And you serve good drink,' Arminius lied with a grin. He related his conversation with Imma to Sigimer.

'You will have put her at ease a little.'

Sigimer explained that they would be meeting his advisors later that morning. His father went to urinate, and then strolled with him through the village. Sigimer had to stop often to speak to the people. He seemed popular, but the limp from his old wound told a different story.

* * *

They met the chief's advisors in front of Sigimer's private chambers. Two men sat on logs in an open-air antechamber. Inguiomer stood at the back.

Caglem was diminutive and stooped, despite being only in his early fifties. He possessed the manner of a Roman small-time philosopher, and squinted at Arminius. Hlutheir was barrel-chested and hairy, with bushy eyebrows and a shadowy beard. Their hair was cut in the Roman style, but they wore the Cherusci tunic and breeches.

Preliminaries were perfunctory. 'We need to know what your purpose is here, Armin,' Caglem stated bluntly. 'Are you Roman or Cherusci?'

Arminius pointed out that, even judging by their own appearance, the line between Romans and Cherusci had blurred.

'That is true,' Caglem said sagely. 'But you should not be fooled by superficial things.'

'Inguiomer said that, yes.'

'You have been sent here by the Romans, and although you are Sigimer's son, we do not know what orders you have, or which side you are on.'

'I was not aware that we are on a different side from the Romans.'

'They are our masters, and our ways are *utterly* different.'

'There are many differences, yes.'

Hlutheir stated in a gravelly voice, 'I watched you last night, and sent my daughter Imma to test you this morning. You were courteous. You seem like a man who still respects us.'

'I do respect the tribe.'

'The people deserve respect,' Hlutheir said.

'The Cherusci are the loyal allies of Rome. That makes my task easier.'

'What is your task?' Caglem asked.

He had to admit that he was not sure. He explained how the assassination attempt on his father had apparently prompted the Romans to reassign him. 'But I do not know what happens from here.'

'Things will stay as they are?' Caglem enquired.

'Rome will continue to build. There is a new governor coming, as you might know. I shall do what he asks.'

'But will you speak for us?' Hlutheir asked.

'I shall.'

'We are happy to cooperate with the Romans, if they respect our ways.'

'I understand.'

Hlutheir continued, 'They let us worship our own gods. They bring us roads that make travel easier; larger trade depots with more goods; bigger farms with more food. I do not deny that. And unlike Inguiomer, I am glad that these things are here.'

Inguiomer snorted at the back. He was still holding his sword.

Hlutheir eyed him, but continued, 'The Romans' innovations do not, however, compensate for our loss. We are no longer a free people.'

'You are free, as long as you obey Rome.'

'There can be no freedom based on obedience and fear. Rome needs to know our limits,' Caglem said, looking uneasy. 'You must help us to tell them.'

'Are you reaching your limits?'

Caglem cleared his throat. 'Some of us have.'

Sigimer was hunched over, seemingly detached from the discussion.

'I am *not* here to be part of a rebellion.'

'There is no rebellion among us,' Caglem replied, exasperated. 'Even Inguiomer fights for the Romans, and is under constant threat of death because of it! We ask only for respect for the people.'

Arminius eyed his father. Sigimer did not make eye contact. 'Tell me of your grievances.'

'There are many,' Hlutheir told him, squaring his shoulders.

'Tell me of the most important,' Arminius said. Caglem's and Hlutheir's eyes met.

'I shall give you one,' Caglem said. 'It might surprise you.'

'Continue.'

'The Cherusci is very… loose. At its basis, it is composed of family groups. They group together in territories, called hundreds.'

Armin nodded.

'These hundreds build only temporary villages. They make decisions through a vote of all their adults, both men and women. However, hundreds cannot defend themselves. Therefore, they belong to clans. Clans used to make decisions through men sent by the hundreds. Clans appointed leaders during war, for the duration of that war *only*. During peace, the women dominated, through ritual and custom.'

Ariminius realised that Inguiomer was glaring at him. He returned the man's gaze.

'Now, let us consider the way the Romans rule us. Hundreds must live in permanent villages. The Romans decide where these villages should be, and they approve the headman. The clans are designated capitals. No more migrations. Our customs may exist only if they do not conflict with their laws. They even license ironsmiths! If you want to fight, you have to join one of their auxiliary units and leave the forest altogether! They pick permanent "big men" to run the clans. Assemblies are few, and closely watched. Our priestesses are either pretending to be mere healers, or they have fled to the Semnones, where the Romans dare not yet go.'

Sigimer interrupted. 'I am one of those "big men". We give the people roads, and goods, and peace, but they are unhappy. The men that tried to kill me were Cherusci. Others will try again.'

'And I too have been attacked, for being a traitor to the people,' Inguiomer said pensively.

Hlutheir added, 'The people are unhappy, and what are we supposed to do? Eventually, they will rebel, or they will embrace Rome and cease to be *us*. Either way, the people will die. What will you do to help us?'

Silence descended, and Arminius considered his reply. Finally, he said, 'I shall serve Rome.'

CHAPTER 11

7 CE (AUGUST)

CASTRA OCTA

THE COMMANDING OFFICER AT CASTRA Octa, Lucius Caedicius, was delighted to meet Arminius, who carried letters of introduction from General Aius Caecina Severus.

Caedicius was jovial, rotund and hirsute. He was also courteous, and immediately offered Arminius a bath.

'The fort has stood for seven years, and we had proper baths installed as quickly as possible.'

The stone bathhouse was luxurious by frontier standards, capable of seating twenty men and composed of hot and cold pools. Slaves stoked the fires under the steaming *caldarium*. 'I would not be able to stand it otherwise,' Caedicius continued as he stripped off his tunic and cast it aside at a slave. She was a foreign import, probably from Asia. It was not customary to have female attendants in a bathhouse, as Arminius pointed out.

'It allays the barbarians' fears. None has *ever* accepted our invitation. Bathing is incomprehensible to them, and they are also obsessed with sex. When one of my predecessors used male attendants, it caused a riot. They have strict rules that men only fuck women and horses!' He laughed, and lay down on one of the benches in the antechamber.

Arminius also lay down, and one of the slaves started applying oil to his back.

'In any event, it is a good change. Slaves are so cheap here that you can buy a new one every month. We normally just screw them a few times and then sell them when they get full-bellied.'

Arminius grunted as the Asian slave scraped the oil off his shoulder blades with a *strigil*.

'When is the last time you had a good wash?'

'Weeks,' Arminius admitted. Romans did not count the odd dip in a river as bathing.

'That won't make you stand out here.'

'Even my father stinks.'

'Indeed. Some of them try to be Roman, but you might as well dress up one of those Iberian apes in a toga.'

Arminius agreed.

They chatted. Caedicius was disappointed that Arminius had not seen the capital in over two years. Nonetheless, the commander had been on the frontier for six years, and news about the theatre, chariot racing and gladiators, and scandal among the rich and noble, made him laugh. He missed reading. 'Mail can only get through during the warm months, and even then, all news is weeks out of date.'

They shaved their beards, and then stepped naked into the hot bath. Arminius swore with pleasure at the warmth. He still remembered the first time he saw a proper Roman bath. The notion of anybody having a pool of hot water big enough to swim in had astounded him.

'I hear that major construction projects are starting,' Arminius noted as they drifted, neck-deep, in the pool.

'Yes. We are getting a civilian governor for the first time. He has big plans.'

Arminius asked whether there were still any problems with the natives.

'There are too many things that we disagree on! I suppose it is the same with all new provinces, but these people are particularly primitive. They have no concept of land ownership, no writing, and no history of administration. Even the Gauls had *that*! We have outlawed raiding, but we *still* find them nailing corpses to trees. They mock us for bathing, while beating to death people who wear the wrong hairstyle! And their women run around as if they own the place.'

'How much fighting is there still going on?' Arminius enquired lazily. He told Caedicius that he had seen armed Chatti tribesmen on the way north, and about the massacre of the Roman detachment.

'We get headhunting, blood feuds, and even human sacrifice. That does not even take into account raids by the unconquered tribes like the Semnones and Marcomanni.'

'And after seventeen years the legions have not stopped this?'

'I shall put it this way,' Caedicius said, raising his hand out of the water and spreading his fingers. Droplets jewelled off his skin in the torchlight. 'Think of our presence here as a hand.' He held his thumb up. 'My arm is Gaul, which has been quiet for over fifty years now, and which started off with far more civilisation than this cesspit. My palm is the Rhenus, which is our main supply route from the south, and the civilised areas around it. Here there are towns such as Colonia Agrippina, Moguntiacum, Neuss and Vetera, up to Vechten. Now, think of my fingers and thumb as the rivers leading west to east or, in the case of the Amisia here, south to north. We use the rivers as our main means of transport. The legions have flat-bottomed boats and even galleys on each river, and roads parallel to all the streams. We can march troops along these axes. But away from the rivers, between my fingers, the forest and marsh is too dense to allow major manoeuvres. So, what do we do?'

Arminius studied the model. 'You make the barbarians live by the rivers, and you build forts alongside them. And you build roads. But you need to patrol the gaps.'

'Numonius Vala, whom you met, runs reconnaissance patrols. The legions proper alternate between a defensive posture in the winter, when they retreat to the rivers, and offensive operations in the summer, when they march east. That is where my legion, the Eighteenth, currently is: killing Semnones on the Albis.'

They discussed other rules: smiths and iron mines were watched, as were metal imports.

'They have few iron deposits here. Some groups even use stone and wood for weapons! We give them every reason to settle down. If they work along with us, we leave them alone but for taxes. If they do not, we send a detachment, *immediately*, and wipe out the village nearest to the problem area. It also keeps the slave markets supplied.'

'Standard procedure.'

'Except for the Unwashed, living in the deep forest eating shit, we are making progress. We are not loved, but most of them stick to killing one another. We are whipping this place into a province.' He eyed one of the slaves. 'Some of us are even having a fair time of it.'

Arminius followed his gaze. He felt relaxed.

CHAPTER 12

ARMINIUS LED HIS BODYGUARD WESTWARDS into the hills. Within a mile, they were back in the dense woods, the only sign of man being the path. In places, Arminius could touch the trees on both sides of the path. Travelling in single file felt intensely solitary. Birds, and the occasional roars of stags, provided the only reprieve from what resembled immersion in a dank, green pool.

After a day, they entered the headwaters of the Lupia. Here, the Roman footprint became more significant. The first sign was a white Roman route marker. A few miles further, the party happened upon a surveyor team with a star-shaped *groma*. The Romans were delighted to meet the auxiliaries – the desolation was turning them feral, they laughed.

A further five miles to the west they encountered local men building the road, under the instruction of army engineers, digging out the sods and tree roots, and laying stones for drainage and gravel and pavestones on the surface. The road crept east to connect Castra Octa to civilisation. The highway ran parallel to the Lupia, and the traffic gradually became more dense, the settlements more regular. Stone buildings appeared – status symbols, given the proliferation of local timber. Herdboys wearing cheap, imported trinkets tended animals on meadows by the stream. Plantations came into view, dominated by sturdy Roman-style farmhouses and worked by gangs of slaves and native tenants under Roman overseers. The atmosphere gradually became more civilised.

Aliso was a surprise nonetheless. The garrison boom town was bigger than Castra Octa, and sprawled by an enormous sod-and-timber fort, protected on one side by the Lupia. Although there were rambling timber slums for the barbarians on the settlement's outskirts, an earthen rampart also surrounded the town proper and its four thousand inhabitants. Inside the town, the streets were of flagstones or logs, the buildings were stone with tile roofs, and there was even a sewage and water supply system. The town featured a temple dedicated to Apollo, and a rambling market. Here, spices from the desert south met furs from animals that lived in the perpetual northern snows. People of every colour and faith in the Empire rubbed shoulders. Merely by riding among the stalls, Arminius heard half a dozen languages over the cacophony produced by livestock and birds.

The fort was named Castra Drusus, after the stepson of the Emperor Augustus, who had died on campaign in Germania sixteen years before. It was as large as the town itself, and attached to its one corner like an interlocking chain. It was the largest building Germania had ever seen.

Arminius immediately gained admission to the fort. His letters of introduction and his uniform – he had put on the regalia of a Praefectus of Cavalry for the last leg of the trip – left no doubt as to his status. He demanded a bath and fresh clothes for his men and himself. He then sent word to the commander that he had arrived.

The opportunity to meet General Sentius Saturninus, supreme military commander of Germania, came over dinner. Saturninus descended from one of the great families of Rome, and he resembled the archetypal senator – his position before the Emperor Augustus had sent him to Germania. He was of towering stature, rake-thin, slightly stooped, and bald. His eyes betokened iron will and penetrating intellect. His subordinate, Legate Marcus Vinicius, Commander of the Eighteenth Legion, was bull-necked and bronzed. His nose had been broken repeatedly, and had set badly.

'We are very happy to have you here,' General Saturninus stated in clipped, patrician tones, as they waited for dinner in the general's antechamber. 'Your letter of introduction merely confirmed reports of you from my old friend Aius Caecina. How goes it in Pannonia?'

Arminius gave a brief, professional account of the campaign to the assembly, ending with 'We certainly cannot attack the Marcomanni within the next three years, Sir.'

'It is that bad?' Saturninus enquired, swirling his wine in his drinking cup.

'Pannonia will draw in most of the army.'

'Not something to tell the barbarians,' Vinicius growled.

'We don't seem to have much to fear from these people, despite the attempt on my father's life.'

'Sigimer is a good and loyal man.'

Saturninus asked him about his time with Sigimer, and he relayed the conversation with the advisors. The general listened carefully. Vinicius took a gulp of wine and beckoned to a slave for a refill.

'These complaints are not new.'

'They hope that the new governor will calm the people,' Arminius replied. He noted a glance passing between Vinicius and Saturninus.

'The *people* are unlikely to get sympathy,' Saturninus replied. 'We are about to experience a major influx of investment into Germania. The new governor will be ruthless to secure that investment.'

He told the story of how the new governor had responded to a Jewish revolt while in charge of Syria. After his legions had slaughtered thousands of rebels and their families, he had crucified two thousand along the road from the coast to Hierosolyma. 'He is a fast-acting, determined man. And the army will follow his orders – whether they are to give babies trinkets or to nail them to trees.'

'I am sure that the Cherusci will accept peace, Sir.'

'Let us hope so,' Saturninus responded, and then adjourned them all to the couches arranged around tables groaning with food. Arminius was included in the top table with Saturninus and Vinicius. He lay down opposite them.

'It is a great change, yes,' Saturninus reflected in response to a question from Arminius. 'But we will adapt to civilian control.'

Vinicius added gruffly, 'The governor has sent an advance party of bureaucrats. They are annoying, but then these people always are.' He took a cut of venison, dipped it in sauce, and gnawed on it. 'At least they have agreed with our strategy.'

'Which is what?'

Vinicius grunted. He took the edge of his white toga, where it fell over his left shoulder, and straightened it. Then he dipped his hand into his bowl of wine and splashed it over the toga. The dashes of red liquid penetrated the fabric, and, as the droplets were absorbed, spread from the centres of impact. 'In the same way, we douse the barbarians in culture and watch it spread. The idea is that the dots will eventually merge. If they resist, we strike immediately and wipe out the rebels.' He shrugged. 'It has worked very well in Gaul and Iberia.'

'Not so in Illyria,' Arminius mused out loud.

'There the problem was tax farming and land grabbing by Romans,' Saturninus said sagely. 'We are not making the same mistakes here. We are giving these savages many incentives.'

'You are,' Arminius remarked, 'but you should not be nailing babies to trees, to use your turn of phrase.' He looked around the table. 'I have just helped crucify thousands in Illyria. It is a filthy business, and whatever the governor succeeded in doing against the Jews, he must not try such methods here. It will lose us ground we have already gained.'

'So what do you suggest?' Saturninus enquired, with patient condescension.

'I was very impressed by Numonius Vala. His patrols should be expanded.' He raised his voice slightly. 'You do not need cohorts lumbering along forest paths to obliterate villages. You need fast action led by proper intelligence. You should eliminate the precise source of any opposition, rather than stoke it. That is the key to building a province.'

There was silence in the circle. Then Saturninus remarked, 'Numonius Vala is a good soldier.'

* * *

Arminius received private quarters and a valet slave, but spent the next day without much to do. It seemed as if the army, having sent him all the way to Aliso, now needed to work out what exactly to do with him.

The fort was busy. The Eighteenth Legion had been garrisoning the province over the summer while the Seventeenth and Nineteenth had campaigned against the Semnones. Now, as autumn approached, the sister legions were marching back to their winter quarters. On their way, they would temporarily join the Eighteenth in Aliso for the big event of the year: the arrival of the province's first civilian governor. A ceremonial parade would welcome Varus. The officers were in a high state of nervousness, and their anxieties easily transmuted into fatigues for the legionaries: polishing, scrubbing and drill.

The weather did not help. Around noon, the first of the autumn storms struck. At first, Arminius, strolling on the ramparts, saw only a black smear along the western horizon. The sky was otherwise virtually cloudless. Air then began to move with increasing speed as the bank scythed towards the fort. It became more humid. Thunder began to play among the billowing cloud pillars. In the parade ground, men and animals rushed inside. Arminius, withdrawing into a guard tower, watched the clouds dominate the western sky. Gusts rippled through the trees.

The storm struck with sledgehammer force. Flags were torn, along with washing left by careless matrons or unlucky soldiers. Trees bent, creaking, and sometimes lost the struggle, whole branches tearing off and adding to the wall of leaves and tepid, heavy raindrops that deluged the settlement. On the river, waves rose as the current, beating into the wind, turned in on itself. A galley tore free from its moorings, and spray and ripples washed into other vessels.

The skies opened. Sheets of water first turned the distant forest grey, and then slashed visibility to a few yards, forcing men behind stout wooden doors, or making them slip in the quagmire of the parade ground.

Arminius hid with a squad of cursing sentries.

'Happens every damn year,' one veteran grumbled, water dripping from his red military kilt. 'Another month of this and then we will get the snow!'

It was an exaggeration, but only just. Within a month, Arminius knew, the temperature would drop and the storms would come from the east.

'Every damn year,' the sentry repeated.

The afternoon brought progress. The previous evening, Arminius had asked Saturninus for permission to peruse the fort's records, housed in the map room. A team of military scribes, led by a retired centurion called Banno, managed the system. Banno, who was missing his right eye from an old arrow wound, explained the system with enthusiasm. They received everything from unit reports to sketches and plans by engineers, and tax records.

'Those ones over there,' he said, pointing out a cluster of men sitting around a particularly laden table, 'are from the governor's advance party.' They were auditing army accounts, the veteran noted with distaste.

Banno warmed to Arminius, and showed him the great map placed on a table in the centre of the room. 'It is the pride of General Saturninus and Praefectus Numonius Vala.' It was a schema of the entire German theatre. Dominating the southern half, just north of the Alps, was the Hercynian Forest, starting in Gaul and disappearing off the eastern side of the map. To the north, the land was described as "open" or "marshy". Vala had indicated the territory of each conquered tribe. The Marcomanni and Semnones menaced beyond the border, which he had indicated with pins and twine – no doubt in the anticipation of moving the pins. Each major tribal settlement and each Roman fort was indicated with different coloured pins, as were points where enemy raiding parties had struck. The three legions, and major detachments, were represented by moveable stone pieces. Arminius was impressed by the detail.

The general had given permission that Arminius could read any document kept in the main map room. Banno enquired what Arminius would like to see first.

'Bring me the tax records for Castra Octa. The district chief is called Sigimer.'

CHAPTER 13

9–8 BCE

ROME

THE INTERIOR OF STATILIUS TAURUS'S house was cool and quiet. Its floors were of stone, its walls smooth and bright. Red potsherds covered the roof. A tranquil garden lay at its centre, and sleek cats lazed there in the summer sun. There were pillars bearing stern stone heads. The boys received a room at the back of the house, where the smell of food was strong. It had a door, but they could not lock it. Slaves took their dirty clothes. The boys were washed, dressed in new tunics, and fed. The old steward watched them all the time.

Frimunt did not sleep well for several nights.

The boys did not speak Latin. All members of the household were instructed to communicate with them in the Roman tongue. They were beaten if they did not learn. They were also beaten if anybody heard them speak Suebic. Armin's name became Arminius. Frimunt received the name Flavus. They were forbidden their old names, even in private.

Frimunt became ill. He had a terrible fever, and thrashed in his bed for a day before they called a healer to see to him. The man wore a necklace with two twisting snakes of bronze. Frimunt screamed until they took the man with the snakes away.

* * *

Quintus kept notes regarding the children's progress. The little one responded first. He was grateful to be fed and petrified of the lash. At first, Arminius was broody and resentful. He remained vigilant, and close to his brother. He had the habit of holding the gaze of whoever spoke to him. This unnerved even Quintus. However, both boys made a rapid, if not enthusiastic, acquisition of Latin. It turned out that they were both bright indeed, especially the older one. Even Arminius started haltingly to ask questions. There was much to learn, and Quintus answered his questions dutifully: free Romans wore a toga, preferably of white cloth, whereas unfree men and the poor wore brown. Children were not fully human, and to become human, they had to be harshly taught. Women were inferior to men: their only role was to serve or bear children. Slaves had no rights. The body reflected a person's morality: daily bathing was vital; and grime, stench, and excess hair had to be removed. Important men did not speak with their hands, and kept their faces still. Your body made clear what happened in your mind. This was *cultus*, which set civilised people apart from barbarians.

Quintus began to believe, by the end of the first year, that the boys were becoming Romans. Then, one day, when the boys were away, a slave brought him a knife, found hidden in the boys' room. The blade was small, about the length of a man's hand, and rusted, but filed sharp. The slave reported that they had also found a small drawing of a pig scratched into the stone next to the little one's bed.

Quintus was disappointed. Little Flavus, with his mop of blond hair that defied the barbers, had been smiling more often. Even his stern older brother had become compliant.

He felt like a fool. He kept the knife. They would not mention the find, and the boys would not be beaten. Instead, he summoned a tutor to the house. Several senatorial families recommended the man, a Latin-speaking Greek called Cleon.

'Are they tractable?' Cleon enquired. He was in his early fifties, and had the grave manner of a scholar.

'They are not completely convinced yet.'

He took Cleon to the boys. When they found them, the elder boy was standing close to the window, staring at the furrowed bark of a poplar tree.

The little boy looked up nervously, while the elder kept ignoring them.

The Greek sonorously announced himself as their tutor. 'You will learn how to use your minds.'

Quintus studied their responses. The youngest boy averted his gaze to watch his feet dangling off the chair.

The elder boy's eyes fixed upon Cleon, and narrowed slightly.

* * *

7 CE (EARLY SEPTEMBER)

The governor was delayed by the weather, and because he insisted that his retinue travel by the new road between Castra Drusus and Vetera.

Days passed. The last elements of the Eighteenth Legion filtered into the fort, until it was bursting with five and a half thousand legionaries and the same number of auxiliaries: Africans, Egyptians, Iberians, and Asians. There was even a squadron of lance-bearing Sarmatian mercenary cavalrymen. The other two legions arrived: first the Seventeenth, then the Nineteenth. Each pitched a temporary fort close to Castra Drusus. Thirty thousand men filled the valley like a human lake. Banners; and the red, green, and blue shields of the three legions added colour. Aliso brimmed with camp followers and diverse refuse.

Among the new arrivals was Numonius Vala. He sought Arminius out the day after his arrival, and found him sitting on one of the logs set by the parade ground, watching hundreds of legionaries drill.

'I hear that you have been frequenting the map room.' Vala looked vibrant, at ease, with confident warmth in his eyes. 'I am impressed. Not many young officers would while their time away in a library.'

Arminius laughed genially. 'I wanted to know what was going on.'

Vala invited him for a drink. As they strolled along the barracks, Arminius asked him how the patrol had fared.

'It was the usual thing: young men eager for a fight, coming up against professionals – no match. The boys brought in a sack of ears.'

They entered the centurions' mess. Vala knew the name of every man he passed, and made small talk. Arminius had been in the army long enough to know that most officers would have received a cold reception in this sanctuary. Instead, the centurions served Vala and his guest *beor* from their own allotment.

'So what did you learn?' Vala enquired as they settled at a corner table. The slab of oak was incised with fifteen years of drunken graffiti.

'You will be disappointed.'

'Entertain me.'

'I studied tax returns.'

Vala took a deep draught from his *beor* and wiped his lips. 'That is *indeed* strange.'

'I wanted to know what paid for all of this.'

'And…?'

'The province is not turning a profit.'

'*My.*'

Arminius pushed on. 'My father pays the tax for his district, his clan; and so do most other district chiefs.'

'And all this does not cover the cost of occupying the place? You are surprised?'

'After eighteen years of occupation? When *is* the province supposed to start paying for itself?'

Vala snorted. 'People have worked this out with far less work. But you should be admired for checking your facts.' He leaned back, draining his cup, and reached for the flagon. 'So, the administration is corrupt. That is normal.'

'Even before the new governor arrives?'

Vala stopped pouring. He stared at Arminius with dark eyes.

'Surely, talk about this man must have spread?' Arminius asked, lowering his voice. 'General Saturninus is on edge. They know what kind of man they are getting.'

Vala sighed and then smiled wanly. 'I shall have to get far drunker before I can have this conversation.'

'You are not the kind of man who gets that drunk.'

Vala put his cup down and leaned back, holding on to the table. He stared pensively at Arminius, and the other let the silence grow. Vala finally said, 'No, I am not. And I do not occupy myself with governors' business.'

'Nor do I; but I am an army man. This corruption is threatening its work. That makes it my business.'

Vala lowered his gaze. He pursed his lips. Finally he said, 'Come with me.'

They did not speak again, but for perfunctory instructions, until they were riding west.

'I am impressed by your reading of the tax records. It speaks volumes for your insight.'

'Gold is the sinews of war.'

'Indeed. So let me reward you, and hope that you do well with the information. The army *is* unhappy. And by army I mean the professional heart, not the hangers-on.' He let the words drift. 'We know all about Varus, and his corruption, and that the Emperor is sending him here to cool down. Perhaps the Emperor thinks that he can do least damage in Germania.'

They continued along the immaculate highway. In the distance, a wagon was approaching.

Vala continued to speak once the traders had passed. 'On the other hand, we receive all the equipment we need, and all the men. Every casualty is made up. Our forts are excellent, and every request for military highways has been approved. Man for man, unit for unit, this is the best army in the Empire – anywhere in the Empire.'

'They left the best legions behind when the rest went to Pannonia.'

'Indeed. However, as with any other military operation, we must pay our costs. And given that this is a bog, with virtually no trade, there is only one way that we can do that.'

They were now half a mile outside Aliso, and as they neared a hillock, Arminius saw a tower. It seemed out of place so close to a major fort.

'We put it here,' Vala said grimly, 'to act as a distraction. When we are attacked one day, they will likely go for these depots first. We will lose a century, but we will buy time elsewhere.'

A great complex came into view. With its palisade of thick trees, its moat, and ramparts, it was half the size of the town itself. It possessed a dozen massive warehouses and jetties. Most glaringly visible from the hillock were the cages.

'Welcome to the *publicania*. The legions, when they returned from the East, brought upwards of five thousand slaves with them. They had captured them across the Albis, or had simply abducted them from villages along the route back from the frontier if they could not make up the numbers. We also sell many natives convicted of crimes.' He paused. 'We ship ten thousand people every year. Plantation owners love them down south. The army receives a percentage of the price. Now, I suppose, the governor will do, too. Do you want to see the cages?'

'I have seen them elsewhere.'

'The *publicania* has become a very important part of our operations here, whether we like it or not.'

'The army exists to win wars. There is of course nothing wrong with slavery, but no self-respecting people will tolerate us dragging their children off on this scale.'

'Certainly,' Vala mused. He seemed to consider his next words carefully. 'But then, the province is not governed for the convenience of barbarians, is it?' He turned his horse away, and started back towards the town.

* * *

The day after seeing the slave depot, Arminius received his orders. He set off to find Vala. The officer was in his office near the library. He received Arminius, but did not take his eyes off his work.

'A *turma*?' Arminius demanded. 'That is fifty men!'

'Yes, it is,' Vala said absently, still not making eye contact.

'In Pannonia I commanded an *ala quingenaria*!' Ninety percent of his command had been cut.

'I know,' Numonius noted, turning briefly to make a comment to a scribe. Then he faced Arminius and said wearily, 'We want you first to get used to the conditions.'

'I did not come here to become a mere *decurion*.'

Vala's lips twitched. 'And there will be greater responsibilities to come, but not yet. The mission I have in mind for you will require nothing more than a *turma*. After the winter, we will reconsider. Now, if you will excuse me, the governor is a day away, and I have a lot of work to do. Find your unit.'

Arminius decided against complaining and turned away, burying his anger.

'One more thing,' Vala called as he left. 'You no longer have access to the library. I want you to focus on being a troop commander.'

CHAPTER 14

PUBLIUS QUINCTILIUS VARUS, GOVERNOR OF Germania, husband of the Emperor Augustus's great-niece, retired consul, past governor of Africa and Syria, the Scythe of the Judaea, marched into Aliso on the day of the Festival of Apollo. He used the new highway from Vetera, alongside which three legions and thousands of auxiliaries drew up. Arminius, mounted on a bay horse at the head of fifty swarthy Iberian troopers, watched the procession approach.

In front rode a *turma* of the governor's mounted guard, dressed in black and gold. Behind them walked trumpeters and men with kettledrums, and banner bearers who triumphantly proclaimed the governor's glory and power. Then followed slaves, who carried booty from his past offices: vases of gold, plumes of ostrich and peacock feathers, lion and tiger skins, and armour from the crushed nobility of Africa and Asia. However, these treasures, and the servants in the costumes of Phrygia, Bithynia, Libya and Judaea, were eclipsed by one thing: an enormous elephant. Its tusks were painted in gold and its saddlecloth was made of red silk. A boy led the beast, which lumbered by, inured to the noise. Local children ran on the riverside of the road to keep pace with the fantastical creature. Behind the exotic animal followed twenty young slaves dressed in white tunics, and with flowers in their hair. The boys carried loaves of bread, sheaves of wheat, grapes and fruit in great baskets shaped like horns. The girls' baskets were flatter, and contained flower petals, which they strewed along the path.

Behind them, riding on a magnificent pale stallion, was Varus, grinning and waving majestically. Each unit of the army came to attention as he passed them. Varus received a stiff-armed salute from every officer, and replied in kind, his face effortlessly moving from grace to stern concentration, depending on whether civilians or soldiers were before him.

As the governor rode abreast of his unit, Arminius barked his men to attention. His soldiers bashed their lances once onto their green oval shields. The governor smiled benevolently.

The new ruler of Germania was followed by great wagons with his possessions and household. Arminius's thoughts turned wintry. He had seen processions like this in Rome. Generals were usually granted them as triumphs, in return for great victories.

'Very impressive,' Sigimer declared that evening to Arminius, Caglem, and Hlutheir. They stood in a reception area lit by torches, thronged by provincial chiefs and nobility, who had come to pay homage to the governor. Different areas had been set up for Roman guests. Dressed in their best togas, their hair and beards shorn in the Roman style, they reasonably resembled Roman gentlemen. Sigimer covered the tattoo from his arm with the end of the toga.

'Any change to being run by the Roman army is good,' Caglem noted. He was enjoying Roman wine from a glass goblet, his eyes lazing over ancient enemies. There were Chatti, some still dressed in their red-and-blue tartan trousers and cloaks, but most clad in togas. Next to them were Sugambri and Ubii tribesmen from around Colonia Agrippina, wearing the most recent fashions imported from Narbonensis. Frisii, mercenaries from the Rhenus delta, eyed the other tribes suspiciously. Hermunduri stood, perfumed and groomed, superficially appearing like Roman men, but still speaking their own tongue as they hugged their watered-down liquor. Bructeri, some still with their front hair shaven, and long locks over their necks, glared at Tencteri, the horse-warriors they had fought from time immemorial. It was an astonishing collection. These men were old enough to remember an age when they had fought one another in brutal inter-tribal wars.

There would be no resurrection of old disputes tonight. Weapons had been banned from the town.

'I suppose you have seen one of those – what did you call it – before?' Caglem enquired.

'Elephant,' Arminius said, his mind drifting. 'I have seen them. They sometimes put them in the arena for gladiators to kill.'

Caglem frowned. 'They hunt them?'

'It is not a hunt. The elephant has nowhere to run, and dies for entertainment. They also bring in bears and lions, and other beasts. Sometimes, they give some bastard a stick and order him to kill the animal.'

'These people are champions?' Caglem asked, frowning with dismay.

'No, they are condemned men or slaves. They also make them fight one another.'

Hlutheir interrupted. 'Come on, you must have heard it being done here, old man. They chain bears and men together to please the legionaries.'

'I always thought that this was just here on their frontier. They do this in *Rome*?'

'Yes, to keep the peasants entertained.'

Arminius had spotted one particular chief, who had just arrived. The man was in his late forties, but his Roman-style hair was prematurely silver. He had a handsome, angular face with deep blue eyes that regarded Arminius from beneath patrician, grey brows. Of all the barbarian nobility in the area, he best succeeded in imitating the Romans. But for his barbarian features, he could have been a senator strolling in the forum. His white toga was immaculate, and he supported its folds on his right arm – the mark of a man who did not have to carry a sword. Like a Roman nobleman, he made no sudden movements, keeping his face stern and calm.

'Cegestes,' his father informed him. 'He is head of the Wolf clan.' He spoke with naked hatred.

'He probably ordered the last assassination attempt on your father,' Hlutheir said hurriedly, as the nobleman started towards them.

'So, this is young Arminius,' Cegestes opened, smiling pacifically. He spoke Suebic, probably not wanting to risk his Latin with someone who had spent sixteen years in Rome.

'Cegestes,' Arminius replied noncommittally. He made the sign of respect, touching his heart with his right hand, but Cegestes merely gave a nod.

'What a fine young man he has grown into, Sigimer!' he continued in his dignified drawl. 'I am *very* impressed. I hope that you can learn from him.'

Sigimer glared back mutely. Hlutheir and Caglem also remained quiet.

'Learn what, exactly?' Arminius said firmly, though keeping his tone polite. He now spoke in Latin. Cegestes's gaze flickered back to him. 'My father is a noble man.'

Cegestes's eyes narrowed and he responded in heavily accented, but accurate Latin. 'He is indeed of a great lineage.'

'As noble as your own,' Arminius said pleasantly. 'A son of the forest.'

Cegestes allowed a smile to flicker at the corner of his mouth. 'It must be strange for you to return here with so much having changed.'

The other three men were looking on uncomfortably. The conversation had passed far beyond their meagre Latin vocabulary.

'It is hardly Rome yet,' Arminius quipped, switching back to Suebic.

'No, but one can hope,' Cegestes concluded in Latin, before also switching to the Suebic tongue. 'Have they told you what they are going to use you for here?'

'To kill rebels.'

'Yes, unfortunately there still *are* many rebels.'

'The Roman army can easily stop them.'

'Yes… and ferociously,' Cegestes said, not losing his restrained Roman manner. 'I do not understand how we ever stood up to them. Do you, Sigimer?'

Sigimer scowled. 'You were there, Cegestes.'

'I was indeed.' Cegestes grimaced wanly. 'Well, young man. I wish you luck with the…' He searched for a word and, not being able to find it in Suebic, said in Latin, '*recidivists.*'

Sigimer swore when the man was out of earshot. 'Now do you see what is going on?'

Arminius stared after Cegestes, sipping his wine. 'Does he have a tutor?'

'He bought slaves to teach him Latin,' Caglem replied. 'And he spends a lot of time in Colonia Agrippina, where his son is a Roman priest.'

'The boy would never make a warrior,' Hlutheir growled.

'He has a daughter called Thusnelda. She is the most eligible woman in the province,' Caglem said, 'and quite a beauty, too.' The girl was promised to the son of the Bear clan's chief. 'The Bear clan have been wayward. Cegestes is trying to use his daughter to bring them into line. When he does, he can easily replace your father as paramount chief.'

'Until then,' Sigimer spat, 'they will just try and murder me. And Cegestes will now try and kill you too.'

Arminius mulled over the revelations. It was a mystery why the Romanised Cegestes had not gained greater favour with the imperial administration. Perhaps the army had wanted a warrior to run things. Now, with the new governor, that might all change.

The conversation died down to bitter recollections of Cegestes. Arminius listened for a short while to the grumbling of the two older men. Then, a slave approached him with a message that the governor wanted to meet him.

Varus stood amid a knot of senior officers, bureaucrats, and cronies. He was gesticulating, grinning, rattling off his sentences. The governor was in his early fifties and of medium height. He was balding and grey around his ears. Large, animated eyes capped his warm smile, but he had small bags under them, as if he slept too little. He wore a white toga with a broad purple hem – the sign of nobility – and a large gold ring.

'It is *fantastic*,' Varus said, waving his hands in an un-Roman fashion. 'I am *most* pleased with the performance your men put up this afternoon. We have an *excellent* army here!'

General Saturninus bowed. The Roman cavalry of the Eighteenth had indeed put on an impressive parade. The Eighteenth's crack 1st Century, First Cohort had followed with a display of arms. Governors everywhere enjoyed such games. Varus, though, felt compelled to discuss them with his commanders. Arminius felt Saturninus's irritation with the governor like a furnace blast.

'I must admit that I came up from Narbonensis with little hope for this province,' Varus exclaimed, speaking so rapidly that Arminius thought he might trip over the words. 'But I can see wonderful progress. What beautiful towns! What lovely roads! The people looked healthy and enthusiastic. Damn good idea to have brought the elephant. What do you think?'

By the time that Arminius realised that the question was directed at him, Varus was gliding towards him.

Varus asked, 'This is the one who served in the imperial bodyguard?' and when General Saturninus confirmed, went straight into 'You must be delighted with the way things went today.'

'It was impressive, Sir.'

'Ah, how beautifully you speak Latin! I have been thoroughly pained by gutter Latin for the last weeks. You speak as if they made you memorise Cicero!'

'They did indeed, Sir.'

'Marvellous! And you still speak your own language?' Varus asked, waving his hand in a circular motion as he ran out of words.

'Suebic, Sir. Yes, Sir.'

'The language of heroes,' Varus noted, winking. 'You can just *sense* the sooty fires of the ancestors as they discuss the day's decapitation; a language like *broth*.'

'Indeed, Sir.'

Varus laid his hand on Arminius's forearm and leaned forward. 'Well, we cannot have that any more! Roads, fields and courts of law – that is the new way of life!'

'And sewage systems, Sir. *Very* important.'

Varus snorted, slapping Arminius on the back. 'Yes! Excellent – I have an interpreter with a sense of humour! Let us go and chat. We still have heroic levels of drinking to do after that.'

* * *

Arminius filed into the library behind the other cavalry officers. It was two days after the governor's arrival, and the army was back to routine.

Vala waited pensively at the far end of the map table. Arminius formed up with other *decuriones*.

'I hope you all had a good time,' Vala opened dourly.

Arminius had indeed done well. After translating the governor's speech to the tribal dignitaries, he had ended up in his suite with the Roman guests, drinking until the early hours. The governor certainly could throw a party.

'Now, we have to settle back into business,' Vala said. 'As the veterans among you know, we have much work to do over the winter while the infantry rests. They have done some hard fighting this summer, and I do not want their work undone.'

Vala explained that the unconquered tribes would conduct raids into the province during the cold months. In addition, there were illicit smithies being set up in the forests while the legions were cooped up. 'We know that the Marcomanni have enlarged their iron mines, and will be continuing smuggling iron.'

The legions could not operate in mid-winter, because there was not enough food and forage available to keep ten thousand men and horses alive in the snow. While they rested, the auxiliaries would patrol and garrison outposts.

Vala spoke to each *decurion* in turn, indicating his area of responsibility on the map, and explaining what he knew about it from spies and previous years' reports. Finally, he came to Arminius.

'You have experience of this type of operation from Illyria, so I have given you a particularly challenging area.' He indicated a zone on the upper reaches of the Albis. 'In the south there are high hills, which mark the border with the Marcomanni. To the east, you have the Semnones. You must eliminate raiders or smugglers from either tribe who enter into this triangle between the hills, the Albis, and the Selas.' He paused, searching Arminius's face. 'I am giving you Hiru, my best tracker. You may also raise some men from the local tribal militia. Rome will pay the men based on trophies delivered. The paymaster prefers ears.'

Arminius studied the map and imagined what the terrain would look like: steep ravines, fast water, and dense forests. 'I would prefer, Sir, to be doing this with my veterans from Illyria.'

'The men assigned to you are very reliable.'

'I am sure, Sir, but I doubt their ability to work in this climate.'

'They are *good*,' Vala said forcefully, before managing a paternal smile. 'I know that you will get the best out of them.'

The next morning Arminius sent one of his German soldiers to his father. 'Tell him to find me fifty Cherusci – men who would rather die than fall behind.'

CHAPTER 15

7 CE (DECEMBER)

CASTRA OCTA

S IGIMER WOKE, AND GASPED AS he sat up, jerking with pain.

'What is it?' Imma asked.

He brushed away her comforting hand, but was captivated by her for a moment: her hair, tousled from sleep, her young face wracked with concern.

'Nothing.' He got out of bed, grabbing his throbbing leg, and steadied himself against a post. He limped around the wicker screen to where the children lay. Dawn drifted through the smoke hole onto Amala's features. The boy stirred.

By the doorway, the guard looked up. His gaze locked with the chief's eyes. Then he looked away, embarrassed not by Sigimer's nudity, but by his weakness.

Sigimer shuffled past the children to the fireplace, where he sat down, grunting, holding onto the old wound on his thigh. After a moment, he reopened his eyes.

Imma had rounded the partition that separated their bed from the rest of the longhouse. She drew her cloak tight. 'Are you sure?'

'You know what it is. Just leave it.' He immediately felt guilty about snapping at her, and beckoned her over. Her bare feet made no sound on the plank floor. She knelt down by his side, and he touched her cheek. 'I am just an old man.'

She kissed his palm.

* * *

7 CE, FESTIVAL OF FAUNUS (5 DECEMBER)

ERZ HIGHLANDS

The tracker crouched, oblivious to the knee-deep snow. They were in a pine forest blanketed in frigid mist. Nearby trees resembled planted spears. Deeper into the mist, the trunks turned grey and they disappeared after fifty yards. Sound was limited to the muffled crash of snow, or men heaving out body warmth.

Hiru barely seemed to notice the cold. His gaze rested on a human spoor. They had been following the tracks for half a day. He raised his mitten-clad hand and, flicking his fingers twice, started forward again. His body was bent as he carefully distributed his weight. He wore animal skins. He spoke little, but one of the few times that Arminius had coaxed him out of his reticence, they had discussed the suit. He would live in it all through the winter. Pointing at different parts, including the boots, the edges of the cape, the soft under-layer, the gloves – tied to the sleeves with twine – Hiru had listed half a dozen species, including deer, wolverine, bison and fox. The Cherusci produced clothes like it, but not in any way as sophisticated. When asked who had made it, Hiru withdrew into a private vastness. With his long, curly black hair, large brown eyes, and elongated skull, he looked unlike either Suebi or Valich. Once, at the fireside and with the help of some *beor*, he had been encouraged to recite a poem in his own language. It had, at first, sounded like gargling, before developing a rhythm that soothed the circle of soldiers like a flame's pulse. Some of the Iberians thought they could understand snippets, but Hiru had smiled enigmatically when asked his people's origins. The poem, he said, was about a time when the forest had been but a sapling.

Arminius carefully placed his own booted feet in Hiru's tracks to make less noise. Before, he would not have considered the crunch of fresh snow to be loud, but Hiru had taught him differently. He had followed the tracker's example and taken to skin clothing, bought from a Cheruscan village. Even his wide-soled fur boots were stuffed with straw to retain warmth. His Cherusci had also come prepared for cold. Predictably, Vala's Iberians, issued only with standard Roman army equipment – including sandals! – had suffered terribly from frostbite. Fourteen were now holed up in the unit's forward camp. In previous years their Roman officers had sheltered with them when the snows came.

Not this year.

The tracker raised his hand again. They had advanced twenty yards. Arminius saw him subtly change the grip on his club. It was made from a single piece of hardwood, with a foot-long shaft and a polished ball head. Against a Roman soldier, it would be useless. Here in the woods, it appeared formidable.

The one moment, Arminius was turning around to signal the file behind him; the next, a volley of arrows and javelins sliced down into the Roman ranks from the incline to their left.

Arminius just had time to see Hiru roll into the snow before a javelin thudded into the ground a finger's length from his thigh. Arminius carried no shield, and he leapt behind a tree before a second salvo.

Pressing his back against the trunk, his heart pounding, he drew his sword and dagger. He waited for the attack.

Above them, and to the front, the enemy howled and mocked. The harshest noise only filtered through his heightened nerves after several seconds: screaming. His men had been drawn out upon the slope. Glancing back down, he saw chaos. The boy who had walked behind him was bawling. A heavy javelin had nailed him to the frozen earth. Blood gushed into the snow. Beyond him, men hid partially behind trees and in the lee of the hill, but two wounded crawled in the open. From the back of the column, he could hear the receding thunder of an avalanche set off by the enemy.

The insults from the Marcomanni grew louder. Some of the Cherusci peeled away from the trees and charged up the hill, roaring. It was too late for him to call them. One made it ten yards before an arrow struck him in the chest. Another was hit in the head by a rock. He spun and thudded into a tree.

Arminius, cursing, rolled from his hiding place. He sprinted up the hill and away from the path, dimly aware that his veterans, particularly Arbex and Obed, were doing the same. He was glad that he had defied Vala and brought them along.

An arrow struck a tree next to him, glanced off, and wheeled out of sight. He changed course, leaping over a log, seeking stretches of thinner snow. Within seconds, he spotted a smear of brown moving away from him. He lost his footing, but scrambled back up to find the man turning around with an arrow in his bow. Arminius kept running, dodging, and when his opponent saw him again and released his arrow, it was too late. Arminius's sword gouged the man's stomach. He was onto the next target even as the mortally wounded warrior sank onto his knees.

Those Marcomanni tribesmen who had set off the avalanche were withdrawing to the crest of the hill. There were six. They wore deerskin coats and trousers, and some quivers on their backs. Arminius caught up with them as they reached the top of the slope, in a small clearing. They fanned into a U-shape, drawing knives, hatchets, and clubs. There was only one man with a buckler – they had been travelling light. Four were big men, and two others, who hung back, were in their early teens. Their beardless faces showed fear and exhilaration.

One of the warriors began to whoop, and was soon joined by the others, leaning forward as they sought a gap in the lone, blood-spattered Roman's defences.

Growling, Arminius hurled himself upon the man to his far right, hoping to draw the Marcomannis' attention away from his veterans, whom he knew would be right behind him. He knocked the tribesman's hatchet away and thrust with his sword at the man's chest. The warrior leapt back, causing him to miss, but Arminius attacked ferociously, his dagger splitting open the warrior's jacket. The man hissed with pain. Arminius parried a determined attack by a second warrior, who was wielding a club. The man struck air as the Roman soldier dashed inside the arc aimed at his head and thrust his sword into his stomach. Even as he stumbled away, Arminius was turning to face another Marcoman – the one with the buckler. The man knocked aside his dagger thrust and nearly found Arminius's jugular. It was too late: just as the Marcoman started a second attack at Arminius's face, a veteran cut deep into the small of his back.

Arminius had no time to thank his comrade, as he had to spin to meet the next assault. He found the Marcomanni fleeing. Snatching a hatchet from one of the dying men, he launched after them, catching up with the slowest. His dagger struck the man in the back. Arminius knocked him down, burying the ungainly barbarian weapon in the man's skull. Splattered with blood, he ducked behind a tree to avoid a javelin. Then he was off again.

The Marcomanni would not stand. They had never intended a toe-to-toe fight, and as the Roman officer, spectral in the mist, raced towards them, they scattered down the opposite slope, crashing through the thickets and deep snow.

Arminius stopped on the crest of the hill, steamy breath blasting from his heated body. Behind him, the wounded Marcomanni wailed as they were finished off.

'Leave one!' he shouted over his shoulder, hoping that it was not too late. He stared down the slope, listening for the receding sounds of the tribesmen. He was livid at himself for having been ambushed.

But there was nothing to be done now. He wandered back to find one of the Marcomanni still kept alive.

'Torture him. Find out where the bastards are camped,' he ordered Arbex. He barked at the Cherusci to form a perimeter.

Four men had been killed and three wounded badly. Hiru had escaped any wounds, as had old Inguiomer.

'They boxed us in,' Arminius said brusquely. 'Any fool could do it. Tell the men to turn and charge up the fucking hill next time, not up the fucking path!'

He found Hiru, where he stood just on the lee of the hill, staring down at the thickets. 'How many were there? Twelve?'

Hiru nodded.

Inguiomer puffed up the slope.

'Provide one man for each of the wounded, and two more to guide them,' Arminius said. 'They can go down into the valley. The rest of us go on.'

Inguiomer looked up. Snow had begun to drift down again. The day was dying. The cold would be murderous once darkness fell.

'We go on,' Arminius whispered. 'They will never expect it.'

CHAPTER 16

8–6 BCE
ROME

CLEON TAUGHT THE TWO BOYS together for three years. Every day, barring festivals, he arrived at the villa with writing implements and books. The boys waited for him in the garden or, if it was cold, in the dining area. He taught them to read and write Latin and his own tongue, Greek. Statilius Taurus, the Emperor's architect, occasionally inspected his charges. He was a thin man with darting eyes. The boys never warmed to him.

Flavus was the easiest to encourage. He saw learning as a game, and delighted in finding the Latin names of first objects, and later birds and plants. He would lie on the floor, his tongue sticking from the corner of his mouth, perfecting his writing.

His brother was a caged leopard. He paced the garden and eyed the sky. He rushed his assignments. He stoically accepted all reprimands and punishments. Occasionally, he would snap at his brother. He continued to use his own language.

Matters came to a head one day. It was summer. Cleon had given the children time to play in the small orchard behind the house. A slave came running to him in the atrium. When Cleon found the children, Arminius was standing over a squirming, wailing Flavus. The latter's arm was broken. Arminius regarded him fiercely. They had played a game and, as Arminius explained blankly, Flavus had refused to obey him.

Arminius was beaten severely, even though Flavus pleaded on his behalf.

* * *

8 CE, FESTIVAL OF TIBERINUS (8 DECEMBER)
MARCOMANNI BOIMIA

Inguiomer was exhausted. They had been running through the forest for three days. His muscles ached. His mouth was perpetually dry. He was hallucinating – flashes of light, shades of colour where none should be. He had long ago tightened his belt. They carried the minimum amount of food, and they snatched water from half-frozen streams. His breath was haggard, his legs screaming when he awoke from the holes they scratched for sleep.

However, even as his torment increased, his determination grew. For this, there was only one explanation.

At the head of the pack – down to eighteen men – and outpaced only by the tracker, Arminius loped tirelessly. Inguiomer's initial attempts to keep up with the youth had been in vain: he had nearly blacked out on one of the sprints up a hillside. His young relative had come back to help him. He had wanted neither kindness nor care, but he had abandoned any pretence of leadership. The young warrior moved along the column to encourage his men. Where Arminius helped to carry the packs of slow men, or scouted while the others rested, Inguiomer could only clutch at every moment of slumber.

Some demon drove the boy.

More amazing was the attitude of the other warriors. He had expected Arminius's veterans to maintain the pace without complaint, but what had surprised him was the determination Armin brought out in the Cherusci. Three days from the nearest friendly face, pursued no doubt by the Marcomanni, sleeping in snow, they seemed to carry on for a mere glance from Arminius, and the excitement of the raid.

What a raid! Within a day of the ambush, they had tracked the Marcomanni to a nearby hamlet. In the dark, they had slipped over the palisade using a makeshift assault ladder. They killed everything in the village. Waiting out a snowstorm amidst the corpses, Arminius had led them back into the bowels of the morning. Instead of rushing back north, they had turned east, and headed to some target Arminius must have chosen long before.

On the way they had found, and killed, an old man and boy travelling together. Their pitiful corpses were buried immediately, to moulder in the warm spring soil. Arminius and Arbex performed the deed. Even Inguiomer, hardened by war, was taken aback by their cold skill. Arminius would have no witnesses to tell of his route, trusting in the snowfall to cover their tracks.

Now, after three days, Inguiomer was squatting amidst pines on a hillside in the heart of enemy land. He would not have thought it possible before. He would certainly not have demanded it of the men himself. However, Arminius had done it.

Lying at the peak of the rise some fifty yards away, flanked by one of his veterans – the black one – and the tracker, Arminius peered down at their target.

A message came. Arminius wished to speak to Inguiomer. Inguiomer dragged himself forward. His relative greeted him with a smile. As Inguiomer arrived, the aboriginal tracker slipped away into the undergrowth, not even rustling a twig.

'Have a look,' Arminius invited him, and he pulled himself onto the lip of the ridge. Below, through the trees, he could see a bowl dug out of the hillside. Through this valley cut a stream. Even through the snow, he could see the iron-bearing red soil. In the upper, narrowest part of the valley, centuries of miners had dug galleries, now flanked by makeshift huts. There were three furnaces, belching smoke. The pummelling of smiths sounded from two lean-tos. Night was pooling in the recesses of the valley, but they counted at least fifty cloaked shapes hurrying with wood and ore to the ovens, or smashing the rock with pickaxes.

'Hiru says that they have been gathering iron here for ten generations.'

'I know,' Inguiomer sighed. 'We used to trade with them.'

'And there are ten other mines like this.'

Inguiomer shifted his aching body. 'Are you going to attack this?'

Arminius nodded in the direction of his remaining veteran. The black-skinned man absented himself, but not before glaring at Inguiomer.

'No.' Arminius gazed into Inguiomer's eyes. Finally, he said, 'We are here to leave Maroboduus a message.' He produced a leather scroll from within his deerskin coat. He laid it on his raised palm. 'This is for Maroboduus. I am going to nail it to the doors of one of his smithies. Then we will leave. He was an officer in the Roman army. If he cannot read it, he can find one who can.'

Inguiomer stared at the scroll. He squinted as he tried to judge its significance. 'What does it say?'

'It says: *I am Armin su eb Hildreth.*'

Inguiomer frowned. There was a long pause before Arminius spoke again.

'If I gave you Rome, could you raise me an army?'

Inguiomer's throat tightened. 'What do you mean?'

Armin gave a thin smile. He said very slowly, 'Do you want to be free?'

'What do you mean?'

'Do you want to be free from Rome?'

Inguiomer's eyes flashed down the incline, where his men waited amidst Arminius's *comitatus*.

'Every one of my men here can be trusted,' Armin whispered. 'They all want what I want.'

'I do not understand.'

Armin touched the old warrior's arm. 'Listen to me.'

'I do not know…'

'If I can promise you a trap for all the Roman armies in Germania, can you give me an army for it?'

Bewildered, Inguiomer glanced again at the *comitatus*. He now noticed how Arminius's men were carefully spaced among his warriors. Their weapons were surreptitiously at the ready. The black man who had just left them stood nonchalantly a few feet from one of Inguiomer's relatives. Arminius followed his gaze.

'Obed wants what I want,' Arminius said.

'He is not even one of us.'

'Even in Kush, we have allies,' Arminius replied.

Inguiomer was too startled to reply. He wanted to reach for his sword, but he knew that Arminius's killers were ready to attack him.. He had seen these men fight. Some were brown or black, foreign-tongued, and some were even Valich. Most were Suebi, but of enemy tribes. They were united only by their love of Armin, who had collected them on his travels. But what answer did Arminius really want? Was this offer a trick, meant to test his loyalty to Rome?

'Do you want freedom?' Armin asked.

Inguiomer hissed through his teeth, and then said, 'Yes, more than anything.' He could only follow his gut instinct, and hope that Arminius had truly turned against the Romans.

'I offer you that.'

'Armin?'

'If I build you a trap for the Romans, will you build me an army to destroy them?'

Inguiomer almost wept with joy, as hope, long ashen and cold, was relit. 'Yes, I will.'

'Thank you.' He grabbed Inguiomer's wrist. 'I am Armin *su eb* Hildreth *ev* Eysle. I am your brother.'

He kissed the old man's trembling cheek.

CHAPTER 17

'IT IS RIDICULOUS!' ARMINIUS EXCLAIMED, hammering his fist on the table over which Vala leaned. They stood in a Cherusci mead hall. Its usual occupants waited outside in the cold while the Romans conducted their business.

'I can understand that you are frustrated,' Vala began wearily.

'No!' Arminius shouted. He was dressed completely in Cherusci winter garb and sported a two-month-old beard. The Tribune had barely recognised his officer when he had first entered the hall, accompanied by his scowling uncle. 'Your Iberians did not last a month! I sent you a message, and you did nothing!'

Vala bit his tongue, and lowered himself onto a stool, his fingertips pressing on the table. 'What happened?'

'They did not even arrive with proper winter dress! The snows started falling, and their toes started dropping off. Soon, half of them refused even to leave the base camp. What kind of a unit did you give me?'

'These men were proven veterans.'

'…Of *what*? I had ten men with me who had fought in Illyria. *They* were veterans. They never complained. And I lost two of them because of these idiots you forced on me.'

Vala gazed down at a scroll. 'From your previous report, you were spending most of your time in the hills.'

'We ambushed them and attacked their camps.'

'In the hills?'

'Yes.'

'And you stayed out several days at a time.'

'Yes.'

'Where would you sleep?'

'We dug caves, or made shelters from branches. My men and the tribesmen were willing, and able, to do this.'

Vala leaned back to interlock his fingers behind his head. He closed his eyes. 'And these extremes were necessary?'

'These *extremes* are what the smugglers manage, *Sir*.' Arminius pointed at half a dozen skin bags, which he had left earlier for the senior officer's inspection. 'As you could see, they were bringing in iron spear-points and arrowheads. Weapons meant to kill legionaries!'

'I know. Were there any raids? Did they try to intimidate loyal villages?'

'Of course there were! What could we do? I lost thirteen men, and many are wounded. They spent nights on end in those hills, starving and frostbitten. I cannot expect them to keep fighting like this, especially with the Iberians just giving up and staying in the fort! How am I supposed to stop raids with men like that?'

Vala kept his peace, so Arminius continued.

'The only way I can get results, is to have my veterans from Illyria!'

'These are the troops serving under your brother?'

'They have fought Marcomanni before. They will do whatever I ask of them!'

'The situation merits that?'

'*Yes*!'

Vala gazed at the great, fur-bedecked figure of Inguiomer. His eyes were rimmed with black, his skin gnawed by the cold. Even Arminius looked as if someone had rubbed ice into his face. With his beard and outfit, he was beginning to resemble Hiru. Behind them waited six similarly wild men, all German. Arminius had not even invited the Iberians inside.

The story sounded plausible. The Iberians, as well as most of the Africans and Asians, hated the weather here. At a time of year when even most barbarians stayed close to their fires, who could blame them?

This was not, however, what he could tell Arminius. 'The auxiliaries will be dealt with.'

'And will I get proper men?'

Vala considered the results. Based on Arminius's own report, a discussion with the leader of the Iberians, and the grisly bag of trophy ears, Arminius's methods had been spectacularly successful. Raids had declined in his sector as against the incidence in the previous year. The problem was that living in the highlands in winter, and taking the fight to the enemy camps, was beyond the Iberians. No other *decuriones* had ever demanded such suffering of them. They were threatening mutiny.

Vala asked the room to clear. He wanted to speak to Arminius alone. To his surprise, Inguiomer simply glanced at Arminius and then acceded to the request. Something had changed between the two men: Inguiomer usually deferred to nobody. It was suspicious.

Vala invited Arminius to sit down.

'I cannot deny your results, so, congratulations. But as you know, it is against policy to bring auxiliaries back to their land of origin.'

'I know,' Arminius said. He was now calmer. To prevent rebellions, auxiliary units were posted away from home. Egyptians served in Gaul, and Gauls in Africa.

'Would Gauls suffice?'

'You cannot have Gauls patrol these hills. Before the Romans came here, the Germans drove the Valich out of these forests. The Cherusci will not fight with them. No, I have five hundred men who can dominate these hills all year round. The Marcomanni are swamping this area with weapons and rebels, so that they can distract our attack on their land! They did the same in Illyria, and now we have ten legions dealing with that uprising! Do you want another disaster like that?'

'We *had* an uprising in this area, six years ago. One of the Cheruscan clans rose.'

'The Bear clan.'

The Roman commander studied the earnest young man. Arminius's few days in the library at Castra Drusus had been well spent.

'You can vouch for these men of yours?'

'Of course I can. They come from all the German tribes. They will fight for money, for hatred of the Marcomanni, and for me, and I will no longer have to watch my back against my own people.'

'You have been threatened?'

'My uncle warned that even the Cherusci might turn on me. They consider me a stranger.' He shrugged. 'It is only because of Inguiomer that they have stayed with me.'

Sending young men into the woods with tribal levies was a dangerous business. Vala had lost Roman officers in the past.

He made a decision. 'Very well, I am standing you down. Take your Cheruscan levies home for now. The Iberians will stay in their fort to teach them a lesson.'

'And my brother and our men?'

'I shall discuss it with my superiors, but there is really nothing we can do until the passes southward open in spring.' He rose from his chair, managing a smile. 'All I can say is, well done. You have confirmed all the good reports we had of you. Indeed, the governor got word of your adventures, and he would like a word.'

Chapter 18

8 CE (February)
Cheruscan District, Castra Octa

Inguiomer pushed the door open and stood in it for a moment, breathing hard. He was worried that he might not be able to contain his joy.

'Close the door!' Andred called from the hearth. She was already walking over, though, even as the rest of the women in the longhouse were just looking up. 'Come inside.' She wore her long, grey hair in a single plait, and wore a tartan woollen dress. He inhaled her scent as he embraced her. It had been too long since he had seen her last.

She guided him into the rush of children, who hugged him in a squirming gaggle, chattering, seeking his attention. He picked up his youngest grandchild, tossed her above the others' heads, and then settled her on his hip. The women kissed him. One took away his sword, and another brought him warm broth. He was laughing.

There was hope again.

* * *

8 CE, Festival of Concordia (5 February)
Castra Drusus

Varus sat by an immense desk, surrounded by piles of parchment. Scribes bustled as he barked orders. Arminius had been let into the library – now the governor's office – for his audience, but Varus was so immersed in work that he did not notice him.

Arminius had never seen any man read so fast. Varus would scan the paper in an instant, and either sign it or hand it back with a growled instruction. Finally, he looked up and spotted the officer, now shaven and in Roman uniform.

'Ah! Arminius!' He beamed. 'You must forgive me,' he added ebulliently as he began to cross the floor. 'I have been working for days, hardly having a wink! It is so exciting to see the province take shape!' He placed his hand on Arminius's muscled arm. 'How are things? Come, and join me here by the fire.'

They wandered over to the hearth. Arminius gave a brief report on the patrol in the Erz.

'Yes, I asked Vala about this. He warned me to expect trouble over the winter months. But apparently,' the governor said, indicating that Arminius should sit, 'you found a solution.'

'It just extended what Tribune Numonius was already doing, Sir.'

The governor asked him to explain, and asked him questions at intervals. The man's command of detail impressed Arminius. He clearly had a phenomenal memory.

Arminius explained his idea of returning his unit from Illyria.

'This force of yours is the only way?'

'It is one option, Sir. The other is to train Roman troops for that kind of warfare. The third is to provide the Cherusci with the equipment to do it themselves. That carries its own risks.'

'Yes. With all respect to the Cherusci, Arminius, we have reached a point where the majority of the people are disarmed and are happy to follow the rule of law. I want as little reason as possible for them to bear arms again.'

Arminius praised the stalwart service of Inguiomer.

'Yes, I know that we have allowed some of the chiefs to retain bodyguards and weapons, and they have worked excellently with us. Nevertheless, the time for militias is past. The army *must* take care of policing duties itself. Whoever wants to retain arms among the populace will have to join the army auxiliaries and leave the province. Those are the rules.'

'But bringing in my old unit will provide a show of confidence in the people, Sir. I agree that we must disband militias, and such a pan-tribal force, under army control, is an ideal solution.' He described his unit's performance in Illyria in some detail.

Varus finally admitted, 'It does sound good.'

'If you give the men, I can cut the Marcomanni off from this province, year round.'

Varus pondered the options, and then said amiably, 'Let us think about it! Now that you are here, I want to invite you to a dinner party tonight. It is for traders and citizens from Colonia Agrippina, but it includes some of your people – a man called Cegestes?'

'I have met him.'

'I do want the two of you to get along. He is a good fellow.'

'I shall be very pleased to meet him again.'

'Good! The servants will give you the details. I look forward to it.' He patted Arminius on the back.

Arminius stepped out into the antechamber where, on simple wooden benches, people waited for an audience with the governor. He recognised one of the supplicants and called out to him.

Sextus, the builder from the march north, shot up from the bench, nervous in the rarefied environment of the governor's quarters. For a moment, he did not recognise the tall soldier. Then his face brightened.

'Arminius!' he exclaimed, then caught himself and, with a bashful squint, scratched his head. He held a collection of drawings that threatened to spill onto the floor.

'How was the journey?' Arminius asked, and laughed as the builder gave an energetic description of their trek across the German wilderness. His family was fine, and he was just about to discuss the governor's plans for Aliso.

'I shall put in a good word for you tonight,' Arminius promised, mentioning the party. 'This town deserves to have a proper craftsman let loose upon it!'

CHAPTER 19

COLONIA AGRIPPINA, "COLONIA" FOR THOSE in the know, had been founded twenty-six years before on the left bank of the Rhenus. During the winter months the Seventeenth Legion garrisoned it, and the rest of the year the Classis Germanica guarded it. It was attracting more money than all its sister towns along the Rhenus combined, thriving on the trade in skins, slaves, amber and wild animals. It was the northernmost city in the Empire, and whatever money came from Germania flowed through there.

'When I saw Colonia, I simply knew that I had not left civilisation completely,' quipped a portly Roman trader over wine.

Arminius laughed affably.

'Have you ever been there?' the businessman asked. He was perspiring from the hearths, but probably glad for it. Since the river was frozen, most of the people who had accepted the governor's invitation to his new quarters had travelled in coaches along the highway.

'I went through there as a child.'

'Really? Are you from *here*?'

'Ah, young Arminius certainly is,' interrupted Varus, beaming. 'He is one of our great hopefuls. I foresee major things for him.' He winked at Arminius before he turned to the wealthy guest.

Arminius drifted off as their conversation turned to the cost of Aliso's new docks. Only about half of the guests had yet arrived, but he could see how the evening would develop. There were only a few token officers: Saturninus had asked to be excused, and those present were young tribunes, eager to make contacts that might later finance their political careers. The businessmen were mostly Roman, with a smattering of Romanised Gauls. They preened, strutted and conspired, flanked by wives, lovers or high-class prostitutes. All the silks and jewellery that Germania could afford them were displayed. Dining tables and couches were ready, the former groaning with the first course – oysters. The most beautiful slaves in the governor's retinue rushed about, providing drinks, while being sized up by the guests for later pleasure.

It was a dwarf version of dozens of parties he had attended in Rome.

The governor went around, joking, flitting between conversations, delighted with everybody. He had a habit of gesticulating, of using his face almost like a comic actor's, and he carried warmth wherever he went.

Arminius caught Varus's last sentence as he caught up with him: 'Yes, of course it is risky, but what is life without risk?' He smiled at the flustered businessman.

'Quite an interesting man,' Arminius noted as the governor moved away.

The businessman drained his cup, and sought the nearest slave. 'Indeed, and extremely optimistic.' He stared into his newly filled goblet – Arminius shook his head when the girl turned to him – and added, 'Even fantastical. You know these people better than I do – the Germans, I mean. Is it feasible that the province will ever extend beyond the Albis?'

'Yes,' Arminius said.

'Are we even safe here, now?' the entrepreneur asked.

'From what I have seen, most people are settling down and enjoying the benefits of civilisation.' Arminius smiled. 'The governor has every reason to be confident.'

'But you said that you have just been in the hills fighting?'

'I fought against bandits,' Arminius said.

'I have heard that Maroboduus of the Marcomanni has a hundred thousand warriors, and that an entire ten thousand of them are equipped like legionaries.'

'Even if he does, he knows better than to use them! Now, tell me something.' Arminius pointed at the room. 'I am looking for a Syrian, the one who owns the slave depots outside the town. Is he here yet?'

The Roman pointed out a small man in an azure toga. 'That is Orontes.' Arminius remained quiet, and the businessman filled the silence. 'He is in business with the governor. They have been friends since Varus was in Syria.' He glanced around before whispering, 'It is rumoured that Varus owes him a *lot* of money.'

Arminius subtly changed the topic of conversation.

New guests arrived, among them Cegestes. With him was a tall, slender girl of about eighteen. Her long, amber hair was arranged immaculately in the latest Roman fashion. She wore a gold necklace set with sapphires. A sleeveless, pure white toga draped from her shoulders, hinting at the shape of her body underneath.

It had to be Cegestes's daughter, Thusnelda, he thought, as he watched the governor approach and fawn over Cegestes. The girl smiled politely, but otherwise remained silent. The governor led them into the hall and summoned slaves to provide them with wine.

Arminius walked over.

'Ah, most exciting – just the man I wanted you to meet!' Varus cried out, taking the girl by the hand and turning her in the direction of the approaching soldier.

Cegestes's eyes narrowed.

'This, young lady, is another of our great successes: Arminius, whom I believe is the son of your tribe's king?'

The girl's cool blue eyes rested upon Arminius. She dipped her head in acknowledgement.

Varus seemed unperturbed. 'Have you had the pleasure of meeting Lady Tiberia?'

'I have not, Sir,' Arminius replied. Tiberia had to be her Roman name.

'Like you, she is fluent in Latin; as fine an example to the other young women, as is her father to leaders.'

'You are too kind, Sir,' Cegestes noted, before looking frostily at Arminius.

There was a pause, after which Arminius asked, 'Does she speak?'

The girl raised an eyebrow. 'I do indeed,' she said, her Latin clear, if slightly polluted by the accents of provincial teachers.

'And you learned Latin around here?'

'My family lives mostly in Colonia,' Cegestes said. 'Tiberia has benefited from excellent tutors.'

Varus nodded emphatically and told Arminius, 'I met her on my way up here. She is very accomplished. You will like her.' He took Cegestes by the forearm. 'Come with me. Let them work out the future of Germania together!' Cegestes was led off.

Arminius let the silence deepen. The girl, though uncomfortable, stared straight at him – most un-Roman behaviour.

'Congratulations,' Arminius began, after he thought the tension had built enough. 'I hear that you are betrothed.'

'And where do you hear this?'

'I believe his name is Bannruod.'

'My father has spoken of this,' she replied evasively.

'And does *he* speak Latin?'

'Does he need to?'

'It seems the fashionable thing to do. It suits you.'

'Learning Latin?'

'Becoming a Roman lady.'

She sipped wine. 'Not Roman enough.' She had switched to Suebic.

'You are doing very well. By the way, what do you prefer me to call you? Tiberia or Thusnelda?' He persisted with Latin.

'Here, Tiberia.'

'They sent me to Rome. Where did you go?'

'Massilia, and then Colonia Agrippina,' she replied guardedly.

'Did you enjoy it?'

'I learned many things.'

'You would not look out of place in Rome.'

'Is that a compliment?'

'That depends upon what you thought of Rome.'

'I have never seen it.'

'You should.'

'Do you think I would like it?'

'That depends upon what you think of cesspits.'

Her eyes narrowed at the dry humour. He turned, so that they stood shoulder to shoulder and looked out towards the room together. 'So tell me; what do you think of this little assembly?'

She raised her goblet to her lips. 'It is as the governor said,' she whispered, '*very* exciting.'

He noticed a devious glint in her eye, and grinned.

Thusnelda snorted indelicately over her goblet. Then she lowered it, and laughed.

Later in the evening, once the hall had filled and some guests had lain down to eat together, the governor beckoned Arminius over. Cegestes stood with him. The governor enquired whether Arminius was enjoying himself, and when he affirmed this, Varus looked pleased.

'Cegestes and I have been speaking about your suggestion of bringing your unit here. He remains to be persuaded.'

Cegestes waded in, 'We all know that auxiliaries do not serve in their home province. Those rules exist for good reason.'

'It is either that, or we strengthen the militias,' Arminius began, but then turned to Varus. 'Sir, this is not the place to debate strategy.'

Varus shrugged.

'We have not had a revolt in six years,' Cegestes said, 'and even that was an exception, born of misunderstanding. I see no reason why we should now bring in five hundred men, on top of the current garrison.'

Arminius shook his head vigorously. 'Everything I saw in the Erz, and what I have heard and read, suggests that the Marcomanni are smuggling weapons into the province.'

'The Marcomanni raid us,' Cegestes exclaimed. 'Why would they give us weapons?'

'To pin down three legions,' Arminius replied calmly. Their voices had risen to the point where nearby guests were glancing at them. 'The same way they did in Illyria. And if we do not stop them now, all the money you are pouring into this place will go to waste.'

At this, nearby guests came to rapt attention.

Varus intervened. 'Good. That is enough.'

'This has to be resolved,' Cegestes said.

'I shall speak to my generals.' Varus began to guide them to one of the tables.

Cegestes resisted. 'I shall not let all my good work to go to waste.'

'Then give me what I ask,' Arminius said.

'Who do you – ?'

Varus hissed, and implored them to move on quietly.

Arminius said in a low voice, 'Let the Cheruscan tribal council meet. We can discuss it there.'

Cegestes bristled, but said nothing.

Varus, still holding their arms, said, 'Yes, yes. Do that. I order it. Now let us enjoy ourselves.'

CHAPTER 20

5 BCE
ROME

CLEON DECIDED TO SEND THE older child to school.

They found a grammar school for boys of equestrian and wealthy families. Cleon accompanied Arminius for the first few weeks.

Arminius stood out among the Roman boys. He was long limbed and a head taller than the others, with light skin and tawny hair. From his first day, the others stared at him. They would sneer when he raised his hand in classes.

'Have you made any friends?' Cleon asked him after a few days.

'No.'

'Try harder.'

Arminius did. He would smile when they sniggered at him. Sometimes he would even joke back, making fun of himself. The taunts continued.

The work, at least, was easy. He would finish well ahead of the majority of the class, and the teachers seemed pleased with him. He began to show his answers to a few boys who were slower. Once or twice, the teacher caught him, and he was beaten, but he did not mind.

Cleon stopped going into the school with him, rather fetching him in the late afternoon and continuing tuition at home. He had other students now. He asked the instructors how Arminius was doing.

'Oh, he is very clever, and pleasant – charming even.'

'And the other boys? What do they make of him?'

'There have been incidents…'

Arminius left his satchel near the gymnasium one day, and returned to find that someone had stood on it, smashing the tablets and implements within. He knew who it was. A boy called Licinius led them. He was big for his age. His father was a senator. Licinius had a brother serving in Germania.

88

Arminius returned one day, carrying his sandals.

'What happened?' Quintus asked him.

'Someone cut the straps.'

'Is this the same someone who put filth on your tunic?'

'Yes.' The boy's jaw was firm.

'Do you want me to do something about it?'

'No. I shall deal with it myself.'

Quintus nodded. He did not mention it to his master. Cleon assured him that the boy was learning very quickly. Besides, he had to learn to defend himself.

In the second year in the school, Flavus joined Arminius. The first day started predictably, with Licinius's mob taunting Arminius. He smiled back, as he normally did.

'Stay with me,' Arminius told Flavus, but of course, Flavus had to go and join the younger boys.

Arminius joined the older children, studying arithmetic. He loved the subject, and completed the work quickly, even though his mind was elsewhere. He showed his wax tablet to the teacher, who commended him. He caught Licinius's gaze: poison.

After the lessons, he looked up Flavus. He found him with one of the house slaves by the gate. Flavus was crying. Someone had put dog shit in his satchel. Arminius helped him wash it out, his face immobile. It had happened to him before. A teacher came over and asked what had happened.

'It is nothing, Sir.'

The teacher, also a slave, took him at his word.

The next day, Flavus was tripped up moving between classes. He landed with his face in the dust. Arminius saw it happen, but did nothing. Licinius did not bother to taunt him any more. Arminius just smiled, and joked, and he was too strong for any of the boys to take on. Besides, he had a few friends now.

Flavus, however, was another matter. A few days later, the younger brother sported a bruise on his arm. He said that he had gained it in the gymnasium. 'We were wrestling.'

'Who did it?'

Flavus would not say. He hesitated, and then told Arminius, 'I do not want to go back to school.'

They did return to school, but by lunch, Flavus came looking for his brother, crying. He was bleeding from a cut to his lip. Arminius knelt before him, and rubbed away the tears with his thumbs. He hugged the younger boy.

Arminius stood up, and walked to the gymnasium. He picked up one of the small weights used in long jumping, and hid it under his tunic. An instructor stopped him as he walked across the central square, asking him about the forthcoming rhetoric competition in which he was participating. Arminius smiled, reassuring him that he was preparing diligently. Then he walked on.

Licinius was walking down the courtyard with a friend. They were on their way to lunch. Arminius turned towards them. Licinius spotted him, and smirked, but continued on his way. The distance closed. Arminius was walking in a leisurely fashion. He averted his eyes as he got nearer to Licinius. The Roman boy opened his mouth to say something.

Arminius exploded into action, his left forearm hitting Licinius's throat and pushing him back two feet against a wall. His right arm swung down, smashing the lead weight into the side of Licinius's knee. The bones cracked viciously.

'You fuck! You barbarian scum!' Licinius swore as Arminius, throwing the weight aside, continued walking. 'Fuck all of you!'

Arminius stopped, and turned. His face was still unnaturally calm. He studied the cursing, whimpering Roman boy.

'We're going to kill every fucking one of you!' Licinius hissed.

Arminius smiled softly, and walked back. Licinius's friend, who had briefly considered defending him, jumped aside. Licinius raised his hands to defend himself, but Arminius, brushing them aside, grabbed him by the back of the neck and, turning his head, smashed his nose into the wall. Licinius collapsed.

Arminius crouched by him, and waited to be punished.

Licinius's father was furious. Only Statilius Taurus's considerable influence, and the payment of a large sum of money, prevented criminal proceedings. Even so, Lucinius's family sent over some thugs, who were allowed to rough Arminius up. He fought them as well. They beat him unconscious.

He went back to school two months later.

* * *

8 CE, FESTIVAL OF TERMINALIA (23 FEBRUARY)
CASTRA OCTA

Arminius dined with Lucius Caedicius the night before the meeting of the Cherusci chiefs. The fort commander was in good spirits, glad to meet 'his old friend', as he put it, and brought out his best food and drink.

'I heard about your good work in the highlands,' Caedicius remarked, as they lay down on one of the dinner couches. 'You have impressed a lot of people.'

'What have you heard?'

'The Marser are very happy. Demand for products coming up the Lupia and Amisia are up now that the Erz smuggling routes are closing, and they have raised their prices. We had to clear up several fights between Cherusci and Marser over prices. However, the Hermunduri have been suffering more from raids.'

None of this surprised Arminius. He asked who the Cherusci brawlers were. According to Caedicius, they tended to be from the Bear clan who, boxed in between rivers and the Erz, had been most reliant upon Marcomanni supplies. 'The Marser really cheat them, yet they are increasingly friendly with Cegestes's crowd. I think that the Cherusci are splitting apart!'

'It would not be bad if it did. The days of the old tribal divisions should end. However, we don't want some of them siding with the Semnones instead.' He saw that Caedicius was losing interest. 'We Romans stuck our hands into a bush when we invaded, and grabbed the end of a beast. We are pulling at it, not knowing how large the beast is, hoping that we can control it.' He shrugged. 'Whatever the case, we must sever the Cherusci from the Semnones now, finally.'

'How large do you think is the beast?' Caedicius asked through a mouthful of mutton.

'I hope to find out,' Arminius replied. 'Across the Albis, the Semnones guard a grove, sacred to all the Germans, which is guarded by priestesses, and is said to contain skulls going back two thousand years. If the beast has a head, it is in that grove.'

Caedicius, splayed on the couch, laughed aloud. 'Human sacrifice and insane women: it all makes sense now!' He groaned as he patted his stomach. 'And when will these harpies strike? When will the monster stir?'

'I think that they are already preparing for their uprising. They are smuggling in weapons from the iron deposits in Marcomanni lands, through the Erz. And somebody is coordinating it all.'

'Maroboduus?'

'Maroboduus is Valich – he is a Celt, a Gaul. His people are mixed: refugees from a dozen tribes. The Suebi will not follow him. No, I fear it is one of my own people, but I cannot prove it yet.'

They discussed the following day's meeting.

'I want to try and flush out the traitor,' Arminius explained. 'I want to present them with the evidence of the smuggling, and I want them to give me men. If I am lucky, I can find out who is planning this uprising. But it will be difficult.'

They talked about what they would do, and came to an agreement. Arminius poured Caedicius wine.

CHAPTER 21

IT WAS THE FESTIVAL OF the boundary stones, Arminius reflected. Wherever Romans resided, men walked to where fields converged to reassert borders and renew friendships. The night before, families had dined together to patch up quarrels and share memories. It was a day for beginnings.

Snow lay heavy, even here in the lowlands. It leeched life from the brittle forest. Deer and boar scratched the ice-covered earth for scrappy plants. Women turned their first nervous eye in the direction of the pantry. Out in Illyria, he knew, Roman killing squads were fanning out, seeking the places where summer's burnt fields and slaughtered herds left rebels gaunt and wild-eyed, gnawing on leather and leaves in their hillside sanctuaries. In Germania, as there, Rome was well fed, but only Rome's friends were secure. Of old, the poor had turned to their chief for food. Now, lines formed by the gates of the Roman forts.

Waiting in the weak noon sun, snow crunching under his boots, Arminius waited for the Cherusci clans: the Wolf from the west of his Boar clan; the Bear from the east.

Caglem entered through the compound's gate. The man leaned on his staff – arthritis made it hard for him even to hold a spoon.

'Is Kuonraet here yet?' Arminius asked.

'He is a short distance away,' Caglem said, exhaling snot. 'Bannruod is with him. Cegestes will move up when he crosses the river. Do you know that in the old days we killed the last man to arrive at a meeting?'

'I do.'

This put Caglem off for a moment. 'They have brought Fruwin, as I suspected.'

Fruwin was a contemporary of Arminius's grandfather Berinhard, who had conquered the Amisia fifty years before. He had moved to live with the Bear clan after the Roman invasion.

'They are almost certain to use him against you. Treat whatever he says with great respect.' Caglem lowered his voice. 'Only the Great Mother demands more honour.'

'I don't want to hear about her,' Arminius said. 'I told the Roman fort commander of her last night. He will be alert for mention of her.'

'He barely understands Suebic. He is a drunk and a rapist.'

'Yes. However, he has spies,' Arminius said, 'and I want them to hear what I want them to hear.'

'Are you going to tell me what you intend to do?' Caglem asked.

'Just support me when I speak. The angrier we make Kuonraet, the better.'

Outside, he heard the tramping of hobnailed boots and clattering of arms. Caedicius emerged through the gate, riding a bay horse and followed by a centurion, twenty legionaries, and scribes. The man was ashen from the previous night's drinking and smiled bleakly as he dismounted. He gave the Roman salute in a clowning manner. Arminius, in his legionary dress uniform, returned the salute as if on parade. Caglem nodded respectfully.

'What a lovely bloody day for a get-together!' Caedicius grumbled in Latin. 'I feel full of the love of my fellow man.'

'We are in for another month of snow,' Arminius replied.

Arminius shared small talk with the commander until Cegestes arrived, accompanied by a retinue of advisors and German bodyguards in Roman armour. Both he and his advisors wore white togas over their barbarian trousers – the latter a compromise enforced by the savage weather.

'Ah, how good to see you,' Arminius greeted him as the older man dismounted. 'How is Tiberia?'

'She is well,' Cegestes replied, his mouth twitching with affected politeness. 'Your father is within?'

'He is. He will be pleased to see you.'

Cegestes nodded gravely, and introduced his two elderly advisors to Caedicius. The formalities completed, he led them into the hall.

Caedicius met Arminius's gaze, his eyes brimming with pent-up humour. 'They try *so* hard.' He coughed. 'I suppose I have to go in there to represent the Senate, or something.'

Arminius awaited the final faction. It did not take long.

Kuonraet arrived on a sorrel charger so large that only Roman stables could have produced it. That was his only concession to Roman culture. He was enormous, his heavy-boned face ringed by an abundant blond beard, his hair long and piled atop his skull, his cheeks tattooed with stylised bear's fangs. He wore a cloak of bearskin, the cape formed by the bear's scalp and face, and a necklace of bears' teeth draped across his Roman-style chain mail. He finished his attire with leather breeches and fur boots.

As his guard rode into the compound, Kuonraet turned his horse sideways and stared arrogantly at Arminius. Behind him was a massive man of about twenty, who could only be Bannruod, Kounraet's heir. He echoed his father's dress, right down to the tattoos.

One other man drew his attention. Whereas all the other Bear clansmen were warriors, this one was shrunken with age, and bent forward in the saddle. Only his eyes retained power. Fruwin.

'You are Armin?' Kuonraet snarled in Suebic, his horse stomping the ice-hard earth.

More warriors entered the compound. Some were on foot and lightly armed with javelins and throwing-axes. They had clearly run alongside the cavalry during the journey. The warriors eyed the legionaries, who had drawn up on one side of the square, with contempt.

'I am,' Arminius called out in Cheruscan Suebic. 'And you are the Bear Lord, Oakson and Ring-giver.' He touched his heart.

Kuonraet just snorted. 'Where is your father?'

'He is inside. Shall I call him?'

Kuonraet whispered to Bannruod over his shoulder, and the son smirked.

'Why waste time?' Kuonraet snarled, dismounting. He strode past Arminius and the mute Caglem. Bull-necked Bannruod followed, spending a moment to glare at Arminius, who felt like a hound circling another dog.

Fruwin approached the steps with painful slowness, maimed by the years. Rheumy eyes studied Arminius. 'You are the Roman?' he enquired hoarsely, his lips trembling.

'I am Armin,' Arminius replied in Suebic, and offered his arm to steady the old man up the stairs. The septuagenarian dismissed him angrily. Arminius watched him mount the stairs, leaning heavily on his oak staff. They followed him inside.

Caedicius assumed the chair, while the three clans each occupied one side of the U-shaped line of benches. Sigimer, Inguiomer and their advisors occupied the left leg, but Arminius walked over to Caedicius's immediate right.

'What is this?' Cegestes exclaimed in Latin. Kuonraet did not know the language, and did not seem to care. His eyes were only on Sigimer.

'The *Decurion* will act as my principal translator and adjutant,' Caedicius responded. 'I have little time, and we have a lot of business.'

'It is unfair to the other clans.'

'The officer is not one of you, but one of *us*,' Caedicius snapped. He sat down.

Cegestes had to obey. A scribe read the agenda. Arminius translated effortlessly.

They sat through reports on roads and taxes, river traffic and imports of wine, complaints about brawls, and gifts to the new governor. A few times, men, mostly Cegestes and his advisors, asked a question. Caedicius presided, heavy-lidded and bored.

Finally, the Roman officer got up and yawned.

'Is that it?'

The scribe nodded.

Caedicius swore under his breath. 'Fine then; Rome is satisfied with what you have achieved. As for me, I am done.' He indicated Arminius. 'The *Decurion* will listen to the rest of your business. He will represent Rome.'

Cegestes swore loudly.

Arminius advanced purposefully.

'Please invite Fruwin to the chair,' Caedicius noted to Arminius, who translated. Caedicius was following his instructions to the letter.

Kuonraet and Cegestes could not sway Caedicius to remain. He left some scribes behind, even though none of them apparently knew Suebic. Then he strolled out.

'Fruwin,' Arminius said respectfully in Suebic. 'Would you please father this meeting?'

The old man, still sitting hunched over by Kuonraet's side, blinked.

'Would you do us the honour?' Arminius repeated, arm over his chest, averting his eyes.

The ancient staggered to his feet and cast his eyes about the room. He received a nod from Kuonraet, Sigimer, and finally, Cegestes. He limped towards the throne. He studied it, and asked for a stool instead. Silence descended as he closed his eyes, and seemed to slip into a trance.

Arminius knew that he had to wait for him to start.

'Eighteen seasons have we, Wood-seed, Tyw's Believers, Men of Men, heard Romans lisp among our hearths,' Fruwin finally began to intone in Suebic. 'Sad the heart beneath Suebic sky, free no more. Swords have melted, spear rooted in rust, shields become worm food. Arrows seek but doe and hare. Our mead flows by Roman leave.' He descended into silence again, his lips pulsing. Then he looked across at Arminius. 'I am Fruwin *su eb* Thuwor *eb* Bjorart *eb* Gaetwan *eb* Borslech, Slayer of the Valich. My lineage is of warriors and sages, back through the Frost Time, back to the first man Mannus, and the flame of Tuisto, God-hero, who first opened his eyes under the Heaven Tree. Who are you?'

All eyes turned to Arminius.

'I am Armin *su eb* Sigimer *eb* Berinhard. I am here for Rome, and for the tribe.'

Fruwin shook the words off, as if he were tossing water from his hair. 'Are you of the tribe?'

'I am.'

'That remains for us to see. Tell us what Rome says.'

Arminius began: 'Elders, thank you for meeting. For eighteen years, we have been under Rome. In that time, we have, on the whole, prospered.' He met with stony silence. 'Rome has brought roads, markets, trade, better crops, and better goods. Our eyes have opened to a great world. Our nobles are respected, and their children are educated as Romans.' He moved unhurriedly, using his hands for emphasis and making eye contact with individual listeners. 'Alas, Rome has not brought peace. Even today, three legions must patrol this province against our enemies.' He lowered his eyes and allowed the silence to deepen. 'This winter, I patrolled the Erz against our old foes the Marcomanni. I saw the damage they do to our lands. I found smithies making arms to kill us. However, I also found smuggling. I found weapons' caches in our lands that could arm hundreds of warriors. Returning to face my Roman superiors, I had to choke the knowledge in my breast, for I did not want their retribution upon you.' He clenched his fist. 'So tell me now, kin. Why are we preparing for a war with Rome? Tell me, before Rome strikes.'

Kuonraet, who sat low on the bench, his great legs extended before him, glared from beneath his bushy brows. His sword rested against his left thigh.

Fruwin shook his head. 'Your question is poison, Arminius. What man can answer it without condemning himself?' He looked around him, challenging any to refute his words.

'I know, but I know on whose lands the weapons were found. I want that man to speak. Who is he for? Is he with the Marcomanni? Is he with the Semnones? Why do smugglers carry iron into his territory?'

Bannruod growled next to his father, who turned his head to quiet him.

'What does Maroboduus promise? Is it alliance?' Arminius asked.

Fruwin glanced at Kuonraet, who grimaced, and then said, 'You know well that there are no borders in winter, and that Rome does not protect against raiders when the snows have fallen. People smuggle. Villages make their own agreements. I do not watch each headman like a hawk.'

'The weapons I saw were not for villages. They were for war, as in the old days.'

Kuonraet snorted. 'He speaks of the old days as if he remembers them! I know that there is smuggling. I do not stop it, for I care for my people. Rome took away their arms, promising them protection. However, Rome does not protect. In summer, it fights our brothers, and in winter, it withdraws to the Lupia. Why should I stop my villages from doing whatever protects them?'

'Are you not a chief to your hundreds?'

'*Chief* is a Roman word, *King* is another.'

Sigimer bristled. 'Don't pretend to be the wise old man, Kuonraet! Just tell us what you've been doing!'

'Do you not rule the Bear clan for Rome?' Arminius enquired again.

Kuonraet hissed, 'I am the father of my people. I am chosen, by their will, to protect them, not to tell them what to do. If war comes, I lead. In peace, I prepare for war. I fill my mead hall with the brave, and give rings to the loyal. That is what a lord is among *our* people. I am not a bureaucrat,' he said, spitting out the last word in Latin.

'Your people arm themselves, and you know nothing?'

'If my hundreds arm themselves, so be it. I shall rather have them buy weapons from the Marcomanni, than have Marcomanni burn their homes.'

'Hoarding weapons is illegal. Rome will hold *you* accountable.'

'Rome burns my villages if they are armed. The Marcomanni burn our villages if they are without weapons. Even our brothers the Semnones despise us and punish us. My clan must have weapons.'

'How will you protect the tribe against Rome's vengeance?'

'If I leave things as they are, there will be no clan for Rome to punish.'

'Rome is too stupid to distinguish one clan from another!' Arminius bellowed. 'If one clan arms itself, all of us will be punished!' When Kuonraet refused to reply, Arminius turned to Cegestes. 'What do you think of this rebellion?'

'There is no rebellion, only self-defence.'

'The law says no weapons, unless you are part of a militia.'

'Yes, and I enjoy Rome's protection, but peoples friendly to Rome, and well-garrisoned forts, surround my lands. My brother Kuonraet faces the anger of Maroboduus, and of the Semnones.'

'You condone illegal weapons, then?'

Cegestes sighed. 'I do not condone them, but I am not the Bear clan's chief. I have my disagreements with my brother, and I have urged him to be careful, but I trust his counsel to his people.'

'And will you fight with the Bear clan when Rome punishes Kuonraet's people?'

'I trust him completely.'

'But trust him to do *what*? Kuonraet, a chief of the old sort, contents himself with drinking *beor*, collecting young warriors, pissing and fighting, and taking his counsel from peasants' councils!'

Bannruod rose to his feet with a snarl.

Arminius continued, 'When those villagers decide, with *beor*-fattened bravado, to rebel against Rome with Maroboduus, will he collect his young warriors, arm them with his buried swords, and attack the legions?'

Fruwin emphatically shook his head at Bannruod, who snorted like a bull, and seemed about to launch himself at Arminius.

Arminius affected laughter. 'Is it just that I do not understand this! Does Rome not speak to Sigimer, and Sigimer, Cegestes and Kuonraet to their clans, and the clan chiefs to the hundreds? Is that not the system under Rome?' He shrugged, feigning confusion.

Cegestes cleared his throat. 'That is how Rome sees it, Armin, but in practice…' He hesitated, casting a glance at Kuonraet. 'The people hate Rome. I wish it were not so, but they do, even among my clan.'

Kuonraet breathed heavily, but his fixed glare remained directed at the floor. Bannruod had resumed his seat. He continued to burn with hate.

Fruwin stepped in. 'Allow me to say it. I care not whether I am punished.' He looked up at Arminius. 'Yes, Rome has created a system, with governors and chiefs. But that is not our way. Your father, or my old friend Caglem, should explain the old ways to you. Villages make decisions together. Headmen do not give orders.' He gave a deep sigh. 'These ways have suited us since very ancient times. Custom and the wisdom of old men and women guide life. Despite Rome's conquest, that is still how the vast majority of us live. We are like a woman living with a boorish man. He boasts, and drinks, and fights, and insults her, but in secret she rules her household, keeping all together, tolerating his excesses and stupidity.'

Arminius nodded deeply. 'I understand, Fruwin, but if the villages arm, Rome will hold the chiefs responsible. I have seen it in other places. Rome will bring fire and enslavement, and our roads will be lined with corpses. We cannot let that happen.'

Fruwin glanced at Kuonraet. 'We try to keep the peace in our own way. Cegestes does it by dressing like a Roman, and bringing his people trade. Sigimer keeps the generals happy, and has you as his son. Kuonraet attempts to keep his people's fears at bay. However, the people still hate Rome. They see legions kill their kin and desecrate their shrines. They see chains of slaves. Roads bring settlers and new ways. They are now taxed, and Roman courts do not respect their traditions. The people fear for their children, and therefore they cannot feel free.'

Kuonraet was nodding. Cegestes ran his fingers across his chin. Sigimer alone was keeping his face blank.

'Even you, your sight dimmed by Roman wealth and education, can see how this will end,' Fruwin said. 'We will vanish.'

Arminius sighed. 'The tribe will not disappear.'

Fruwin shook his head. 'What are we to do? If we fight, we are extinguished; if we do not fight, we fade. What man would see his world depart without resisting?'

'I am proof that we can live with them.'

'You are proof that even our finest can be turned against us.'

Arminius's eyes searched the lake of faces.

Fruwin continued. 'Allow me to give you some advice, Arminius. Rome wants kings, but the tribes will never tolerate them.'

Cegestes added, 'And this is why we won't give you the warriors that you asked from the governor. I have told Kuonraet of your suggestion to Varus, and we are in agreement.' He glanced at Sigimer. 'I can guess what your father wants. His ambitions have been clear for a long time.'

'As always, jealousy rules Cegestes,' Sigimer snarled.

Arminius shot a firm glance at Sigimer. The chief halted. Arminius had warned him beforehand not to lose his temper, and he had posted grim Inguiomer next to him, just in case.

'I ask for five hundred men. I can bring peace, and the villages will not have to arm themselves. We can avoid being drawn into a revolt by peasants.' He met with menace. 'I respect the old ways. I am not here to force people to become Roman, but the customs that served us before Rome will destroy us now. Rome is nervous about Maroboduus. If our villages arm themselves with Marcomanni weapons, the legions will strike! Thousands of us will die! If you will not tell these people what to do, you must let me keep them safe, so that they need not think of war. It is the only way.'

Kuonraet laughed derisively, shaking his head. 'Ah, the boy has his father's silver tongue! I remember eighteen years ago, when the Romans came, that Sigimer spoke as eloquently. Resist, he said. We can beat them back and hound them through the forest. And when the battle started, where was Sigimer? If he fought, I have heard of no great deeds being told of him. I know but that my father died, and two of my uncles, and my brother, and that while I searched for their corpses, Sigimer took his sons and sold them to gain favour with Rome.'

Arminius had expected Kuonraet to mention that day at some point. He had given his father dire warnings not to rise to the taunt. Moreover, he had given Inguiomer instructions to remove Sigimer if the taunts proved too much.

'Sigimer, the great warrior, became the Romans' favourite! A man who had been the least of the clan chiefs now became their "king"!' He jabbed his hand at Arminius. 'And now I am asked to trust his son?' He bared his teeth. 'I can see the fever of kingship in your eyes.'

Inguiomer exclaimed, 'I have seen this man fight!' and, pointing at Arminius, 'I believe that he can do anything he says.'

Kuonraet's eyes narrowed angrily. 'I am not giving men over to this *creature*. What do you think he will do if he is allowed to become a warlord?'

'If you cannot protect your own villages…'

'*Damn you*!' Kuonraet exclaimed, rising to his feet. 'Of all the people in this room, *you* should know Sigimer!'

'This is not about Sigimer,' Inguiomer said calmly. 'This is about avoiding another war with Rome.'

Kuonraet began to speak, but then abruptly caught himself as he remembered the Roman scribes in the room.

'I do not believe,' Inguiomer began, 'that Cegestes wants to fight Rome, regardless of what his peasants want. I know that Sigimer has made peace with them. In your lands, though, the peasants are arming themselves. What is next? Will you invite the Marcomanni in?' He pointed at Arminius. 'As much as I hate Rome, I shall not let your peasants draw me into another hopeless battle with the legions. Give him men, or maintain the peace yourself. That is your choice.'

Kuonraet's gaze turned towards Cegestes. The assembly waited.

'You have to decide now,' Inguiomer pushed him.

Kuonraet hissed, 'I shall *not* give Sigimer's son men!' His eyes did not waver from Cegestes.

Sigimer said authoritatively, 'Then you must keep the peace in your territory, or be deposed.'

'What do you say?' Kuonraet asked Cegestes.

'I shall keep my people at peace with Rome. But I, too, shall give no men to Arminius.' He turned to Sigimer. 'And if you threaten Kuonraet again, you shall have me to reckon with. We are not your servants.'

Kuonraet grimaced. 'Good, then that is settled. Tell the legions they must protect us, or we will protect ourselves.' He looked towards Fruwin. 'I take my leave.' He stalked out, followed by Bannruod and his retinue. Fruwin remained a moment longer, studying Arminius. The young officer's face was harsh with tension.

'Sigimer,' Cegestes said in farewell, as he too rose, and offered his arm for Fruwin to lean on. They departed together, with the Boar clan representatives watching their receding backs in silence.

Arminius relaxed only when the doors closed behind them. He turned his back upon the scribes. Warmth crept into his eyes. The meeting had gone exactly according to plan.

CHAPTER 22

8 CE, EQUIRRIA (27 FEBRUARY)
CASTRA DRUSUS

'I AM RATHER DISAPPOINTED IN THEM,' Varus noted before draining a bowl of water. He had been drinking heavily the night before; depressed by the interminable darkness. 'I expected them to have more sense.'

'They refused flatly,' Arminius declared. 'I, too, expected more. But what can one do?'

They sat by the governor's desk in the library. The scribes had been dismissed. Numonius Vala leaned against one of the pillars, his arms folded, his brow furrowed.

'I cannot ignore it,' Varus growled, aware of Vala's eyes on him. The intelligence chief had insisted on slipping a scribe who could understand some Suebic into the Cherusci meeting. The slave's report, made before Arminius had even arrived back at Aliso, corresponded closely with the young officer's version. So much, Varus thought, for Vala's disquiet about Arminius.

'We have no idea how much weaponry has been smuggled into the area. Nor can we find most of the caches. The land there is wild and broken up,' Arminius told them. 'But storming in there with a legion and trying to force the people to give up the arms will be like hitting a gnat with a tree. It will simply make the province go up in flames.'

'So, what do you propose?' Vala demanded.

'First, we need to give them year-round security. Second, we need funds to encourage informants. Third, I need some means of controlling Kuonraet.'

'What about just replacing him?' Varus snapped. 'The man is clearly a rebel.' He immediately raised his hand in apology. 'Do not worry, I know. Subtlety is the best way.' He sighed. 'What about building him a new gathering hall? That or a market that he can tax.' He waved his fingers dismissively. 'I have done so with other barbarians; it works.'

Armin commended the governor on his idea.

'We can work out the details later. For now, I can confirm your request.' Varus shot Vala a warning glance, lest he intervened. 'I shall send a courier tomorrow requesting the transfer of your brother and your unit here.'

'Thank you, Sir. My father can furnish another few hundred if need be.'

Varus nodded. His head began clearing as he scratched down a note. Even Vala's baleful stare did not bother him. 'Moreover, I am ending this silly situation of you being a mere *decurion*. You clearly know what you are doing, so I am restoring your rank to praefectus. You will still follow Vala's directives and report to him, but do whatever is necessary to end his… problem.'

Vala shifted uncomfortably, but did not speak up.

'Thank you for your confidence in me. I shall need funding to get things going.'

'Money is available,' Varus said.

'And I need you to take care of another matter, which will improve our position.'

'What is it?' Varus asked, tapping on his desk.

'I would like you to keep Lady Tiberia, Cegestes's daughter, here at Castra Drusus. Cegestes has promised her to Kuonraet's son Bannruod.'

Varus produced a boyish grin. 'She is a beautiful girl. You have an interest in her?'

'I do,' Arminius replied, returning the smirk. 'But her value goes deeper. The meeting confirmed my suspicion that Cegestes is using her to ally with Kuonraet.'

'And why should I not allow this? Cegestes can only have a good influence on this Kuonraet.'

Arminius smiled. 'Because such an alliance will mean my father's death, and I would no longer be your *devoted* servant.'

Varus sized him up. The young officer, tall and handsome, seemed relaxed. Beneath his skin, though, he was like a coiled snake. Even shaven, and with his hair in neat Roman fashion, he possessed an ineradicable wildness. He reminded Varus of a pet cheetah he had owned in Africa. For years, the beast had eaten from his hand. Then one day, it savaged a child, tearing it apart. Varus executed the beast himself. He said, 'The lady will live here. I take it that she is not to be the only hostage?'

'My father has two young children.'

Varus was taken aback by the offer. 'Is it necessary for him to leave a hostage?'

'It is probably not, but the tribe will notice, and the children require education anyway.'

They shared a weak joke, only Vala remaining aloof. The intelligence chief requested final orders and then, stiffly, left. When the doors closed behind him, Varus winked in Arminius's direction. 'He does not like you, even more so now that you have shown his work to be *patchy*.'

'That was not my intention.'

'It does not matter. I like you.' Varus grabbed a winter cloak, and invited Arminius to walk with him. They left the library by a small side doorway guarded by two sentries. The soldiers – burly, scarred Africans from the governor's bodyguard – saluted smartly.

'I miss Africa,' Varus mused as they crossed a courtyard. 'The Africans are civilised. Their cities were edifices. There is a proud past. This place is so crude.'

'I know how you feel, Sir.'

'You saw Africa?'

'I served in Aegyptus and I also travelled to Leptis Magna, Sir.'

'And compared to Syria, even those places are hovels!' They passed down the outside of the gubernatorial quarters through a square. Legionary stable-hands tended horses on the opposite side. 'Oh, the East! What magnificence: spices and silks! The music could hush any heart. And gold! This place is *shit*. But we, Arminius, will bring civilisation to it. And we are starting with proper courts of law!' He pointed to the squat, red-tiled buildings ahead. 'As you know, I have set up an appeals court here where I personally dispense justice. The military courts are fine, but this is the real *Pax Romana*. We have to show the natives how Roman law works!' He punched his fist into his open palm.

He led Arminius into the torch-lit interior of the court building. Scribes were copying documents and filing records – the new bureaucratic machinery already dwarfed that which had preceded Varus. Every room housed officials and shelves. The drone of distant voices permeated every cranny.

'And this is my public,' Varus drolled. The court was held in an open yard. The judge sat under the awning. Even in this cold, tribespeople filled the yard: a mass of brown, grey, and green cloaks with a smattering of blue. As Varus entered, the audience was prompted to stand by a blast of a trumpet. There were thirty legionaries standing by.

'We have a rather interesting case today,' Varus noted, as he took his seat and invited Arminius to stand by his side. 'The charge is breaking the peace, but there is a complication. The victim and accused come from different tribes.' He smirked, noting offhandedly that he could hardly distinguish between male and female barbarians at times, 'never mind one bunch of thugs from another.'

The shackled prisoner was led inside and a murderous hiss rose from the mob. He was heavily bruised and shackled. His accuser, a Cherusci, followed. This man received cheers from most of the crowd. A smaller knot of people, standing close together, glared and muttered. Varus invited Arminius to interpret for the prisoner and his representative.

Even before the torrent of words commenced, Arminius knew that the prisoner was Chatti. He was dressed in the tattered remnants of blue-and-red tartan trousers, and blue tattoos ran from his cheeks to behind his ears. His elderly representative, a chieftain, followed Chatti fashion even more strictly: he sported a great moustache instead of the Cherusci beard, and a massive bronze torque with ends the shape of bulls' heads. The Chatti worshipped the aurochses, the wild bulls of the forest. They spoke Suebic with a thick accent. Every time the Chatti man spoke, the Cherusci crowd hooted, and Varus had to threaten to send in his legionaries.

'The Cherusci man says that his homestead was attacked by Chatti. They killed his brother, who tried to defend the women and the cattle. The Cherusci chased the Chatti, and they captured this man. They brought him to you as the father of both the tribes.'

'And what says the other man?'

Arminius struggled to make sense of the testimony. The Chatti also claimed to be the aggrieved party. They, too, had been raided and their fields burned. They had merely retaliated against the Cherusci village they knew was responsible. 'They demand that their man be set free.'

Varus was pinching the bridge of his nose. He asked for more detail about the difference between the tribes.

'They are Valich and they have a different religion and language from us. They are family of the people the Romans call the Gauls. The Marcomanni are also mostly Valich.'

Varus became more attentive the moment the Marcomanni were mentioned.

'The Chatti used to occupy land further north. My grandfather pushed them over the Lupia, but even though he took one of their princesses, my grandmother, as his woman, the Chatti have never forgiven us.'

Arminius looked out at the crowd. The legionaries had confiscated the weapons of all barbarians in the yard, yet he knew that hidden daggers had probably escaped the Romans. The Chatti would have to be escorted by Romans to their homes.

The Chatti speaker let out another torrent of complaints.

'He is called Adgandes. He says that he was your guest when you arrived here.'

'Tell him that I remember him, and that I appreciate him returning on behalf of his people, who are friends of Rome.'

Adgandes seemed little softened by the words.

'He says that the fort, and the town, stands on Chatti land, and that since the Romans built their settlement more Cherusci had crossed the river. He blames my father for invading Chatti lands, even though the Romans promised to maintain tribal boundaries.'

'Tell him that I regret that he still thinks of the Cherusci as his enemy, even though both tribes are children of Rome.'

The Chatti retorted that Rome had not stopped Cherusci raiding. 'He demands compensation for his cattle and for the children the Cherusci have stolen.'

The Cherusci spokesman responded acidly that he too wanted compensation.

Neither side appeared interested in Roman justice unless it involved *wergild* – that is, the price that was on every person's head.

Varus listened to these demands with distaste. 'And, I suppose, if I do not allow this, they will continue fighting?'

The Cheruscan stated guardedly that he would use whatever means necessary to defend his people. 'He says that although my father has tried to mediate, the governor alone holds the solution.'

Varus pursed his lips. 'Tell them that I regret the violence. I had hoped, as all of Rome does, that the protection of our army and courts would make such feuds unnecessary. Rome is determined to provide peace.' He paused. 'Tell them that the *wergild* cannot be allowed. It is not the Roman way. Rather, both sides have admitted to breaking the *Pax Romana,* and both sides should be punished. I do, however, give them a chance.' He paused, waiting for Arminius to communicate the message, and saw the ire rise on both sides. 'Tell them that I am letting you decide their fate.' He then sat back, before saying under his breath, 'You have my permission to continue.'

Arminius felt the attention of the assembly shift directly and exclusively onto him. Even the legionaries, who had heard Varus's command in Latin, gazed at him.

From the moment that they had entered the courthouse, Arminius had suspected that the governor was going to test him somehow. 'What is the punishment for breaking the peace?'

'He has admitted to the murder of at least one Roman subject, and he has forfeited his life.'

Enough people within the crowd could translate the governor's words for the Cherusci to mutter approval. The Chatti looked even more outraged.

Arminius stepped closer to Adgandes. The old man was not hiding his distaste for Arminius. The officer placed his right hand over his heart and inclined his head. To his relief, Adgandes copied the traditional gesture.

'Father, this young man here is a relative of yours?'

Adgandes nodded. 'He is Vegates, my sister's son.' His Suebic was so thick that he could have been speaking with stones in his mouth.

'And he does not deny that he raided the Cherusci?'

'He does not. He defended his people.'

Arminius related the information to Varus, who returned a blank stare.

The centurion in charge of the legionary guards gave Arminius a nervous glance as the Cherusci section of the mob edged closer to the Chatti. Arminius asked for quiet.

'It is clear that a crime was committed here,' he said in Suebic, speaking slowly so that the Chatti could follow. Another interpreter relayed his words to Varus. 'Neither side denies that they broke the *Pax Romana*, and both sides are to blame.'

This caused a furore. The legionaries snapped to attention and Arminius roared at the soldiers to step down. The troops obeyed instantly, even though the centurion had not given the order himself. Arminius snapped at the centurion to do nothing without his permission. The man went pale.

'The law of Rome is the law of the land. By that law, this man Vegates must die. However, if I kill him, I must also demand from the Cherusci the youths that raided the Chatti. So my verdict is this: Vegates is sentenced to die, but his sentence is commuted to slavery.' Hissing issued from the crowd. 'I shall be his master, and he shall serve me in bringing peace between Chatti and Cherusci.' Vegates stared at Arminius in horror. For a warrior to become a slave was the ultimate disgrace. 'In return, the Chatti will receive compensation from the Cherusci. The Chatti will set the compensation, and I shall ensure that it is paid.' He glared at the crowd. Some of the tribesmen shook their fists, and the Cheruscan spokesman cursed. Some people were picking up stones.

Arminius did not bother to consult the centurion: a single, thunderous bark and the legionaries were at attention. Another command and swords were drawn. The power in his voice and the legionaries' reflexive obedience did as much as the show of steel to quash opposition.

'I am Armin *su eb* Sigimer *eb* Berinhard, who married a Chatti,' he bellowed in Suebic. 'I am a Praefectus of Rome! *I* say that the war between Chatti and Cherusci is over! We are *all* under Rome! If you break Rome's peace, you break my peace! I shall raze your village myself.' He glowered at them, singling out individuals. 'Tell your kin.'

He snapped his fingers at the guards to remove the prisoner. The governor regarded him thoughtfully, tapping his fingertips against his lips.

'Your Grace.'

Varus nodded before getting up. He placed his hand upon Armin's shoulder, a smile in his eyes.

As the two men departed, Vala detached himself from his hiding place in a nearby building and headed straight for Saturninus's quarters. The general was busy with paperwork.

'He pardoned him, as I expected,' Vala told the general. It had been his idea for the governor to set the test.

'And what did Varus do?'

'He lapped it all up, but, I repeat: Arminius is dangerous.'

Saturninus sighed. 'He does what we tell him, and he fights well.'

'It is a ploy.'

'What evidence do you have?'

'You have to trust me on this, Sir.'

Saturninus shrugged. 'I would, Vala, but this man comes with very powerful references.'

'I know, I know. He guarded the Emperor. He arrived with recommendations from General Caecina. It does not matter.'

'Prince Tiberius also vouches for him.'

'It does not matter. I want to make my own enquiries.'

'Very well,' Saturninus said after a moment. 'I shall mention it to the governor, but you have my approval.' He sat back and studied his spymaster. 'What do you think he will do?'

'I do not know. He is extremely cunning. He studied our methods and our records, before I stopped him. He knows the province inside out. And he knows that if he strikes us while Illyria is aflame…'

Saturninus nodded. 'Do nothing openly until you have evidence.' He smoothed a sheet of paper. 'Use Cegestes to help you.'

Vala agreed. 'The governor is set on summoning Arminius's brother here, even though it has always been our policy to keep tribal mercenaries out of their home territory.'

'We could ask for hostages,' Saturninus said. 'We could do it tactfully, but he will understand the consequences of any treachery. I understand that his father,

Sigimer, has a wife and two young children? We could make sure that they are under our control.'

'I would still be uneasy,' Vala said.

'Surely, we can control him once we hold his family?'

'Why would he care for these children?' Vala said. 'He has only met them recently, and in truth, they challenge his right to inherit Sigimer's position.'

'Would you sacrifice the children if you were Arminius?'

'There is so much at stake that he might just be willing to risk his family in order to lull us into a false sense of security. Children, even his own half-brothers and sisters, will not stand in the way of this man getting what he wants.'

Saturninus smiled and leaned forward. 'But it will stop Sigimer from betraying us. It will make him watch Arminius very closely.' His eyes searched his subordinate's features. 'You are a father, Vala. Do you think that Sigimer will risk us harming his children? Surely, he will hand over Arminius in an instant to save them.'

'I am not sure what Sigimer will do, Sir.'

'We are both fathers, Vala. I think we know what Sigimer will do. Still, I understand your concerns.' Saturninus folded his hands and looked down. 'Make sure that we can punish any treachery on Arminius's part with a blow to his family. I shall speak to the Governor, and we will take as many hostages as are necessary.'

'Thank you, Sir," Vala said.

'Put your mind at ease. But I think, Vala, that if Arminius is so monstrous that he will begin to sacrifice his loved ones, then his own family will destroy him.'

'We shall see, Sir.'

'Let us consider his next move. Let us imagine that he is planning to fight us. What do you think he will do next?'

'If I were him, Sir, I would contact Maroboduus.'

CHAPTER 23

ONE DAY, CLEON TOOK ARMINIUS out for a walk. He wanted to speak to him alone, to explore his thoughts. They headed down to the forum, where Cleon liked to go to look at the art. He asked Arminius how he felt about school.

'They laugh at my hair and skin, and my tribe.'

'You are no longer of your tribe. You are a Roman.'

'Then why do they mock me?'

'They are children. Ignore them.'

'Do adult Romans respect me? You are a Greek. Do they respect you?'

'I am a slave. You are free.'

'*Do* they respect me?'

Cleon sighed. 'Some of them never will.'

'Then I shall continue to fight them.'

'Fighting will not work. You must earn their respect.'

'And how do I do that?'

'People respect those who most perfectly are what they want themselves to be.'

'Romans respect only force.'

'Romans respect bravery. Romans respect toughness. They respect those who serve the City, and make it great.'

'I respect Hannibal.'

'The Carthaginian?'

'One of my tutors said that Rome is great because it defeated such a great man as Hannibal. He drew the battles for us in the sandpit. Hannibal was very clever.'

'Do you want to be Hannibal?'

'Hannibal lost.'

111

Cleon laughed at this, and told the boy not to reveal these thoughts to Romans. They strolled onwards.

'It does not surprise me that you hate them, but I do not want you to hate Rome because of schoolboys and snobs.'

'They defeated my people.'

'They defeated *my* people too, and yet I know that Athens is superior to Rome. I know it every time I look at their buildings, or attend their theatre.' They ambled into the forum, where they stared up at the gaudy coloured vaults of the Temple of Concord. 'Your patron, Statilius Taurus, found this city made of brick, and he is turning it to marble. And he is inspired by Hellas. Compared to Hellas, you come from a base people who can only benefit through conquest.'

'You say this, yet you are a slave. There is no dignity without freedom, and no life without dignity.'

Cleon displayed a ghostly smile at the dramatic statement. 'Yes, I am their property, like the statues they took from our homes and temples. But *you* are free, and in a position to rise.' His eyes narrowed. 'If you wish to defeat them, let them take you into their hearts. When they love you, they will be vulnerable.'

'Do you think that they deserve to be destroyed?'

Cleon weighed his words carefully. 'One day, if you are in a position to destroy them, think this: is mere freedom from the worst of Rome, worth losing what is most beautiful of Rome? Is freedom worth the loss of progress?'

They never mentioned the conversation again.

At the age of sixteen, after eight years in the architect's house, Arminius came of age. On the Festival of Liber and Libera, the household assembled. They dedicated his children's clothes to the household gods. Statilius helped him put on his pure white *toga virilis*. He was now both a man and a full citizen. The architect accompanied him to the Tabularium, where he was registered. They continued to the forum, where Arminius was introduced to nobles and senators as Statilius's adopted son. That evening, the architect gave a great banquet in his honour. Two hundred Romans attended, including the Emperor's son, Prince Tiberius.

* * *

8 CE, EQUIRRIA (27 FEBRUARY)
CASTRA DRUSUS

'I was surprised by your leniency.'

They were relaxing in the governor's expensive new bath chambers. Arminius sat naked on a bench. A slave girl threw water onto the red-hot rocks in the room's central pit. It released a fresh hiss of steam to drive the temperatures even higher. Another girl was massaging the governor's back. The masseuse was dusky, with curly black hair, and had accompanied the governor from Rome. She was attractive, expensive, and judging by Varus's occasional groans of pleasure, skilled.

'The Lupia has been a war zone too long,' Arminius replied, leering at the girl who tended the steam. She was probably a Gaul; with very light skin, and flaxen hair falling halfway down her slender, naked back. She kept her eyes averted, and the masseuse ordered her around. Arminius beckoned the girl towards him and lazily ran his fingers over her thigh. 'It is our major transport route towards the Rhine, and the most civilised section of the province. These people have to behave.'

Varus stared with sleepy fascination at Arminius's toying hand. He noted that Arminius's leniency would be unlikely to solve the problem.

'Oh, I think it is worth a try,' Arminius said.

'And what do you intend to do with him?'

Arminius's hand had moved to stroke the girl's belly. Being a slave, she made no attempt to stop him. He explained that he would keep the youth with him. 'I have to avoid humiliating him. Let him earn his freedom, and let him see the benefits of civilisation.'

Arminius's hand slipped down between the girl's legs. She squirmed slightly. He did not need to look at her face to tell that she was terrified. Then again, his attention was really focussed on Varus, who now swatted the masseuse's hand away and turned upon his side. He was grotesquely aroused, and made no effort to hide it as he leered at the young woman. His pale, sagging gut drooped.

Arminius removed his hand from the girl and stood up. He patted her on her buttocks. 'I shall see you in the *tepidarium*, Sir.' He sauntered out. Varus barely noticed him.

A short while later Varus strolled into the *tepidarium*, where Arminius sat with his legs in the lukewarm water. His skin was flushed. He idly rubbed his crotch with a blanket. A lazy grin spread across his face. 'At times like this I *really* appreciate the fact that my wife hates cold weather – the bitch.' He joined Arminius. 'Do you have a wife?'

'I have a woman in Rome, and a little boy. His name is Gracchus. But I have not seen either in two years. She lives with her family.'

'You are free then, to pursue the Lady Tiberia?'

'I am not sure that I need the complication!'

'I think you do. She is an attractive woman, and you explained the political benefits.' Varus sighed contentedly as he lowered himself into the pool. 'I would mount her like a billy goat myself!'

Arminius grinned in agreement.

Varus groaned and leaned back against the side of the pool. Arminius sipped some wine, and remarked upon how good it was.

'We got that from Narbonensis. It is decent stuff. I hear, though, that even the Gauls are starting to produce wine now.' He yawned. 'Imagine that! Two generations ago they were headhunters, and now the bastards are aping us.'

'If only we can do the same here.'

'Oh we will, though it might take a bit more time. These Germans are incredibly obtuse.'

'I know,' Arminius remarked. He told Varus that he had been asked by his father to undergo the Cherusci manhood ceremony.

'And this is important to them?'

'It is, if I am to be seen as my father's successor. The traditionalists are adamant.'

Varus asked what form the initiation would take.

'Nothing serious, my father claims.' He laughed light-heartedly. 'Just some light circumcision. His brother, Inguiomer, has agreed to be my guide through it.'

Varus shrugged. 'By all means, do it. Silly barbarian customs!'

CHAPTER 24

8 CE, Festival of Mars (March)
Castra Drusus

VEGATES REMAINED IN THE GAOL at Castra Drusus for several days, before Arminius brought him out into the open. The first scent of spring was in the air. The Lupia was swelling with snowmelt.

Arminius met him on an empty parade ground, away from prying ears, yet visible to onlookers – Chatti, Cherusci and Roman.

Vegates squatted. His wrists were chained together and a rope, the mark of a slave, was tied around his neck. His filthy red hair hung over his face, and he shivered in only a tattered cloak. Two Roman guards stayed with him, as much to protect him as to prevent his escape. Although famished and chilled, there was still fight in the Chatti. The glare he shot at Arminius spoke of pure hate.

'Be careful, Sir,' the one legionary said. Arminius dismissed the guards nonetheless. Then he, too, squatted, and faced the prisoner.

'Vegates,' he said reassuringly, glancing across the man's shoulder to see whether anybody was within earshot.

The man's stare did not waver.

'I am Armin *su eb* Sigimer,' Arminius said softly in Suebic. There was no reply. 'I am here to make you an offer.'

'I am your slave.'

'Yes, but you are the son of a great people.'

Vegates was barely twenty. He had freckled pale skin, and green eyes. Auburn bristles coated his jaw.

'I hear that you tried to kill yourself,' Arminius said.

'What else would you have me do?' Vegates replied.

'I am glad that you did not succeed. And I beg you not to try again.'

There was a flicker of confusion in the Chatti tribesman's eyes. He studied Arminius's face. Finally, he said, 'What do you want from me?'

'Your help.'

'I am your slave.'

'Yes,' Arminius replied. 'But you are also my kinsman through my grandmother. And you are helping me by wearing the rope around your neck.'

Vegates looked at his shackles that bound his wrists.

'I am here to ask for your help,' Arminius continued.

'*Ask* me? I want to kill you, and them.'

'I know.'

'I can kill you.'

'You might kill me, and perhaps, one or two of them, and then you will die, having achieved nothing. We have had enough empty deaths, Vegates.'

'The Chatti would celebrate your death.'

'The Chatti can have far more than me.'

Vegates snorted, and kept his eyes averted.

'Accept the rope, Vegates, and by it, you shall hang them all.'

* * *

Lady Tiberia came to Castra Drusus with three wagons of possessions. They had travelled by the highway, as the river was glutted with floodwater and the boatmen would not travel up from Colonia Agrippina. With her came eight servants. She received rooms in the newly expanded governor's palace inside the fort.

Arminius went to see her the day after her arrival. A tawny youth opened the door. Two other servants, middle-aged women, bowed as he entered the main corridor. They were flitting about with vases and other domestic items in a determined attempt to create a home.

The lady emerged. Her tall frame was draped in an expensive, white, Roman-style stola. The servants had braided and swept up her golden hair, piling it upon her head to bare her neck.

'How dare you come here? I know this is your doing!' she shouted at him in Latin.

He attempted a greeting.

'I know what this is! My father is furious!'

'There is no need,' he told her, using Suebic and raising his hands in his defence.

She glared at him, surprised by his use of the barbarian language. She began to speak, and then halted and lowered her gaze, the tip of her tongue flickering across her lips. 'Am I not a hostage?' she asked icily in Suebic.

'I do not want to talk about this in front of slaves.'

Her eyes narrowed, but she relented and, barking at the servants to continue their work, led him to her private chambers. The room was by far the best decorated of those he had passed – he noted a kitchen and a private washing area – with a low bed in the Roman style, covered in expensive linen. Chests lined the one wall, and the other featured a polished metal mirror. A pair of ornate chairs completed the furnishings.

'The governor's messenger demanded that I come here.' She had switched back to Latin. 'He was polite, yes, but it was clear that there was no choice. It is outrageous!'

'You are no more a prisoner here than you were in Colonia, Thusnelda.' While she hesitated, he let his eyes wander across the room. 'I do not know what you are used to, but this is not bad. It is better than what a prisoner could expect.'

'But I am not free.'

He did not reply.

'Why are you here, Armin?' she asked in the barbarian tongue as she sat down in one of the two chairs. Unlike him, she spoke Suebic with only a slight Latin accent.

'I am here to ensure that you are well looked after.' He did not seat himself, waiting instead for her invitation. It did not come.

'You do not deny that you had me brought here?'

'Nor am I ashamed of it. This is the new capital of the province. A lady of your status should be here. Others will follow soon.' His eyes flitted, taking in small details: a favourite linen dress on the bed, a comb with an exotic handle, a scattering of jewellery on a table. By the mirror was one incongruous item. He walked over to look at it.

'What are you doing?'

He bent forward to study the small toy. It was a wolf cub, about the length of a hand and carved out of wood, its tail curled under its belly. The edges of the toy were smooth from years of handling, and grime had accumulated in the hollows where the barbarian artist had tried to suggest fur.

He asked her what it was.

'It is not your business to know.'

'Please, tell me.'

She sighed. 'My mother gave it to me when I was taken away from home,' she said softly.

'They allowed you to keep it?'

She did not answer. He took a few moments to look at it, aware of her eyes resting on him. Of all the things in the room, it was the only one clearly not Roman.

'How old were you?'

'Six. But you are trying to change the subject.'

'What is the subject?'

'Why you thought it your right to have me brought here.'

'Oh yes,' he told her, turning away from the bed, with a faint smile playing across his face. 'Colonia is not the place for you, and nor is the hearth of Kuonraet.'

'I knew that had something to do with it! What? Are you jealous?'

'I hardly know you, Tiberia.' He continued before she could go ahead with a retort. 'But I *do* know that your betrothal to Bannruod is not in my own interest.' He approached her, and was happy to see that she did not back away even when he was within arm's reach.

There was fire in her gaze. 'My father warned that you would be trouble.'

'Yes,' he laughed, 'your father, who has agreed to marry you, the finest of Roman ladies, to the most brutal of barbarians. What is the point of all of this,' he said, indicating her Roman dress, 'if you are to live out in the woods? Is that your vaunted freedom?'

'It is in the interest of the tribe.'

'Is it? Are you going to Romanise the Bear clan all by yourself?'

'Our arrangements do not concern you.'

'They do. They concern me, my father, and Rome.'

'Don't pretend…!' she began, then hesitated.

'What?'

She ground her jaw, and then said, 'Are you here for Rome?'

He lowered his gaze, and softened his voice. 'You do know what they are doing to you?'

'Of course I do,' she whispered.

'And you do not object?'

'It still does not give you the right…'

'Do you object?'

'What can I do?' she glanced down at her folded hands.

He went down on his haunches and whispered, 'Your father's plan will not work. I have spoken to the governor. You will be sent to Bannruod for nothing.'

'And you prefer to lock me up instead?'

He let the silence drag on for a moment. 'Stay here for now. Nobody will take you from here without my permission. Stay here, and think, and when you have decided, tell me, and I shall respect your wish.'

He smiled gently at her, and then went over to the bed, where he picked up the sleeping cub. He held it in his palm. Then he mused, 'I knew I would find something like this here.'

She seemed transfixed. He tenderly replaced the cub. 'I hope that you are comfortable here. I am sorry that this is necessary.'

She had closed her eyes now.

'I shall not come back without you inviting me,' he said. 'But I hope that we can speak again. We can start with you telling me which name you prefer me to call you: Thusnelda or Tiberia.'

He bid her a good day. She remained motionless.

Chapter 25

8 CE (Early April)
Aliso

Arminius waited for his brother at Castra Octa. It was spring. The passes to the south had opened, and Roman supplies and reinforcements could push through. Numonius Vala and Arminius's father joined him, to the delight of Caedicius, who entertained them. On the fourth day of waiting, Flavus's contingent arrived.

Flavus wore his full uniform, including the red cloak and plumed helmet. The men – nearly five hundred on horseback – cheered when they saw Arminius.

The two brothers greeted one another with a bear hug. Sigimer wept as he embraced the child that he had not seen in seventeen years.

'To Germania!' toasted Caedicius in the officers' mess that evening. Outside, the men were sitting down to their own feast, as Arminius had insisted. 'May your men haunt the enemy!'

Flavus's hair had grown into blond curls during the journey. This, and his beard, he would soon cut. He would order the men to do the same. 'We cannot let things slip, especially now that we are back in the land of their birth.'

Vala enquired after conditions in Illyria.

'It was hard after Arminius left,' Flavus said with a glint in his eyes. 'He is a charm to the troops!' Losses had mounted steadily as the troops had harried rebels in the back-country.

'Is there any sign of the rebels giving up?' Vala enquired.

'Not a chance – they are definitely receiving help from Maroboduus.'

Vala studied the younger brother. He was as tall as Arminius was, though he was not built as powerfully. He spoke Latin in a more sophisticated manner, and he spiced his conversation with references to events in Rome.

'You do not mind coming up here?'

'I am pleased to serve. And I hear that the new governor is an epicurean.'

Vala merely smiled.

Vala watched the next morning as Arminius inspected his command. Arminius spoke to nearly every man, often using their names, and regularly asked to see specific items of equipment. Occasionally he turned to Flavus and enquired after a detail: the supply of boots, the quality of new weapons and horses. The men seemed to be accustomed to it.

The day after inspection, the unit broke up into *turmae* and started patrolling into the wilderness, led by Cherusci scouts. While they were away, a cohort of legionary infantry arrived from the south. They were replacements for losses the legions had suffered during the last summer's campaigns.

Vala was furious. 'I ask for new men, and they send me raw recruits!'

'Experienced men go to Illyria. You should be lucky that you received even these, Sir,' the commander replied.

'Where are they from?'

They were from the deep south of Italia – dark men used to olive groves and sunlight. They already looked miserable amid the woods. There had even been attempts at desertion. As the commander rattled on, Vala began to suspect a budding mutiny. He ordered Caedicius to marshal a cohort of his own legionaries on the parade ground, in full battledress. The two units faced one another in the weak midday sun. Arminius observed, flanked by Flavus, as Vala addressed the troops:

'I am Praefectus Numonius Vala, the eyes and ears of Rome in Germania! You have marched from your homes, through mountains, marshes, woods. At night, wolves howled while you lay in your tents. Familiar sights have faded, and you, new to war, feel yourselves an island. I am the eyes and ears of Rome in Germania, and I tell you that there is but one thing to fear in these lands: Roman arms.'

Vala called to an aide, who brought up two shields and a spear.

'These things were taken from barbarians we fought but a month ago.' He took one shield. 'This is made of wicker!' He cast it aside and took a smaller buckler. 'This is made of planks with cowskin over it. It does not even slow down our swords!' He held up the spear. 'The man who carried this could not even afford metal, only wood! They are fighting us with sharpened sticks!'

He hurled the spear into the earth by the newcomers' feet, and pointed at the veterans. 'Each of these men, each one of you, is sheathed in iron. You carry spears of iron. You carry a sword of steel. Each one of you, down to the humblest *tiro*, carries more iron on your bodies than their kings.' He grimaced. 'The men you will fight will be big, wild, but naked!'

Armin glanced at his brother, who stood with folded arms.

Vala summoned a prisoner. Two legionaries dragged the man forward. Barefoot, with long, tangled hair, he was big even by barbarian standards.

'This man is of the Semnones, a tribe that still fights us.' He asked the words to be translated to the savage, and then asked the man's name. 'He is called Brunald. I am giving him a sword and shield of the quality used by his people's chiefs. I shall fight him without my armour. If Brunald kills me, I promise that he will be taken home unharmed.'

There was a delay as Brunald was told of his fate. The barbarian was untied and received a slashing sword and barbarian shield. Vala took a sword and shield from one of the new legionaries.

Brunald was confused, and a translator had to repeat the order to him. Seeing the sea of Romans, he displayed panic, then resignation.

'He is just a peasant,' Arminius muttered.

Vala hoisted the legionary shield onto his shoulder. It covered his body from chin to knees. He kept his sword low.

The barbarian advanced. His first blow was high, aiming at Vala's skull. Vala took it on the rim of his shield. The barbarian grunted at the impact. A nick had been taken out of his blade. He advanced again; smashing his shield into Vala's. Vala stayed low, his sandals sliding in the dust as he was pushed back. The barbarian sliced in from the left, trying to get around the shield.

Vala countered.

The barbarian lunged at Vala, hissing with effort, his hair flying as he wheeled a blow at Vala's temple. Vala burst forward, his iron boss thudding against the savage's shield. The barbarian yelped and retreated. Blood was coming from his side. Vala's stabbing sword was coated red to an inch from the point.

'See his fear!' Vala exclaimed.

The barbarian glanced at his wound with horror.

Vala slammed his shield into the barbarian's shield. The man countered, but winced as he stepped aside. Blood dribbled down his leg. Vala bashed his shield forward again. The man moved to his right, his sword only half raised. As Brunald lifted his shield, Vala danced to the right. The left edge of his shield hooked around the barbarian's rim and yanked it aside. He jabbed hard and low. The man screamed; he had three inches of steel in his gut.

Vala pushed forward as Brunald tried to drag himself off the blade, keeping him off balance. He twisted the sword, ripping the man's stomach.

Brunald stepped back, mewling like a hurt child, pushing his forearms against his belly.

Vala studied him as one would an animal.

'I care not about Brunald's dignity or his dreams, about his children, or his home. I am here to strip him of everything, and to make him an example to his kin, that they shall not *fuck* with Rome!'

The veterans cheered.

Brunald wept.

Arminius glanced at Flavus. 'This is sickening.'

'Of course,' Flavus replied, not making eye contact, 'but necessary.'

Vala killed the prisoner and, turning him onto his back, slit his chest and throat. Then he ordered each of the recruits to step forward in turn, and dip his fingers into the blood.

* * *

That evening, when the first detachments of Arminius's *ala* returned, Vala sought out Flavus in the stables, where he was overseeing the stable-hands.

'How did it go?'

'The men will have no trouble adapting,' Flavus replied. He was leaning over a beam, twirling straw in his mouth. Vala settled in beside him.

'That was an impressive display: the duel.'

Vala shrugged. 'The man was not very skilled.'

'Nonetheless… it impressed the recruits.'

'Good.'

'My brother is quite a swordsman.'

'What about you?'

'Not really!'

'What are you good at?' Vala enquired pleasantly.

Flavus laughed. 'Architecture! Our patron in Rome was an architect. He let me work with him. But Rome doesn't need German architects.'

'You could attempt engineering. We need engineers here.'

'They barely have any towns.'

'Castra Drusus is bigger. And Colonia Agrippina is a fine place.'

Flavus regarded the cavalry commander doubtfully. He indicated that they should leave the stables. They stepped out into the torch-lit street.

'Your brother seems to like it.'

'I am sure he does,' Flavus snorted. 'He is at his best sleeping in the woods.'

'Arminius told the governor that he has a son in Rome, and a wife.'

Flavus nodded. 'Caecilia. They are estranged. She is of decent stock.'

'He suggested that you stay at Castra Drusus and join the administration.'

'If he can spare me.'

'It seems that he can,' Vala noted. They caught sight of Arminius, surrounded by junior officers from his unit. 'The men seem to love him.'

'He gets things out of them that no other man can.'

'Including you?' They strolled down the lines.

'Oh yes.'

'And this does not bother you?'

'Why should it? He is my brother, and he defends things worth fighting for. Art. Progress. Learning.' He remarked that he had been invited to Sigimer's hall that evening again. 'My father wants to catch up.'

'He seems very proud of you.'

Flavus excused himself.

'I shall find an assignment for you at Castra Drusus, with the governor.'

'Thank you.'

Vala wandered back to the commander's quarters.

Flavus was interesting.

CHAPTER 26

8 CE (APRIL)
ERZ HIGHLANDS

ARMINIUS SQUATTED IN THE CIRCLE of soldiers. They stood over a model of the surrounding valleys, made from stones and branches. 'There is a large village over here. They use it as a base, and we raided it during the winter.'

Vala watched as Arminius's officers made suggestions. He listened to each of the men and opened up ideas for discussion. The men spoke freely and with confidence.

The unit was camped at the base of the Erz, on the Hermunduri side of the border. Vala knew the area well. It was a good first outing for Arminius's *ala*.

'Arbex is correct,' Arminius noted. 'That river will channel them to here.'

Vala had warned himself to reserve judgement, but he was impressed by Arminius's *ala*. The men performed fatigues without complaint. They drank hard in Castra Drusus, and they wore their equipment for battlefield utility rather than parade-ground conformity, but on the mission, they behaved faultlessly. They were almost supernaturally quiet for a force of five hundred.

In previous years, Hiru had rejoined Vala in early spring, appearing as mysteriously from the forest as he had vanished into it that winter. This year, Hiru remained by Arminius's side. Vala was unsure whether he should demand the tracker's return, but the situation bothered him.

'Sir.'

Vala's attention returned to the discussion. He nodded emphatically as Arminius explained the plan to him.

'You assume that they already know that you are here?'

'I would.'

'And you can catch them off guard?'

125

'They will attack here once we taunt them,' Arminius said, pointing at a rock on his model. 'The Hermunduri say that the woods between us and that point are impassable to horses.'

'Are they?'

'We are not attacking them there.'

Vala glanced at Inguiomer, who sat menacingly upon an overturned tree trunk. Inguiomer had been following Arminius closely of late, as if he were one of the lupine hounds waiting nearby.

'Where do you want me to be?'

Arminius gave instructions. Inguiomer watched.

* * *

Two days later, the Marcomanni launched their first big raid of the season. They headed for a Roman caravan bringing supplies to Aliso from the south. A hundred auxiliaries and three hundred Hermunduri guarded two hundred mules laden with gold, steel, spices, cloth, olive oil and wine.

It all proceeded as planned. The Marcomanni hit the convoy in one of the highway's narrow, densely wooded sections. The Hermunduri ran, and the auxiliaries fell back. The Marcomanni ransacked the convoy.

Arminius now watched a line of Marcomanni enter the clearing. The tribesmen were a morning's walk from their nearest village. Some of them were singing. They slowed down to lessen the burden on their shoulders and to blink at the rare sunlight of the glade.

Arminius motioned to his trumpeter. As the man sounded the attack, Arminius exploded into the glade. A hundred men followed.

The Marcomanni turned into a sleet of missiles. Arminius's axe caught a startled man in the face. He shouldered the barbarian into the grass, yanking the blade from his flesh. Almost immediately, the axe found the back of a fleeing youth, sticking in the squirming body, and Arminius drew his stabbing sword as he parried a blow with his buckler. All around, axes, javelins and clubs flew. Shields butted.

The Marcomanni in the clearing died. The survivors scattered. Those foolish enough to rush for their homes would collide with a picket Arminius had hidden to the east.

Arminius slashed the throat of a tribesman, his hand in the warrior's face, his knee in his chest. The man thrashed, blood bursting from his artery.

He looked up and found Flavus sinking his dagger into another fighter's side. The task done, his brother caught his eye. Flavus looked dismal, like a man putting down a horse.

Arminius nodded at him and surveyed the slaughter. Surprise had been total. From the woods beyond came the sounds of further fighting.

'Armin?'

He glanced at Inguiomer. He had released the dogs and their Cherusci handlers into the thickets.

'We have done it,' Inguiomer said bitterly.

'Vala will not be satisfied,' Armin replied in Suebic. He studied the sun, trying to guess how long the light would last.

'And Flavus?'

They watched the younger brother rush into the brush after one of the detachments. As ever, Obed shadowed Flavus, along with four other trustworthy men.

'He will not join.'

* * *

The men were celebrating. The ambush on the returning Marcomanni had worked perfectly. Arminius had lost eight men. In return, he had killed eighty-nine Marcomanni.

Vala, Arminius, Flavus, and Inguiomer sat around one of the fires. They were safe in Hermunduri lands. *Beor* flowed.

'I am impressed,' Vala told Arminius. 'I could not have done it better.'

'Thanks for agreeing to the plan…' Arminius passed him a skin. Vala took a deep swig. Arminius continued, '…and for allowing the pyres.' He had insisted that his casualties be given the burial of chiefs. Arminius had lit the pyres himself. 'It is the way we did it in Illyria.'

Vala's eyes slid over the company. Arminius was leaning forward, hands folded, eyes on the fire which was tended, as ever, by the silent Hiru. Flavus sat straight-backed, rolling his head as if nursing his stiff neck. Inguiomer was watching Flavus.

'I was disappointed by the Marcomanni,' Arminius noted.

'They are peasants and savages,' Vala said.

'True, but any Roman force could have broken that ambush.'

'I have caught them a dozen times.'

'Do we ever see their real warriors?'

'You mean Maroboduus's mythical legion?'

'Enough people have seen it.'

'Yes, but if he ever brings it into battle, we will crush him. We will soon have ten legions in Pannonia, and when that is dealt with, we will take on the Marcomanni.'

'When?'

'Two or three years.'

'Good.' Arminius stared pensively at the flames.

'And then you will be ruler of Germania.'

Arminius snorted. 'The governor rules Germania.'

'Varus will go. The next man could be more hands off.'

'It will never happen.'

Vala accepted the *beor* again. He could play this game. Nowadays, he took a long time to get drunk.

'Being back here must be awakening memories.'

Arminius looked at his brother. 'Yes, and they are piss poor compared to Rome, once you have seen it.'

'Maroboduus did. He was a soldier with us.'

'In some provincial fleapit. I do not understand that man.'

'He is insane,' Flavus slurred. 'He was offered a *gift*, and he refused it. He makes his people live in hovels, shitting in their own water, rather than embrace civilisation.'

Vala suggested, 'But his people are free.'

'No! Maroboduus is a tyrant! If his people knew the benefits of Rome, he would be out on his arse in a day,' Flavus said loudly.

Vala glanced at Inguiomer. The conversation had been going on in Latin. The old man was patting one of his hounds.

'What about Hiru?' Vala asked.

'What about him?' Arminius replied.

'He knows Rome, yet he prefers to wander the forest.' Vala looked at Hiru as one would at a playing child. The man showed no sign that he understood their conversation. 'Is there dignity in being what he is?'

Flavus nodded emphatically, before gulping down more *beor*.

'What about the Lady Tiberia's freedom?'

Arminius's eyes narrowed.

Vala continued matter-of-factly. 'She seems happy. She has her trinkets, her nice clothes. People treat her with respect. Yet she is a bird in a cage.'

'What is your question?'

'Would you have her kind of freedom?'

Arminius accepted the liquor, but did not bring it to his lips.

'Would you choose servitude, if it brought comfort?' Vala asked.

Arminius snorted. 'Hell, given that I've been sleeping in mud for years, I'd give it a chance!'

CHAPTER 27

'THE HERD IS IN THERE,' Hiru told them. He wore only a skin loincloth and was barefoot.

Arminius asked how many animals. It was a small herd, with a bull, at least five cows, and calves. Hiru squatted and, using his fingers, sketched the terrain: a bowl of wood and marsh draining into a north-flowing stream.

There had been a lull in Marcomanni raids. Arminius and Vala had shifted the *ala* north, to the upper Albis. The legions would soon move to the river from their winter quarters, and the *ala* would join them to fight the Semnones. This morning, while patrols combed nearby hills and valleys, Vala had invited the two brothers and Inguiomer to go aurochs hunting. He brought some Iberians – 'Men used to fighting the black bulls of their homeland' – and Arminius matched him with three of his veterans.

'The bull is the only one worth killing,' Vala told them.

They stood behind a ridge, upwind from their prey. The land fell into a thicket of willow, alder, osier and aspen – trees betraying boggy ground. The morning breeze tugged at the leaves. It was impossible to see anything within the wood.

Flavus was thoughtful, turning the hunting spear over in his palms. It was solid, with a broad, seven-inch long stabbing head. A barbed javelin was stuck into the ground by him.

'Are you ready, Brother?'

'Of course.'

Arminius winked and then rolled his shoulders. As always before a fight, he was bursting with energy.

'Have you hunted aurochses before?' Inguiomer growled at Flavus in Suebic. When the younger man said no, he added, 'It is worse than hunting man. Give it space to run and you are finished.' He spat in his hand and rubbed his palms together.

'Let us go,' Vala said, nodding at his Iberians, who followed Hiru into the undergrowth. The Iberians mouthed an insult to some Germans as they walked past: they were using their own language, but the meaning was clear. The Germans retorted in Suebic, afterwards glancing guiltily at Arminius.

Arminius grabbed his weapons and fell in with his brother and Vala. Inguiomer brought two of the dogs: hip-high, granite-coloured beasts. The rest of the hunters were a mix of Roman officers, auxiliaries and Cherusci.

They descended through the bracken into the bowl, into a tangle of nettles and saplings. Hiru was unhurried. The file of men halted regularly as he sniffed the air. Soon, the upper branches cut off most of the sunlight, and they were immersed in the mesh of branches and stumps. Each man focussed only on the next noiseless step. The ground became sodden. Reeds appeared around puddles. Arminius was glad that it was not yet hot enough for mosquitoes.

Inguiomer, the beaters and hounds broke off early. They would form a wide arc behind the herd. The hunting party appeared to have lost most of its members.

Arminius came upon Hiru, hunkering down in the leaf mould behind a storm-shattered alder. Hiru had already sent the three remaining Iberians to the left, where they now squatted, spears ready. Arminius knelt by the tracker.

Ahead, in a minor clearing, appeared the sun-dappled back of a huge, reddish-brown creature. Its skin jerked at parasites and its tail moved languidly. The beast raised its head, chewing as it regarded the forest edge to Arminius's right. Its great horns curved forwards and inwards and were as thick as a man's arm. It shook its head, causing more ripples through its russet skin. The aurochs snorted, and vapour billowed from its light-coloured snout. It was heavily muscled and stood a third bigger than any domesticated cattle. Its fierce black eyes told of savagery long since bred out of its tame cousins.

Another shape appeared – a calf. It brushed through the grass, pausing to nuzzle the brown cow.

Arminius raced to find the other members of the herd. He spotted three other cows. The bull was not visible. Using sign language, he asked Hiru for help. The tracker indicated a stretch of trees and shadow that, to Armin's eye, revealed no animals. The tracker's hands flitted instructions.

Arminius felt a rush of blood. He inhaled sharply. Vala and his hunters were similarly excited.

Vala nodded at Hiru for the drive to begin. The tracker disappeared into the bushes. Shortly thereafter, Inguiomer blew the horn.

The noise reverberated through the herd. The old cow looked over her shoulder. Her chewing ceased. The calf dipped its head and sought the protection of her flank. Other cows appeared from the long grass, where they had been ruminating.

The shadows moved. At first, Arminius thought that a rampart of earth had shifted position. Then branches were pushed aside rowdily, saplings snapping. The bull emerged. It was jet black, except for its light saddle patch and snout. It stood a foot taller than the cows, the height of a tall man. Its curved horns were savagely sharp, the tips two feet apart.

The herd started moving to the right, but the bull, tossing its head, moved against the current. It grunted and then sniffed the air, pawing the ground.

More cows hurried from the left, their abrupt appearance from the thickets seemingly impossible for such massive creatures. The bull snorted again, its undersized black eyes wide, mucous dripping from its nostrils. It appeared to be counting the herd funnelling through the clearing into the far wall of willow and osier by the brook's banks.

Vala tapped Arminius on the shoulder. The men rose at his command and moved in a half-crouch, parallel to the herd. Their eyes were on the bull, which had wheeled around when the last calf passed him. Arminius looked back guardedly.

The beaters hooted in the distance.

The old cow bellowed. She was on the right flank of the herd, and gazing in Arminius's direction. The bull's head swivelled towards the new threat. Arminius's blood ran cold as he estimated the density of the brush between him and the brute. It would take the beast a heartbeat to reach him.

The hounds burst through the undergrowth to the left. It took the bull but a moment to swing his colossal forequarters about. The dogs slid to a halt, snarling. The bull, roaring once, tossed its horns in warning, and then followed the lowing throng of brown cows and calves.

One of the hounds took a chance, rushing for the bull's hind limbs. The bull kicked back disdainfully, splashing mud. The dog tried another trick, dashing forward to draw the bull's attention. A second hound rushed in.

The bull was too experienced. The second hound, half the height of a man, ran straight into a raking right horn. Barely uttering a sound, it smashed against a tree, crushed.

'This way,' Vala commanded. The auxiliaries were trying to get between the bull and the cows. Arminius darted to the right after Vala, dodging branches. As he leapt over a stump, an agonised howl sounded behind them. Another dog had died.

The hunters nearly ran into the old cow. She stood between two alder trees, front hooves resolutely spread, head lowered, covering the calves' retreat. She locked eyes with the hunters.

Vala jumped over a mossy trunk to the animal's side. The cow, blinking, changed position. Moments later, Arminius was racing to her other flank, weaving through saplings, javelin ready.

He launched the weapon at fifteen feet. The missile sliced into a willow, sending grey-yellow bark flying, and bounced against the cow. It elicited a bellow but did not pierce her skin.

Vala did better, storming between the thick branches behind the beast to thrust a spear into her haunches. It did not go very deep, and he yanked it out.

Most animals would have sought safety at this point: the cow charged.

'Arminius!'

He twisted just in time to see the bull coming from the opposite direction, its horns bloodied from the dogs it had gored, a javelin trailing from its side. Splinters and leaves scattered as it smashed through the trees. Arminius ran, branches raking his arms and face.

Behind him, the bull and cow met. For a moment, their muzzles almost touched. Then they turned outwards, the bull roaring.

'Hold them there!' Vala shouted, barking for the hunters to fan out. The remaining hounds yelped.

Hiru appeared. He grimaced at Arminius. 'They are too strong on hard ground.'

Arminius looked at the earth. Where the bull now stood, the soil was firm beneath the top few inches of loam, leaves and mud, but about ten feet behind the animal, slightly down the slope, the ground was boggier, with reeds protruding from oily pools.

One of the Cherusci moved in, his bare legs and chest spattered with mud. He hurled his javelin. Again, the branches deflected the weapon. His fellows hooted as he retreated, and the man, shouting over his shoulder, decided to try a second time. This time, he went in on the run. He got to within ten feet. The javelin bit into the bull's forequarters, but as the Cheruscan tried to fall back, the animal charged. The man skidded. The aurochs's horn caught him in the shoulder and bashed him against a tree. Screaming, the man tried to crawl away. The bull finished him off with its hooves.

However, the fleeing Cheruscan had inadvertently taken the bull down the slope. The bull slipped as it began to move back up to the cow and level ground.

Arminius rushed in the direction of the bog. Flavus followed him. The bull's gaze stalked them.

At the top of the slope, the old cow made a fatal mistake. A javelin had caught her in the neck, causing her to bleed profusely. Enraged, she charged one of the Iberians. The soldier dodged behind an alder sapling. The cow tried to smash through, but one horn caught a branch, twisting her head. By the time she recovered, another Iberian had thrust a spear between her ribs. Dark blood gushed. A second spear struck. The cow lowed. Her legs began to buckle.

The bull stormed up the slope. A javelin struck it, but fell out. The hunter, another tribesman, tried to take cover, but the nimble bull wove through the trees to clip him on the arm. The limb snapped, the man yelling in agony. He tried to flee, but the bull shouldered a sapling and struck him from the side, ploughing him into the earth.

Arminius, now standing knee-deep in the water, watched the bull rampage. It was on level ground again and moving at speed. It possessed an uncanny ability to judge the thickness of trees that it could smash. The hunters were scattering.

'It is too strong!'

The herd had disappeared. From the east, the beaters appeared, but stayed safely out of reach.

Only Inguiomer advanced.

'In here!' Arminius shouted.

The older man nodded as he entered the marsh, holding two javelins.

The bull was trying to break out towards the herd again, but Vala contained it at desperate risk.

Arminius handed his spear to Flavus and tore off his olive-drab tunic. Taking the spear back, he tied the rag to its shaft.

The bull had paused by the collapsed cow. She was dying, her limbs jerking. She was bleeding profusely, the wounds sapping her strength. It sniffed her body. Then it noticed Arminius downhill, emerging from the reeds.

'Once it charges, everybody attack!' Arminius shouted, waving the rag at the animal. The bull's head bobbed as it assessed the target. Then it launched at the human.

Arminius fled into the marsh, thrusting the spear-point into the muck as he hit the water, so that the rag stuck out. He heard the bull avalanche at the reeds and he half fell behind a clump of plants. He turned just in time to see the bull, chest-deep in the water, rake at his head. He rolled away. The bull persisted. Arminius crawled frantically through the muck. The bull rounded the reeds and waded towards him.

Inguiomer's javelin struck the animal in the ribs. The bull swung noisily to the new danger, spraying water. Weighing a ton, it was being sucked into the mire. A second javelin sank into its flesh. Arminius came to his feet, dripping with mud.

'Kill it!'

Flavus lumbered forward, one of half a dozen spearmen. Among them was Vala. Arminius watched as the circle closed, the animal thrashing and sweeping its horns, trying to head back to dry land. It was futile. An Iberian struck first, and barely escaped as the bull rounded. The man stumbled away, cradling a broken hand. A second spear drove into the bull's left side. Flavus's weapon penetrated almost as an afterthought.

The bull began to slow down. Its great neck seemed incapable of raising its horns. Blood frothed at its lips.

Arminius, collapsing on a tuft of reeds, watched the beast succumb. For a short while, it still attempted to charge. Then, as the mud sucked it down and its blood ebbed, it just moved its massive head. Finally, the bull merely stood, surrounded by silent hunters.

'It is yours,' Vala told Arminius, handing him a thrusting spear.

Arminius went in for the kill.

They dragged the bull from the marsh and butchered the aurochses. The skins and skulls would go to the governor. That night, they lit pyres for the dead hunters, and cooked the meat on separate fires. Vala insisted that Arminius be washed in the bull's blood, but he refused the honour, granting it to the Iberian who had thrust the first spear into the creature. The young man beamed as his friends smeared the blood on him.

Afterwards, Hiru approached Arminius in front of the other hunters. He bore a torch in one hand, and a soggy orb, the bull's eye, obscured his other palm. He offered it to Arminius. It was customary among his people, he explained, for a great hunter to eat the eye of a beast that had fought well. Arminius dropped the eye into his mouth, where it burst. The men shouted approval.

* * *

The following morning, Hiru appeared at the encampment with his family. There was a tiny, dark-haired woman in her early twenties – his wife – two small children and a youth who he explained was his brother, Bjec. They were dressed in animal skins and were dirty and emaciated. The woman, whose only clothing consisted of a deerskin skirt and a primitive necklace, carried one of the children on her back. She seemed petrified and avoided eye contact. Bjec, who carried a spear with a bone point and a small bow, was hostile.

It had been a rough winter, Hiru explained to Arminius. They had lost a child and his wife's mother during his absence with the Romans.

'It is time that we settle.' He asked for protection.

'You want Rome's protection?'

'Your protection.'

Arminius ordered food. The woman, whom Hiru called Aba, masticated the meat and fed it to the children.

'I am but a servant of Rome,' Arminius explained in Suebic. 'Perhaps it is better if you went to Vala.'

Hiru explained that the Romans did not understand.

'Understand what?'

'How old the land is.'

'And I do?'

'You learn.' Hiru gazed at the woman. She held the sickly child on her lap and rocked it as she pressed food between its lips. Her dark eyes flickered to Arminius. She had black facial tattoos – wavy lines, like flames, that accentuated her sharp cheekbones.

'Good,' Arminius said. 'I shall protect you, but I must warn you: safety outside the forest is not worth surrendering what you have within the forest.'

'What is that?'

'Dignity. Freedom.'

'Freedom means nothing if you are starving.'

'Still, be careful.'

'We can always return to the forest.'

'I hope so.'

Chapter 28

THUSNELDA SANK HER FACE INTO her palms. She sat on the edge of her bed. On the bed lay a dress.

'Are you ready?' Berhilda enquired from the door. She was a matronly forty, and had been the girl's nurse since birth.

'What is the point? There is nowhere to go.' Thusnelda rose and began to pace around. 'What am I supposed to *do* here?'

'We could ask the governor to bring your friends over again.'

'How can I do that to them? They know that I am a prisoner here!' She folded her arms, bending over.

'You have to make the best of it.'

Thusnelda pursed her lips. She had been in the quarters at Castra Drusus for nearly two months. At first, gifts had flooded in from her friends in Colonia – merchants' and bureaucrats' daughters. Two had even visited to help decorate her gaol. Letters still arrived, but there seemed nothing more to say.

'Something new came for you. It is from Arminius.' Berhilda tried to discern interest in her charge, but Thusnelda just hugged herself more tightly. 'I shall fetch it.' It was in a box, which she placed next to the forlorn dress. When Thusnelda paid no attention to it, she opened it, and exclaimed.

Thusnelda looked up.

'A wolf cub – carved from wood.' Berhilda's eyes travelled to the worn toy by the bed. 'He remembered what it looked like. It is almost exactly like it.'

Thusnelda dismissed her nurse.

It took her some time before she picked up the gift. It indeed resembled her treasure.

The gift did little to calm her. Even her servants were edgy. They were used to the bustle of Colonia, the parties and ceremonies, the banter with other slaves, the market. Castra Drusus was impoverished. They suffered guards at the entrance of Thusnelda's quarters, and constant, discreet observation from the governor's staff. She had no facilities to entertain. What passed for her new female social circle consisted of three wives of minor administrators – anybody important had allowed their spouses to remain in civilisation upon their own deployment. Her father visited occasionally, but although he ranted and promised to have her returned home, the governor politely ignored him.

'What is his explanation for *this*?' she had asked Cegestes.

'He is concerned about your safety.'

'Am I under threat?'

'No more than before.'

Her father railed against Sigimer and his son, and she listened. She suggested, once, that her father forget the idea of marrying her to Bannruod, but his response was caustic.

'But he has not even visited me here.'

'He does not like the Romans.'

'Then why are you selling me to him?'

'I am not *selling* you to anybody! Think of what good you can do for the tribe.'

She had heard it all before.

'Am I then to forget all my education and move to the forest?'

'You will be allowed your freedom.' She might continue living in Colonia.

'What man would allow that? I see no middle way. Either I become all Cherusci, or he becomes all Roman.'

'There is a middle way. We are proof of it.'

'What if the people do not agree? I do not see them wearing Rome's fashions or speaking Latin!'

'They will.'

He could not convince her. Every time she entered the town, Romans leered at her, and sometimes they laughed. Barbarian men glared at her. Women averted their eyes. Her servants told her that graffiti about her had appeared on the walls of the settlement. They called her Varus's Cunt. They burned dolls of her, or punched sticks into them and hung them like dead magpies from branches.

'And this is in the Roman army's headquarters!'

Perhaps she *was* a whore. Every few days, the governor summoned her to dine with him. His invitations were always written in his own hand. She would even receive an expensive dress for each occasion. Usually, mercifully, the two of them would share the evening with officers or visiting merchants, or cronies like the Syrian. But the company was overwhelmingly male, and they invariably got drunk. Sometimes they made lewd comments, which she brushed aside with a smile. The governor never intervened, even though he regularly praised her.

Occasionally, however, Varus would appear alone, scented and dressed in his finest, to make excruciating conversation, get inebriated, and stare at her breasts. She could not tell her father this. He would be in an impossible position. She carried a hairpin on her for self-defence. She was grateful that she had never needed to use it.

Varus would typically begin the evening asking about her quarters, and she would thank him for his care and make small requests, which he would usually grant. After some wine, he would become talkative, his thoughts racing as he described his most recent grand ideas for Germania. She would flatter him. He tried to impress her with his achievements during his governorships in Syria and Africa. He recalled parades, expeditions, even parties. He boasted crassly about sexual conquests. He had a fantastic memory for detail and was easily distracted. Once, he spent an entire main course gleefully describing a particular woman's intimate parts. He would also outrageously flatter Thusnelda's blonde hair, her eyes and her curves.

'Gods, if I were younger,' he began once, 'you would make a lovely fuck.'

Between invitations, he episodically showered her with expensive gifts. But once, she made the mistake of asking to be returned to Colonia. There was an abrupt change in his manner.

'Are you not happy here?'

'It is a comfortable place, but...'

'Do you not *see* what I have done for you here? That you are *safe*?'

She thanked him profusely.

'You do not appreciate your *role* here! You are the symbol of the Empire! You *are* everything that is beautiful about Rome!'

'I understand...'

'You devalue what I am doing! You people want comforts and trinkets, but you will not work to better yourself!' He slammed the table. 'You lazy blonde bitch!'

He dismissed her. However, the next morning he arrived at her rooms, burdened with gifts, to grovel.

'Beautiful women should not be spoken to like that. I am a fool! I work too hard and my temper snaps! I should have more regard for others' feelings.'

He then held a party in her honour, ordering guests from Colonia to attend.

'My wife…' Varus explained once at a private dinner, 'I have not seen her in a long time.' He smiled dejectedly. 'You *have* to forgive me. I am very fond of you, but you should not be afraid.'

She still took the needle with her.

One day, a second gift arrived from Armin: pressed marigolds. She could just about detect a scent.

'He is certainly not spending much,' Berhilda mocked.

'That is not the point.'

'The others are sending you expensive things. He sends you wood and flowers.'

One of the rooms in her quarters had stored presents from admirers, including the governor's most important clients. A few days before, an exquisite gold chain had also arrived from Bannruod.

'It can fit around my ankle.'

'You should be happy that you are being pursued.'

'Even by the man who gives me mere flowers?'

'Well, despite his cheap tastes, he is becoming important.'

'The governor likes him.'

'More than that: the soldiers like him. They even say that he is a hero.'

* * *

8 CE (MAY)

UPPER ALBIS

Cegestes arrived at the hilltop log fort just before noon, accompanied by thirty hefty bodyguards. He demanded to see Arminius, and paced furiously before his tent while the commander was fetched. The first man to arrive was Arminius's younger brother.

'Cegestes!'

'Don't talk to me like that, pup.'

'How can I help you?'

'I am here to see your brother. You don't make any decisions around here.'

'Nonetheless…'

'Are you part of this conspiracy?'

'What conspiracy?'

'I know that something is going on.'

'I do not understand what you mean.'

Inguiomer lumbered up, scowling.

'Are *you* part of this scheme,' Cegestes repeated, switching to Suebic, 'the pursuit of my daughter?'

Inguiomer just snorted and leaned on his staff. Cegestes turned his rage back onto Flavus, who tried to calm him. Arminius took an age to arrive. He was mud-spattered and tired.

'Yes, I am after her,' he said.

'She says that you have sent her gifts!'

'I have, yes.'

'I refuse you permission!'

Arminius looked at him blankly.

'First you have her locked up, and now you are chasing her!' Cegestes continued.

'She interests me.'

'She is promised to another!'

'Then you have nothing to fear.'

Cegestes paused and then growled, 'I *know* that this is part of something else! Your father has been scheming against me for years, but with you here his ambitions – '

'I can't tell what you are implying.'

'You want *this*. All of it!' Cegestes stretched his arms.

'It all belongs to Rome.'

'You cannot fool me! You want to be king!'

'There is no king here, only the will of the Senate and the people of Rome.'

Flavus interjected, 'My brother has been fighting the Marcomanni...'

'Don't be *naïve*!' Cegestes snapped, not taking his eyes off Arminius. 'My daughter shall not be a part of this! I *demand* that you have her released!'

'She is safest where she is.'

'You shall *not* use her to destroy me!'

'I mean her no harm, and you no harm.'

'Then release her and leave her alone!'

'I cannot, and I do not wish to.' Arminius produced a smile. 'Let us be reasonable. You are welcome to be our guest, or, when Vala returns, you may dine with him.'

Cegestes refused, and remounted. 'I know that you are planning something, Armin! I shall have you!' He raced off.

CHAPTER 29

8 CE (MAY)

CASTRA DRUSUS

I NGUIOMER MET SIGIMER IN HIS tent outside Castra Drusus. Dignitaries had been invited from all over Germania to celebrate the start of the summer campaign season with the governor. The brothers had left their *ala* at Castra Octa. The barbarian encampment sprawled outside the town, beside the menacing presence of the three reassembled legions.

Inguiomer grunted as he sat down and accepted *beor* from his brother.

'And he was angry?' Sigimer enquired after Inguiomer told him of Cegestes's visit.

'Mad.'

'Is there anything new?'

'It is the same as before. Armin is trying to keep the girl from Bannruod. We are waiting to hear what she thinks.'

'Nothing else?'

'No. Should there be?'

'The governor approves of Armin and her?'

'Armin says so. What have you heard?'

'The governor likes Armin, but Vala has been asking questions. He is suspicious.'

'Of what?' Inguiomer asked.

'I do not know. That is why I am asking you.'

Inguiomer snorted. 'Vala is jealous of Armin having the *ala*! Your boy is the best soldier that I have ever seen.'

Sigimer was pleased. 'Tell me if something new happens.'

'I shall.' Inguiomer steered the conversation towards the forthcoming celebrations. Perhaps it was wrong to keep secrets from Sigimer, he thought, but he was sure that Armin was not telling him everything either. He did not mind. Armin seemed to know what he was doing.

They discussed Frimunt. 'He is different from Armin,' Inguiomer said. 'In love with Rome, but for different reasons.'

'He spoke to me about art and buildings, and the sea he had seen,' Sigimer said. 'I did not understand most of it. But he loves Rome. That cannot be a bad thing.'

'No.'

'And he fights well?'

'He does.' Inguiomer spoke of the ambushes and the aurochs hunt. Young Lamar stood close by to hear and he invited the boy over, placing his arm around him. His mother hovered nearby. She was excited, Sigimer told him, about having received an invitation from the governor.

'We might all move here,' Sigimer explained.

'Will you?'

'Imma would meet Roman ladies, and the children need education.'

'Frimunt – Flavus – will be happy to hear that. He has mentioned it to me.' Inguiomer asked Imma what she thought.

'It is wonderful. This is a much bigger place.' She described the market and strange people excitedly.

'It is nothing to Colonia Agrippina,' Inguiomer guffawed, hiding his disquiet. He hugged his nephew.

Flavus arrived shortly thereafter. Arminius, he said, was with the army, discussing the latest patrols. He spoke Suebic more haltingly than Arminius did.

'Do you like your new posting here?' Inguiomer enquired.

'It is not as hard as Illyria, but less civilised.'

Flavus accepted a cup from Imma, but took only a small sip. He glanced at the woman, who still dressed in barbarian fashion. He asked whether Lamar was learning his Latin.

'We were just discussing that,' Sigimer said. 'He speaks a bit, but not enough. I think we will bring him here. It will be good for him.'

Flavus nodded approval. 'This is the only place to be if you want influence.' He continued, 'Cegestes is in town already. Are we going to take any precautions?'

'No more than usual. We shall be polite.'

* * *

'It is good to see you,' Thusnelda said.

The big warrior looked ill at ease within her quarters. He eyed the furnishings sceptically.

'Are you well?' Bannruod replied in Suebic. He looked around for a place to sit, but the chairs were too puny for his frame.

'I am as well as can be expected. The fort is a small place.'

He was physically handsome, and someone had told him to tone down his tribal paraphernalia. Gone were the excesses of furs and leather. He wore a shirt and trousers in the barbarian style, and a necklace of bear canines. He had oiled, if not washed, his hair. He still reeked.

'You received my gifts?' he asked after an uncomfortable silence.

'Yes, thank you. They are beautiful.'

He casually looked for them. He noticed a jewellery box that he had sent her.

'I have been told that you are being chased by another man.'

'I am?'

'Armin.'

'Who told you this?'

'I am here to find out whether it is true.'

'Oh.'

He tugged at his beard. She let the silence draw out.

'He has sent you gifts?'

'He has.'

'Are you accepting them?'

'I accept gifts from many people.'

'But not from others with his intentions.'

'What are his intentions?'

'It is to have you.'

'Are these your intentions?'

'I have been promised you,' he said.

'That is not the answer to my question.'

'I have been promised you, by your father.'

'Are you here to claim me?'

'Yes.'

She did not reply.

'Does this mean,' he asked eventually, 'that our agreement is over?'

'My father made the agreement. You should ask him.'

He remained surprisingly calm. She had no idea what she would have done if his rage had taken over. He stood there momentarily. Then he walked out.

* * *

General Saturninus kept Vala behind after the briefing. Reports had been mostly good. The Semnones and Marcomanni had suffered significant casualties over the winter and spring, their raids frustrated by rapid-reaction patrols. Unrest within the province was lower than in previous years. Saturninus had praised Vala in front of the legates.

Now that they were alone, however, Saturninus turned to Vala with concern.

'Have you found anything on him?'

'I am still waiting to hear from our contacts in Illyria and Rome.'

'You will not find anything. I have received a letter from General Caecina, on behalf of Prince Tiberius, enquiring after Arminius's performance.'

'It has been exemplary.'

'It has.'

'But we cannot stop watching him.'

'Yes. How is that going?'

'I am having his men spied on, but we are struggling to infiltrate the *ala*.'

'They are a very close-knit group.'

'Someone always talks.'

Saturninus hummed and pressed with outstretched fingers on the map table.

'The younger brother seems loyal to Rome,' Vala said, 'but the men follow Arminius, not him. I am building up a relationship with the brother.'

'You think that he will betray Arminius?'

'He talks of nothing but Rome. It is pitiful, really.'

Saturninus paused and then declared, 'Be careful. We cannot afford to offend our allies, or the governor.'

'Nor can we ignore suspicions because they are awkward.'

'I know, and I shall disband this *ala* of his at the first sign of trouble.'

'He will reveal himself.'

'Just be careful.'

'I shall, Sir.' Vala asked to be excused and rose to leave.

'And Vala…'

'Yes, Sir.'

'I meant what I said. You are doing an excellent job. Thank you.'

'Thank you, Sir.'

* * *

'It is impressive,' Arminius remarked. He checked the plans on the table against the building being constructed. 'You can be very proud.'

Sextus beamed. Arminius had just wandered down to the building project in the town. The site was hard to miss: a massive stone market, dominated by the settlement's first great civic building, where the governor's staff would one day reside. It recalled placid old provincial towns throughout the Empire.

Arminius enquired after the plans and about sourcing materials. The army was mining the stone and transporting it down the river. It was even providing legionaries to do some of the building. Sextus thanked him for his help and references.

Armin was pleased. He changed the subject. 'What has happened to that slave I lent you, the Chatti nobleman?'

'I expected him to run away, but he has worked well.'

'May I have him back? He has served his time here.'

Sextus sent a boy to fetch the slave.

Arminius inspected the building work again. 'You are doing really well for yourself.'

'Thank you. I am very happy.'

'Excellent,' Arminius said, patting Sextus on the back. 'Tell me if there is anything I can do for you or your family.'

Vegates arrived. The young man now wore a Roman-style tunic and went barefoot, but he seemed well fed. Best of all, Arminius noted, there was still pride in his eyes. As they walked away from the building site, Arminius asked him how he had fared.

'I am well.'

'I was afraid that you might run.'

'I am patient.'

They crossed an open stretch between the town and the fort. 'Did you get a good look around?' Armin enquired when they were out of earshot of passers-by.

'I know the town like my own hand.'

'Good. You are now going to be my personal servant. Study the fort. Your day will come.'

* * *

Imma was crying. 'I feel humiliated!'

Sigimer tried to comfort her. They had just returned from the governor's party to their temporary quarters in Aliso.

'They treat me as if I am an animal!'

'You are being too sensitive.'

She collapsed on a chair and buried her face in her hands. He placed his arm around her, but he did not know what to say.

'I saw the way they looked at me. It is awful.'

'They are just not used to – '

'They will *never* accept us! *Never*!'

'They accept Armin. Look at how well he – '

'I am not him! I cannot speak like them. I look stupid in their dresses!'

'You are a very beautiful woman.'

She threw up her hands, tears coursing over her cheeks. 'I just cannot be like them. I just cannot do it.' She broke down.

He held her, allowing her to exhaust her tears against his chest. 'It will take time, my love. It will take time,' he whispered.

CHAPTER 30

THE WEATHER WARMED. CONVOYS CROSSED the passes and plied the rivers. Soon, the legionaries would lumber east.

First, there would be celebrations. The field to the west of the citadel, intended to provide defending legionaries' bows with a killing zone, was now turned over to the festivities. Two lines of fire pits had been dug, about two hundred yards apart, and lit as the afternoon ended. Cattle, sheep and swine were slaughtered. Rough timber tables were constructed and burdened with food – partly from the army and governor's own reserves. Most importantly, sacks of *beor* and amphorae of wine stood ready. People would sit on the new grass, or on stumps. Thousands were expected to attend, including the town's inhabitants, and tribespeople from all over the province. A gaudy pavilion had been erected for the governor near one of the fort's minor gates. Expensive acrobats and performers had been brought in from Massilia.

'This will put them in a good mood,' Varus mused. The field was filling with attendees. 'Families spending time together, little blonde children frolicking, savages getting pissed – delightful!' he clapped his hands. 'The army is ready?'

They were. Elements of all three legions were posted surreptitiously within the fort. Thousands of additional soldiers were on standby in the nearby camps, in case of trouble.

Arminius and Flavus, both dressed in togas, stood before the half-filled gubernatorial pavilion. Separate facilities were set up here to receive important guests. They watched as Thusnelda arrived in the company of Marcus Vinicius, commander of the Eighteenth Legion.

'She *is* beautiful,' Flavus noted.

Arminius nodded. Many eyes would be turning towards her, and some to him.

'Cegestes does not look happy,' Flavus remarked.

The clan chief, standing about fifty yards away, had just lost the thread of his conversation with some Roman merchants. He glared icily at Arminius, who ignored him. Bannruod and his father, Kuonraet, were not present yet. One of his men had informed Arminius that Bannruod had visited Thusnelda briefly and had left angrily. He could only imagine the conversation that had transpired.

Arminius turned to Vegates, who was now dressed in the fashion of a respectable Roman head slave. 'Do you see your kin?'

'I do.' Vegates had already made eye contact with Adgandes.

'Shall we go and speak to him?' Arminius suggested, turning to Flavus before he left. 'Go to her now.'

His brother nodded and strolled to the Lady Tiberia.

Adgandes dismissed the men around him as Arminius and Vegates approached. He restrained his joy at seeing his young nephew.

'He is fine, as I told you,' Arminius said.

'Are you?' Adgandes asked suspiciously. Vegates nodded with a firm gaze.

'I have given him a dagger to defend himself,' Arminius said, keeping his voice low.

Vegates tapped a bulge on his hip under his tunic.

'What are you going to do with him? This cannot go on.'

'I shall free him as soon as it is possible. As I said, I am not trying to humiliate him.'

Adgandes frowned. 'I do not understand what is going on.'

'You do not need to,' Vegates declared. 'For now, I am his servant. I am going to the Albis with the legions. After that, the governor will consider a pardon.'

'It is all arranged,' Arminius added.

Adgandes regarded the young men in turn, puzzled. 'You are planning something.'

Vegates bowed humbly to the elder, as Armin had told him to.

Arminius said, 'Just be patient.'

They parted ways, Vegates remaining two steps behind Arminius as they approached one of the serving tables. Arminius had some *beor* poured, and drank it, while Vegates remained vigilant. He would let the old Chatti chieftain in on the conspiracy soon. Vegates had wanted to tell his uncle the moment he had found out, but there were still other details to attend to first.

Flavus sauntered back. 'What a delightful girl!'

'What happened?'

'She was polite. She says that you may come and speak to her later. That might be difficult with her father lurking nearby.' He glanced at Vegates. 'Are the Chatti happy?'

'Yes.'

Flavus spotted his father and his young wife, who was, for a change, dressed in a civilised way. The two brothers joined Sigimer by the pavilion. Thusnelda's gaze briefly met Arminius's.

The governor arrived to much fanfare, and the entertainment kicked off: horse racing, precision manoeuvres by legionaries, Iberian troopers whirling torches in the gloom. The highlight was a ferocious mock charge by armoured Sarmatian mercenary cavalry, who, in a shower of chaff and splinters, rode down a line of straw men armed with Suebic shields. The governor handed out trophies to the commanders. Then the evening settled into drinking and dining.

'Lady Tiberia.'

She turned around. Warmth flickered in her eyes. 'Arminius.'

He continued in Latin. 'Did you enjoy the display?'

'It was *thrilling*.'

They shared a laugh. She held a cup of wine, which she hardly sipped. There was a diadem in her hair and she wore an expensive necklace. Both, she revealed, were gifts from the governor. He enquired whether she had received his presents.

'They were very thoughtful.' She followed the last word with a long silence. 'They showed perspicacity.'

'Oh, I place little faith in my insight.'

'Am I that mysterious?'

He did not answer. Cegestes, currently conversing with General Saturninus, was glaring at them.

'Have you decided by which of your two names you want to be called?'

'What do you wish to call me?'

He thought about it for a moment. 'Thusnelda.' He rendered the name with the correct Suebic enunciation. 'That is, if you agree.'

'Why did you choose that one?'

'It is a beautiful name and it suits you best.'

'The governor will be disgruntled. He prefers Tiberia.'

He chuckled. 'We shall not tell him then!'

She peered at him over the rim of her cup.

Cegestes had broken free from Saturninus and was striding over. Thusnelda was not surprised when Arminius stood his ground.

'I do not want you to speak to her!' Cegestes hissed. 'I told you that!'

'I am sorry, Greatfather,' Arminius replied in Suebic, using an honorific usually reserved for the elderly. 'We mean no harm.'

Cegestes's eyes narrowed. 'Liar!' he growled in Suebic. He faced his daughter. 'Keep away from him!'

'Am I to speak to Bannruod then? I do not see him here.'

'I heard what happened between you two,' Cegestes snapped. 'You are causing trouble.' He glared at Arminius. 'Stay away from this man; I know his secrets. He will just harm you.' The soldier met his gaze without unease.

'Thusnelda,' Arminius said gently, bowing his head. He walked away.

The festivities were picking up. The Romans lit more torches, and the barbarians gorged on the mountains of food. Arminius saw one man staggering already.

Inguiomer intercepted him. 'Kuonraet and Bannruod are here.' He gave Vegates, still a few paces behind Arminius, a brief look. Arminius told Inguiomer that he could talk in front of him.

'Are you sure?'

'I trust him.'

Inguiomer remained cautious. 'Expect trouble. People I trust say that the Bear clan will come for you tonight over the girl.'

'I shall be careful.'

The smell of roasting meat pervaded the air. Children played tag. Here and there, Roman settlers wandered, watching the tribesmen with a mixture of bemusement and trepidation. Alcohol began to break down barriers. Arminius noticed a knot of Cherusci, who were playing a drinking game. Men were attempting to balance cups of *beor* or mead on their foreheads to the rhythmic clapping of hands. First one, and then another of the Romans were roped in. They failed – drink spilling over their tunics – but the laughter was fraternal. Just behind one row of people, two Cherusci fondled one another. The woman's hand reached to the man's groin to indicate that it was time for privacy. Nearby, another barbarian woman patted a man draped across her lap as he drunkenly sucked on her breast. A female companion passed her *beor*. Romans glanced at them with bemusement.

By one of the fire pits, a wiry old man in animal skins told a story to children. He twisted his body and produced masks and props from the folds of his outfit. It was the oldest story of all. Arminius stopped to listen.

The ancient told of how the World Serpent, Jossfir, surrounded the old world, Nifhem. The Serpent was older than the mountains. In its hunger, it consumed all living things, until the gods left and the world was icy, dark, and void. Giants, who could eat ice and rock, wandered this wasteland. Only one god remained: Nerthus, the daughter of the moon, who tended the last remaining hearth. The Serpent, growing cold, coiled around the hearth, but Nerthus sang to keep it away. As the fire settled into embers and ash, the snake drew closer, no longer frightened of the light. However, Nerthus reached into the dying fire and, mixing the ash with milk from her breasts, formed a human shape. At the heart of this new being she put a glowing ember. Then, she breathed into its mouth, creating Tuisto. She taught Tuisto to dance and sing to keep the Serpent at bay, and fed him with her milk. When he had learned to dance, she transformed herself into the oak Yggdrasil, the greatest of all trees, the Grandmother of the Forest. From Yggdrasil's roots ran four rivers of milk. Tuisto took her branches and fed the flames, as she had told him to do. The Serpent was frightened and withdrew to the edges of the world. Yggdrasil's roots spread over the earth and her branches reached to Heaven. Her first acorn became the first mortal woman, Embla. Her second was the first mortal man, Mannus. From Yggdrasil grew the whole forest. Each tree in the wood is like a hair on Nerthus's skin.

Somewhere behind Arminius, a drum began to beat. It was a great, flat drum of animal skin stretched over a round frame. Its musician struck the rhythm of a relaxed heartbeat. He held the drum above his head and his eyes were on the ground. His black hair draped over his shoulder blades and upper arms. He was naked, and his body was a thicket of animal tattoos. The man stood near the middle of the field, by one of the fire pits, so that the flames played over the perspiration beading his frame.

A girl appeared by him. She had long, brown hair that fell to her lower back and partly covered her face. She was unsteady with drink. She raised her hands and began to clap in rhythm with the drum, swaying her hips.

From the growing crowd surrounding the musicians, another drummer stepped forward. His drum had the circumference of a man's outstretched arm. A third arrived, his instrument possessing a bulky chamber and suspended from his neck by a leather strap. They took up the beat, amplifying it. More women began to filter from the crowd, some young, others wizened, and took up the swaying dance. Many merely clapped their hands to the pulse, which extended over the field and fires.

Arminius caught sight of Bannruod through one of the bonfires. He surreptitiously pointed the man out to Vegates. Bannruod glowered. Then he was lost among the crowd. Arminius peered around, to see Inguiomer a short distance away. He, too, had spotted Bannruod.

More drummers emerged. The beat was now so booming that Varus, standing by the gate to the fort, turned around to gaze at the source.

A great semicircle, composed of hundreds of people, had widened around the musicians and dancers. Into this circle stepped a man. He carried a heavy stave, and he had stripped off his clothing and unbound his long hair. Across his back was an immense tattoo of a tree. Its base was just above his buttocks, and its trunk rose up his spine to branch out into his shoulders, neck, and arms. Its roots flowed over his legs. Lifting his stave above his head with two hands, he shouted over the crowd. The drums and clapping ceased immediately. The man waited and then roared another sentence, to which the whole crowd replied in a stock phrase. A third time he shouted, and this time only the men replied.

Arminius, standing on the outer edge of the crowd, searched it for Bannruod. Vegates looked longingly at the dancers.

The crowd fell back to open a larger space, and into this came young Cherusci men, each bearing a stave: they had expected the dance. They stripped down and, in pairs, undid one another's hair-knots, before forming a single line on either side of the first dancer. Here they stood, their staves held in both hands, their eyes cast down.

The biggest drum rumbled a rapid three beats. The line of thirty dancers lifted their staves in unison. Another three beats, this time taken up thunderously by the other drums, made them take one stride forward with their left feet and lash out at the air with a guttural bark.

Bannruod appeared. He was about thirty yards away, backlit by a bonfire. Arminius could not make out his face. He checked for Inguiomer, Flavus, and Vegates. The latter's loyalty would now certainly be tested.

The drums kept rattling out the three beats, the interval between each set becoming slightly shorter. The crowd grew, with more people surounding Arminius. He tried to work his way to the back again. Vegates was a few feet away, but people separated them. Inguiomer had become lost. Flavus was struggling to keep up.

The dancers leapt and pounded the earth, roaring, jumping, twisting, then landing in a feline crouch, their faces contorted, their staves extended. The crowd clapped with the drums.

A scowling tribesman knocked into Arminius. Another, seeing his Roman-style hair, refused to step out of his way. A woman glowered at him and pushed her child aside.

His eyes wandered over the crowd, trying to find Bannruod. Eyes made contact with his. Hateful glares; bared lips; simmering resentment. It had been a stupid idea to wear the toga. It was designed to obstruct a man's sword-arm, to enforce good manners. With his left hand he traced the dagger strapped around his waist.

The dancers now separated into opposing lines, each man eyeing a partner. Like a phalanx of rutting stags they clashed, pushed, parted, staves whirling and smashing, hair flying. The drums beat faster, the three-beat sets melting into one continuous sequence.

'This way!' Flavus shouted over the people's heads.

A hand tugged at Arminius's toga. Another, from behind, ripped it. He twisted to see, but the culprit was gone in the crush of bodies.

Bannruod loomed before him.

The dancers' sticks collided.

Vegates was moving towards Bannruod, speaking to him over the people. Arminius could not hear what was being said. Bannruod remained immobile. Arminius tried to push towards Flavus, but the crowd would not budge. Bannruod's eyes shifted to Vegates, who was now repeating a single phrase. Then the Cherusci warrior glared back at Arminius.

Where was Inguiomer?

Flavus swore stridently. Excrement had been wiped on his toga. He turned away, distracted.

Arminius headed straight for Bannruod, who stood with head lowered like the bellicose aurochs bull. His heart pounded.

'Do not do it!' Vegates was saying. 'Leave him!'

Bannruod's lips warped. He reached inside his shirt.

'No,' Vegates said.

Arminius closed in.

Bannruod's malevolent eyes flickered to his right. In doing so, he gave away his companion, who was approaching Arminius from the rear. Arminius darted aside just as a dagger sliced at his lower back. Grunting, scowling from the pain, Arminius stumbled. He knocked a woman aside. As he twisted around, he drew his own weapon. People shrieked, knocking one another down in an attempt to escape. One man remained, crouched, ready. He was stocky, his face shrouded by his loosened hair, his knife held low.

Arminius could feel blood starting to well out of his wounded side. He fought against the pain. A few terrified scurrying bystanders now separated Bannruod from him. People were screaming and shouting. In the confusion, Arminius parried another, rushing attacker, breaking his nose with a jab of his empty fist. The man staggered back.

Arminius faced the remaining knifeman. The man shifted on his toes, trying to calculate his chances. The circle around them had widened. Bannruod could clearly see what was happening.

Arminius tossed his knife up and deftly recaught it by the blade. He extended the dagger towards the attacker.

The man's eyes widened.

The offered knife did not waver.

Inguiomer's club smashed down on the back of the prospective assassin's head. The man crumpled.

Bannruod faded into the crowd, as did the man with the broken nose.

'Get him out of here *now*,' Arminius ordered Inguiomer, his hand reaching for the slice in his back. 'Hide him.' Inguiomer began to deal with the unconscious knifeman.

Flavus rushed through the crowd to his brother. 'Are you – ?'

'Yes!' Arminius snapped. His hand, which cupped the wound, was soaked. 'We have to go!' He cursed as Vegates and Flavus made way for him through the onlookers.

Chapter 31

'H ow bad is the wound?' Vala enquired. Outside, the festivities continued. Arminius sat on a bed in the fort's hospital, bandages wrapped around his middle.

'It bled, but it is not deep.'

'You are lucky.' Vala's gaze flitted to Flavus, who was standing by the room's door. 'I hear that there were two of them.'

'Yes.'

'Any idea about who sent them?'

'There are so many possibilities.'

'And they got away?'

'I hit one in the face.' Arminius touched his back. He winced.

'You did not catch either?'

'The crowd was dense. Most people there wanted them to get away.'

Vala hummed. He knew that Arminius was lying. His men had been watching Arminius, and knew that Inguiomer had struck down one of the attackers. What had happened to the assailant, they could not say.

'Very well, then,' Vala said. 'I shall ask around. Tell me if you get closer to the truth.' He eyed Flavus, whose complicity he found surprising. 'Heal quickly.'

'I shall be travelling with the army tomorrow,' Arminius said.

'Good.'

* * *

A few hours later, Bannruod, travelling back towards the east, was confronted by the unlikely sight of his captured knifeman, Carnoth, reappearing. The man was bedraggled and walked unsteadily from the blow he had suffered. Otherwise, he seemed unharmed. He even had a horse.

'They took me into the woods,' Carnoth explained hastily.

'Who did?'

'Inguiomer,' Carnoth added. Carnoth had been a blood brother to Bannruod since childhood. Bannruod trusted him more than he did any other man, except his father. 'They roughed me up a bit, but they were just waiting for Armin to appear.'

'How bad was his wound?'

'He was walking.'

'And then?'

'He knew that I was one of your men, and told me to bring you a private message. We spoke alone.'

They let the rest of the party ride on a short distance.

'These are his exact words: "Forget her. Do you want freedom from Rome?"'

'What? Did he want a reply?'

'They gave me a horse and told me to find you.'

Bannruod thanked his companion, told him not to speak of Armin's words, and let him ride ahead. The assassination attempt had gone badly wrong. His father had advised him to flee lest the Romans arrest him. They would deny everything.

He had been mulling over details of the attack: the Chatti nobleman's mysterious appeal, Armin's reversal of the knife. Armin's message further confused matters.

He needed time to clear his head.

* * *

8 CE (JUNE)

CHERUSCAN HIGHLANDS

The army departed from Castra Drusus along the military highways. They marched in strict order, as laid down in military regulations, to maximise speed and minimise risk. First went units of lightly armed infantry and cavalry. These fanned out beside the road, checked for ambushes and seized high ground or fords ahead of the column's route. It did not matter that the province was pacified; the army took no chances. Second was the vanguard: the Eighteenth Legion and its cavalry. Then came camp surveyors, pioneers to clear obstacles, and the Eighteenth Legion's general, Marcus Vinicius, who organised the march. The combined remaining cavalry of the legions, and then General Saturninus and the governor's party, rode behind them. Then marched the legions, headed by its commander, and the camp followers: sutlers, tradesmen, and women. Finally marched the auxiliary infantry and a rearguard provided by the heavy infantry of the Nineteenth Legion. With the camp followers, the force consisted of twenty-five thousand people. They bore east, towards the Semnones.

Arminius, riding with the vanguard, watched from an outcrop as the column slid through the hills. Every infantryman wore hobnailed sandals. Together with the noise of clanking equipment, these produced a grating, clashing din on the stone road that drowned the forest sounds.

'Quite a monster,' Vegates remarked. He was now armed like a Roman auxiliary.

'Wait until you see it fight.'

Arminius had already explained the details. At the end of each day's march, the three legions would build one massive temporary fort. The next day, they broke it down, leaving ruins useless to an enemy, but easy to reconstruct the next time they travelled by the highway. Watchtowers with signalling equipment and relays of cavalry provided regular communication with nearby permanent forts, and with the headquarters at Castra Drusus.

'And the secret to it all is the road system,' Arminius concluded.

'Do they ever leave the roads?'

'Not if they can help it.'

* * *

'This is ideal for freeing you from those stuffy rooms!'

Thusnelda smiled at the governor, and thanked him again for suggesting that she accompany the legions east. It was the fourth morning of the march. They stood by the luxury wagon.

Today, the Seventeenth and Eighteenth Legions were responsible for breaking camp. The Nineteenth, who would lead the march, stood arrayed on parade. They had removed the leather covers from their shields to create a rippling red hide. They were about to engage in a daily ceremony: the Worship of the Standard.

Thusnelda watched absently as the senior *signifer* brought the legion's eagle forward. There were other standards: one of the Emperor's face and another with a bull on it.

She wondered where Arminius was. She had not seen him since the journey east began. She had been horrified by the assassination attempt. He had sent her a message welcoming her on the march – nothing more.

She searched the crowd for him.

A soldier kissed the bull banner, and then led the whole legion in saluting the eagle. Five thousand men moved in perfect unison. It was impressive, but she disliked it. They seemed like little toy men – moving without thought. They gawked at their gold bird. When the head centurion bawled at them whether they were ready to fight, they all shouted yes.

She stifled a yawn.

'It has been some time since I travelled this far to the east,' she told the governor after the parade.

'What do you think of it?'

'It is savage – not as beautiful as the land around the Rhenus.'

'I love it when you speak so disdainfully!' he roared with mirth. 'It makes you sound like a real Roman lady!'

She hesitated before asking him whether he had seen Arminius.

'He is off in the woods somewhere,' Varus replied, but then he winked at her. 'I thought you were still angry at him.'

'Why?'

'For making me lock you up.'

'Oh, that turned out to be a good thing.'

'It gave you time to think?'

She nodded.

'Does this mean I can invite him over to my tent again? You will not snap at him?'

'I never did.'

Varus guffawed.

'You are an infuriating man, governor.'

He laughed. 'I pity any man who gets on the wrong side of you, girl. Fine, I shall have him over for dinner. I think he's man enough for you!'

* * *

8 CE (JUNE)

WEST BANK OF THE ALBIS

Marcus Vinicius pointed with a stick at the sand model. He indicated the flow of the Albis, its likely depth, and the geography beyond it. The officers of the Eighteenth Legion, tasked with the crossing of the river, asked questions.

It was the classic summer campaign. The three legions stood along the west bank of the Albis. The Eighteenth and cavalry would build a bridge and punch through into Semnones territory. The Seventeenth and Nineteenth would provide flank protection, guard supply lines, and build roads.

'The Semnones will defend the river, and if we are lucky, will give battle. Most likely,' Vinicius explained, 'they have learned not to take us head on. Our plan is to choke their river trade, take slaves and, in the process, kill as many of their warriors as we can.'

Vala, who had reassumed his summer command over the cavalry, described the land further east. The weather was dry and the ground hard, allowing long-distance cavalry operations.

After the meeting, he came over to Arminius.

'How is your wound?'

'I can manage.'

'Take it easy, though. I see that you brought the Chatti nobleman with you.'

'He is still my slave.'

'You have armed him.'

'I am trying to build a relationship. Besides, he helped save me from the assassins.'

'It does not seem as if you are punishing him for his crimes.'

'The Chatti are proud. They can accept punishment, but not humiliation.'

Vala enquired after the assassins. He had heard nothing new. 'There are just too many candidates. My father suspects members of the tribe. If that is so, we will deal with it ourselves.'

'That is not the Roman law.'

Arminius stopped in mid-stride. 'No, it is not, but if not handled properly, it will set off a blood-feud, and we *cannot* risk that.' He took his leave. He had a dinner appointment with the governor.

* * *

'How good it is to see you!' Varus gushed as Arminius and Flavus entered the tent.

Lady Tiberia rose to her feet. Her hands flitted over the fabric of her white, sleeveless dress. It dropped straight from her shoulders to her ankles. Her hair was intricately arranged.

'Thank you for inviting me.' Arminius's eyes had already sought out Tiberia's gaze.

'No need to introduce you to my lovely companion.'

'No,' Arminius whispered. He took Tiberia's extended fingers and kissed her softly on the knuckles. 'Lady.'

She dipped her head.

'You remember my brother? You spoke at the celebrations at Castra Drusus.'

'Indeed.' She exchanged pleasantries with Flavus, and then turned her gaze back to the elder brother.

'I am sorry about being so scarce,' Arminius said to Varus. 'The march is a very busy time.'

'I am sure, I am sure,' Varus replied, offering the two brothers wine. 'And you are recovering from your wound?'

'It is not serious.'

'I would crucify the culprit if I found him,' Varus growled. 'Wouldn't you, Lady Tiberia?' He had to repeat the question.

'Yes, of course.'

Varus laughed.

'Have you seen a cruxifiction?' Arminius asked.

'No. I haven't.' She averted her eyes.

Varus guided them to the couches. The tent was decorated luxuriously with small statues, carpets, and valuables worthy of any prince. Varus started a spirited conversation with Flavus about a particular statue.

Arminius sat down opposite Thusnelda. He smiled tenderly, and asked her whether she was comfortable on the march.

'It is better than my quarters.' She smiled delicately, and spoke in Latin, 'It is good to be out of Castra Drusus. Did you ask the governor to bring me?'

'He did not require much convincing. It is not dangerous.'

'I know.'

'Your father is angry, though.'

'I do not see much of my father at the moment.'

'I am sorry.'

She shrugged and looked away. She asked him again about his wound.

'It is healing fast.'

'We *know* who did it,' she whispered in Suebic.

'It does not matter. It is important that it *should* not matter.'

Varus glanced over to the couple as Flavus inspected a Syrian brooch in his collection. Tiberia sat on the edge of the one couch, legs swept sideways, cupping a glass of wine. Her free hand stroked her forearm. Arminius was leaning forward, slowly swishing his wine in his goblet.

They were speaking in Barbarian.

She laughed at something he said.

CHAPTER 32

T HE TRIBUNE NODDED. THE LETTER of introduction was indeed from Statilius
Taurus, the Emperor's friend.

'Well, as the boy comes so highly recommended, I see no problem,'
the tribune replied to the dignified old slave. He glanced at the fifteen-year old.
Unlike many young men with noble connections brought to his office, this one was
strapping, already near his full height and filling out with muscle. He had a severe
look in his eyes that would fare well with troopers.

There was only one problem.

'We can, of course, not place you in charge of Roman soldiers.'

The boy did not visibly react.

The house slave replied that a proper command of regular troops was of course
not expected.

'You will probably end up commanding an auxiliary unit – if you are good
enough.'

'Cavalry?' the boy asked. His voice had broken. He spoke with confidence.

'We will see. For the moment, we will give you basic training. My legion is
currently in Pannonia. It is quiet, but you will learn the ropes.'

* * *

8 CE (JULY)

WEST BANK OF THE ALBIS

The clearing resembled an enormous timber yard. Hundreds of legionary lumbermen
and carpenters laboured over logs.

163

Vegates was amazed. 'The Semnones *must* know that the Romans are going to cross here.'

'But they cannot stop them,' Arminius remarked. The bridge would be up in less than three days. He had seen it done a dozen times before.

They rode on. Separating the timber yard and the river was a copse that made observation from the other bank difficult. Within this copse were rafts and boats, either prepared on the spot or confiscated from nearby villages. The vessels were covered in brush. The river was broad, turgid and shallow. Only heavy rain upstream could cause problems.

Arminius imagined Semnones warriors clustering nearby, waiting. They would be afraid.

* * *

The night before the crossing, the engineers cut down the trees between the lumber yards and the river. Just before dawn broke, the ballistae and catapults fired incendiaries en masse at the opposite bank. As the forest erupted in flame and smoke for hundreds of yards on either side of the landing position, teams of legionaries launched boats. Their shields were covered in vinegar-soaked skins to avoid being set alight by fire arrows. The first boats dragged ropes across the river before the enemy could respond. Slower, more exposed rafts then operated like ferries along the ropes. By the time that the first sleepy Semnones, their eyes burning from fire smoke, launched a few desultory arrows, two hundred legionaries were across and lining up behind shields and pre-cut stakes.

By now, the biggest Roman artillery pieces rained missiles over the legionaries' heads, into the wood. The empty boats returned for a second load of archers and light infantry, who crossed the river and formed up behind the heavy infantry. By the time the sun peeked above the trees, five hundred men were across. By mid-morning, rows of pylons had been hammered into the riverbed upstream of the landing site to break the force of the current. By noon, the first great A-shaped frame stood on the near bank. The sun sank over blackened trees and a river half-spanned by Rome. A sod-and-timber fort dominated the far bank.

The Semnones had melted away.

* * *

Vala explained. 'The villagers on our side of the river say that a lot of traffic came downstream recently. The men they described were Marcomanni. They also heard that the queen of the Semnones has collected extra food. It looks as if they are going to fight all summer this time.'

'How many warriors do they have?'

'Up to one hundred thousand, but if they mobilize them all, they cannot farm this summer, and they will starve come winter.'

The cavalry officers exchanged comments. Vala waited for them to finish.

'The governor wants a battle.' They all noticed the pause. 'The Semnones have a sacred grove. He is letting the Semnones know that he will march upon it if they do not negotiate.'

'Sir.'

'Yes, Arminius?' Vala had expected that the barbarian would speak.

'That grove is sacred to all the German tribes. Does the governor know this?'

'He does.'

'If he burns the grove, everything between here and the Rhenus will erupt.'

'We are taking the grove into custody for all the Germans.' Vala grimaced. 'The original plan has therefore changed. Two legions will march on their capital, and this grove, while a third guards the bridges.' After three days of work, two timber spans existed, guarded by a massive fort on each bank. 'The cavalry are going ahead to reconnoitre and distract them. If all goes well, the legions can force them into a set-piece fight.'

'This is a mistake, Sir.'

'Thank you, Arminius. I suggest that you go and tell the governor that.'

Chapter 33

I T WAS TWO YEARS AFTER joining the army before Arminius saw Flavus again. He arrived at the house in Rome one day, unannounced and in uniform. His brother embraced him joyously.

'It has been boring without you!'

Arminius was taller, his skin bronzed. He sported a beard and scars.

'What is the army like?'

'I cannot imagine a better life.' He made himself comfortable in the garden, where the household came to greet him and listen to his stories.

He had been stationed in Pannonia with a unit of German mercenaries under Roman officers.

'How much fighting did you see?'

'A few scraps with hill tribes. The barbarians across the river are difficult.'

'Your letters said that you fought in a battle!'

Arminius laughed. 'It was not quite as impressive as that! They stood up to us once…'

'What happened?' Flavus demanded excitedly, when his brother paused.

'We cut through them like steel through milk, of course.'

* * *

8 CE (JULY)

SEMNONES TERRITORY

'Get ready! They're coming!' the horseman shouted as he careened down the line. Arminius cursed. The Roman cavalry were in file, extended along a landscape of copses and abandoned peasants' hovels.

Vala had to show his worth now.

Far ahead, he heard the doleful carnyxes of the Semnones. Roman bugles bleated out orders, and Arminius relayed them to his contingent. There were only fifty of them. Vala had ordered the rest of the unit, under Flavus, to help protect the baggage – he had not even let them cross the Albis. Vegates had also been forced to stay inside the province.

Inguiomer reined his horse in beside Arminius. He had unsheathed his long-hafted battleaxe. 'What do we do?'

'We're deploying into a *cuneus*.' Arminius disliked fighting from horseback. He felt vulnerable, unable to hear, see and balance as well as he could on foot. He preferred to travel fast and then dismount.

The five hundred horsemen in the patrol had pushed ahead of the legions. Ostensibly, the Semnones had shifted forces to intercept the Romans, but Arminius suspected that Vala had gone out looking for a fight.

As Arminius brought his men into the back of the dense triangle that was the *cuneus*, he spotted Vala. The cavalry commander was at the front among the heaviest cavalry, a unit of fifty Sarmatians. Not only were the men covered in metal scales down to their ankles, but their big horses were also monstrously mail-clad. Each Sarmatian carried a heavy two-handed lance. They would form the nose of the triangle. The majority of the cavalry were Romans or Iberians, armed with swords and javelins.

There was a patch of grassland ahead. The baying from the Semnones was becoming louder. Arminius tried to see them over the other cavalrymen, but he was too far to the back.

'Get ready!' the order came at last. At the front of the pack, Vala hoisted a red banner.

The flag dropped. The charge began at a walk. The men cheered. The formation speeded up into a canter, and the horses began to separate. Mud and hoof-torn tufts of grass spattered the ranks.

There was a roar from the front: the boom of Semnones awaiting the charge.

The Sarmatians' lances dipped. Men readied their swords. The hoofbeats made it impossible to hear properly, to see…

A volley of javelins and rocks rose over the front ranks and then curved down, slicing into the cavalry. Men spun out of their saddles. Horses twisted, tripped, and fell. Arminius jumped a thrashing, riderless mare. He glimpsed a corpse, skewered by a lance, cut to ribbons by swords.

The ranks ahead opened around spotted trees. A barbarian spearman was jabbing at the passing cavalry from behind a trunk. The blond warrior struck a horse in the flank just ahead of Arminius, sending the animal careening and its rider flying.

The next moment, Arminius's mount gave an agonised whinny. He felt the horse go down and he jumped free, slamming into the ground. He staggered to his feet. The churned-up landscape was littered with corpses from both sides. Some barbarians that had survived the charge were racing in. More savages were appearing from copses flanking the line of advance.

A young barbarian appeared close by, rufous, naked but for a loincloth. He carried a slashing knife. Oblivious to Arminius, he leapt like a cat at a severely wounded Roman still holding desperately onto his mount. The horse's legs buckled and then, freed from its rider, it hurried off. The cavalryman squirmed on the ground as the barbarian hacked at his face and arms.

Arminius started forward.

Howling Semnones bounded across the shredded land. A few spotted him.

'Arminius!'

It was Inguiomer, holding a free horse. Arminius mounted swiftly and raced after the older man. They passed dead men, shattered shields and broken weapons. The charge had petered out a few hundred yards further on. The bugle was barking out new orders.

'How stupid!' Inguiomer snarled in Suebic. 'What were they thinking?'

'Peasants,' Arminius said hoarsely, but his eyes were frantically scanning the nearby forest. Something was wrong. 'Look!'

Others had already spotted the problem. Down the entire right side of the field, just inside the forest, was a barricade of brushwood. Behind it, more barbarians massed.

Arminius looked behind him, to see ground sloping away, ever so gently, into beds of reeds.

The booming war hymn had restarted.

'Damn!'

The bugle sounded for the cavalry to reform. Arminius joined one of the hindmost ranks. Behind them, in the direction from which they had come, a screen of several hundred Semnones was forming among the trees. The barbarians crouched behind their wooden shields, chanting, jabbing with their javelins.

Stones were flying from the barricade.

'Damn it!' Inguiomer cursed.

They were in a trap. The line they had just smashed was the bait.

'He is going to try and charge straight through,' Inguiomer growled. Vala was riding among his troops, shouting orders at his officers. They were to ride parallel to the barricade and directly at the barbarians manning the gap.

'Straight through, you hear me! Straight through! They will not stand!'

The barbarian rearguard, closing the trap behind them, was growing ever more numerous. There was no going back.

The horses began to move. Long-haired heads bobbed above the barricade.

The pace increased. The barricade drew closer. The Romans' animals were bunching. Arminius saw a javelin strike a trooper in the neck. A stone collided with his shield. Mud from the other cavalry obscured his vision – the marsh drew ever closer to their left.

The horses slowed. There was a bottleneck ahead.

Inguiomer's leg touched his. 'Don't do anything stupid, Armin,' he growled. 'We need you!' He glared at his nephew, raising his shield to protect him.

They reached the narrows, where the Semnones' barricade reached towards a rocky outcrop on the marsh's edge. A gate, now smashed, had closed the gap. Dozens of men were fighting murderously among the stakes. Riderless horses, many bleeding, careened back into the formation. But most men had broken through, as Vala had predicted, sweeping the barbarians from the barricade, driving them from the blood-smeared outcrop.

An enormous mêlée was commencing beyond the barricade. The Semnones' main force was charging out of the tree line. Half of them were mounted on ponies, and alongside them warriors ran on foot, holding onto the horses' manes. Vala's cavalry smashed into them.

Arminius did not see the outcome of the charge.

'They're coming from the back!'

Semnones infantry were now charging from behind, keeping between the barricade and marsh. They were about four hundred feet away. Warriors who had manned the barricade were joining them. They would arrive before the Roman cavalry could all feed through the narrows. The Romans on the barricades would be slaughtered.

'Turn around!' Arminius shouted in Suebic.

The men from his unit obeyed immediately.

'Turn!' Arminius repeated in Latin, calling the name of a nearby *decurion*. 'Defend the gap!'

The junior officer, seeing Arminius's rank, began to order men to dismount and follow. Arminius leaped off his horse. 'Hold the gate!'

The barbarian wave sped up.

Grunting, Arminius planted his feet apart and punched his shield forward. Inguiomer's shield locked with his. Obed moved in on the other side, muttering in Kushite, his grimace ivory against his sweat-beaded skin.

'Don't give way!'

The Semnones warriors whooped as they crossed the final fifty yards.

'Hold!'

The barbarians smashed into the Roman formation.

The gate became a death trap.

Afterwards, when he led his gore-covered men back past the barricade, now held by cheering Romans, Arminius felt ill. Around him, exhausted men retched at the butchery.

Obed was crouching over his dented shield. Arminius stopped by him and lay a bloodied hand on his shoulder. Obed looked up. His lips were quivering. 'I did not come here for this.'

'I know,' Arminius said. He bent down and their foreheads touched. 'I know.' He closed his eyes, his hand reaching behind the man's neck. Then the noise of the barbarians began to intrude again.

'They are reforming,' Inguiomer said behind them. Arminius stood up and ordered his men through the gate, where their horses waited. A lot of his troopers were wounded. Several were now dead upon the field.

On the other side of the gate, the fighting had been equally intense. He counted many Roman corpses. However, the barbarian charge, which had tried to crush the Romans as they filtered through the gate, had died on the steel of the Roman troopers.

Somewhere, the barbarians were again singing, trying to work up their courage for another attempt. Vala had to get his men out soon.

'Charge, crunch, and then single envelopment– beautiful,' one of the *decuriones* boasted of Vala's tactics as Arminius remounted. He pointed out the place where the barbarian chief had made his last stand. 'Courageous bastard. He would not retreat. You know what these people are like.'

'I do,' Arminius replied.

CHAPTER 34

VALA SWORE AS HE STUDIED the documents. He had asked for the agents that he had sent south to enquire about Arminius, to bring the information directly to him on campaign. It was too pressing a matter to wait.

'Is it as Saturninus expected?' asked Gnaeus Silius. Silius, his second-in-command, was lounging in a campaign chair, staring up at the tent's ceiling.

Vala read the record. 'Served two years in Illyria. Received his first command after one year. Elected to remain in the army.'

'What else was he going to do? He is a Hairy.'

Vala glowered. 'He volunteered for service in Moesia as a trooper. He served one year, after which time he was *ordered* to accept promotion to *decurion*. He chose to serve on the Upper Nilus, beyond Luxor, for one year.'

'Is he insane?' Silius exclaimed.

'He attracted the attention of Prince Tiberius, then visiting Memphis, who assigned him to his bodyguard for an expedition to Armenia. There he won the oak leaves for courage. Twice upon his return to Rome, Tiberius got him assigned to the Emperor's bodyguard.' He rattled off the rest of the record, which included more service in Pannonia.

'He volunteered for that too?'

'When the rebellion broke out, he asked the Emperor personally for an assignment to an auxiliary unit.'

'He went from guarding the palace, to mucking it in bloody Pannonia?'

'It appears so.'

'Fuck. You have a true hero here.'

'He is highly decorated.'

Silius laughed. 'And you honestly think that he is up to something?'

'I do.'

'You will sweat to prove it!'

Vala just grimaced at the papers.

'What exactly do you suspect him of?'

Vala sat back. 'He is planning a rebellion.'

'He is going to kick us out of Germania?'

'Yes.'

'And you are basing this theory on…'

'He lied to me. And if I were him, it is what *I* would do.'

* * *

4 CE

ROME

'This is the new man, Your Imperial Highness,' the officer announced.

The Emperor's German bodyguard: fifty men strong and dressed in black and purple, stood in parade formation in the palace. All the men were exceptionally tall, and handpicked for their loyalty and skill at arms.

'Good, I like to know all their faces.'

Augustus was of short stature, handsome for a man of sixty-nine, with a body that retained some of the proportions of his youth. When he smiled, he bared bad teeth, and a birthmark on his throat peeked from under his toga. However, he undeniably radiated power; and so he should have – he was the most powerful monarch in the world.

'He is called Arminius, Sir.'

The Emperor studied the man, who remained at attention, his eyes in the middle distance. 'Oh, yes, my son Tiberius speaks highly of you.'

'Thank you, Your Imperial Highness,' the guardsman replied.

'He was raised under the roof of Statilius Taurus, Your Highness.'

'I remember, yes. Very good,' the Emperor muttered, gazing at the guardsman's face, as if he could discern something in the man's handsome features of the mind beyond. After a moment he said, 'Arminius, I need not tell you that my life depends upon your vigilance. I have many enemies. Can I rely on you?'

'You can, Your Imperial Highness.'

Augustus took a moment more to study the young barbarian. Then he nodded. 'Thank you.' He turned to the officer. 'I am satisfied.'

* * *

8 CE (July)

<small>Semnones territory</small>

Arminius peered into the distance. He stood outside the governor's tent. Around him, the great camp bustled with two legions.

'Has he arrived?' Varus asked, out of his hearing, inside the tent. He stood over a map table, surrounded by Saturninus, the two legionary commanders and Numonius Vala.

'He has, Sir.'

'Good, let him wait a moment longer,' Varus said, before returning a stern gaze to Saturninus. 'General, I understand that you want a fight, but my instructions are to secure the province, by whatever means.'

'We need a battle, Sir. These people will not listen to anything else.'

'I know, General; and normally I would just march on their capital, but I am thinking further. I want to use the legions for internal duties, rather than endless fighting with unconquered tribes.'

'Before we crossed the river, Sir, you said that you wanted a battle. We have beaten back all their attacks. Our supply lines are secure. We are ready.'

'Yes, at the outset I did intend a battle, and I still do, if necessary.'

'Take their capital, Sir. Teach them a lesson. Then negotiate,' said Marcus Vinicius.

'Their capital is a collection of stick-and-mud huts. They can abandon it like *that*.' Vala snapped his fingers. 'No, I want to offer them negotiation and split them from the Marcomanni.'

'And where will you get your cheap slaves from, Sir?' Saturninus asked sarcastically. He felt the eyes of the governor's Syrian associate fix on him from across the room.

Varus noted the barb, but shelved the anger. He would punish Saturninus later.

'The Semnones will get them for us. The forest goes on forever, and there are dozens of tribes beyond them. If the Semnones are raiding them, they will not be raiding us.'

'And you will use this grove as leverage?'

'The Sacred Grove is the equivalent to the German tribes of the Temple of Delphi to the Hellenes, or our Temple of Vesta. Unlike their capital, they cannot abandon it. Praefectus Numonius Vala here knows where it is.' He glanced at Vala, who nodded. 'If they want to fight us for it, so be it. All we ask for is access for our Germans. We will send Arminius to deliver this ultimatum.'

Saturninus hissed; his eyes lowered.

Vala interjected, 'According to the Cheruscan Cegestes, Arminius's mother is an important priestess in this grove.'

'Oh, Arminius told me about his mother some time ago,' Varus said impatiently. 'It just proves that if anybody can negotiate with them, it is he.'

The soldiers glanced uncomfortably at one another.

'We will send a trustworthy Roman with him,' Varus said. He shrugged. 'If it does not work, *we've* lost nothing.'

CHAPTER 35

ARMINIUS STARED THROUGH THE CROWDED trees at the pond. Its waters were black, its depth uncertain. Leaves peeked from the amber-hued shallows. At intervals, projected over the pond, were stretched horse skins, the poles stuck like backbones through the base of the attached skulls. Flies settled on drying eye sockets.

His Semnonian guard did not explain what it signified. Arminius did not ask.

Inguiomer had hugged him when he heard of the mission. 'It is good your brother is not here – he would have wanted to go along.' Deeper feelings had welled in the old man's eyes.

The exchange with the Semnones had taken some negotiation. The tribe had provided a chieftain as hostage, but Arminius had declared it unnecessary, and the man now returned with him. He had two Romans with him: Silius, Vala's friend and envoy; and the man's servant. The Semnones would take them straight to the capital, two days from the legions' last marching camp.

The gloomy forest gave the impression of ever-greater antiquity as they travelled east. Arminius had seen what some people called the trees' eastern edge, in Moesia by the Pontus Euxinus. Others said that the treescape continued, unbroken, north of the vast grasslands above the Bosphoran kingdom. His people said that the forest had been born here, close to the Amisia, in the Grove.

Occasionally they passed through ruined villages or overrun fields, destroyed in earlier battles with Rome. The guides would touch their foreheads when passing mounds – he assumed these were mass graves. Onwards, the land turned healthier and the woods opened to reveal hamlets with fields of flax, barley, and wheat.

The Semnones were the oldest and most numerous of all the Suebic tribes. The capital lay on a river near a series of small lakes. It was unfortified. He guessed that five thousand people lived in the warren of huts, hovels, and longhouses, together with their animals.

A vast wooden longhouse, as high as seven men and as long as an arrow-shot, dominated the town. It incorporated enormous oak pillars carved with the shapes of animals and plants, and was encircled by oak trees, upon which fluttered thousands of scraps of fabric, alongside animal skulls nailed to the trunks.

'I hope you know what you are doing,' Silius whispered.

Arminius scowled. He hoped that the Roman would behave. 'Respect them and they will respect you.'

'This is a suicide mission. Fuck these people.'

Arminius wanted to kill the man right there.

They dismounted and were taken into the cavernous hall. The air was laced with smoke and the moisture from many lungs. Arminius needed a moment to become accustomed to the murkiness. He felt like a man trapped in a dark cage with a leopard. Then, shapes became apparent, and eventually faces. He advanced across the dirt floor towards the far end of the hall, where the warlord and council waited.

She was with them.

He immediately recognised her. With the passing years, her body had become fuller and more matronly, but there was no mistaking her eyes, or her auburn tresses.

He could not keep his eyes off her.

'I am Armin *su eb* Hildreth *ev* Eysle,' he announced in Suebic. 'I have returned to my people.'

* * *

She regarded him from across the table. Her arms were tattooed in black whorls, and more patterns covered her chest and neck. Two lines, like the lashes of an owl, rose over her cheeks.

'I knew that you would come here.' It was a statement of fact. It contained no discernible emotion.

'They must have told you that I had come back.'

She said nothing.

'Frimunt has returned as well.'

She did not answer. They sat, alone, in a hut some distance away from the great hall. It was night. He had sent the Romans to bed. He stared at the stone lamp between them. It produced a golden glow and the rich aroma of burning animal fat.

'Frimunt is more Roman.'

'…Than you are?'

He gave a wan smile.

'Do you come here with your father's blessing?'

'He does not know.'

'The governor sent you.'

'I convinced him.'

'Why?'

'I wanted to speak with you.'

'Rome's demands are no more palatable coming from your throat.'

'I know.'

He hesitated, looking into her powerful grey eyes. They *had* changed since he had last seen them, seventeen years ago, just before the battle. She had been magnificent, praising the warriors, encouraging the women to sing them on and to bind their wounds. She had kissed him, and sent him off to hide, while she strode off to war.

'I am not here for Rome.'

She did not weaken her gaze. He realised that he feared her.

'How much have your people told you about me?' he asked.

'My spies? They have told me that you are a hero,' she said sarcastically. 'That you have killed hundreds for your masters.'

'That is true. What else?'

'What more needs to be said?'

'What *else*?'

She hesitated at the force in his voice, and then spoke more slowly. 'They said that the governor favours you, and intends great things for you.'

'And what do you think?'

She smiled bitterly. 'That you are your father's son.'

'What does that mean?'

'He is a slave. You are a slave.'

He lowered his gaze. 'You left him because of Frimunt and me?'

'I left because he surrendered.'

Armin clenched his fists and forced himself to look up. '*I* never surrendered.' He did not want to weep in front of her.

'You were but a boy.'

'I *never* surrendered.'

'If you say so.'

'When I said I had returned to my people, I meant it.'

His mother leaned back from the table, until only her fingertips touched its edge. 'What about your brother?'

'He is lost.'

'What do you mean?'

'He serves Rome.'

'Whereas you – '

He dared to interrupt, even though he was shaking. He had waited nearly twenty years to tell her. 'I am the enemy of Rome.'

'What do you mean?'

'I am the snake in their heart.'

She shook her head, still uncertain whether she understood him correctly. 'What is it that you intend to do?'

It was the first time he would say it. He had not even dared tell Inguiomer or Adgandes. 'Destroy the legions.'

'All three of them?'

'All three, at the same time.'

He expected her to ask him to explain his plan immediately, and he was fearful that he would stumble. There was still so much uncertainty.

'Why?'

'*What*?' He was confused.

'I asked, *Why*. After seventeen years under their roof, seeing their cities and roads and their empire, shedding blood for them and having them as your brothers – *why*?'

'They were *never* my brothers!'

'You are avoiding my question.'

He did not know what to say. He had always imagined that at this moment she would simply be proud of him.

'Freedom.'

She snorted. Cynicism rippled across her mouth and the corners of her eyes. 'What do you mean by *freedom*?'

'I mean: having dignity; making the Romans leave.'

She nodded slowly. 'And then?'

'We can be ourselves.'

'We will be as we were before?'

'Yes!' he stammered.

She simply stared at him.

'I am giving you a chance to get rid of them!'

She smiled gently, indicating that he should settle down. 'How well do you know *our people*?'

'Well enough to know that they hate Rome!'

'Let me put it another way. What will things be like after the Romans leave?' She saw his hesitation. 'Good. To make it easier, what will *you* do after the Romans leave?'

'They will come back.'

'And you will stop them again?'

'We will need an army.'

'You will be the warlord?'

'They *will* come back.'

'Yes. What else can you offer the people?'

He searched for words. 'Laws, peace.'

'Who will make the laws?'

Again, he wavered.

She continued, 'Who will maintain the roads, towns, fields, trade, and all the other things that "our people" are becoming used to?'

'We do not need these things.'

'We will all go back to the old ways?'

'The people prefer freedom to trinkets!'

'Perhaps.'

'They will make sacrifices.'

'That is freedom?' she said pensively.

'It is better than being slaves. Like you said…'

'We can never return to the way it was.'

'We will…'

'The old ways are dead. If we go back, we will be too weak to beat them when they return for vengeance.' She held up her hand when he started to speak. 'Is that not true?'

After a moment, he nodded with regret. 'Yes.'

She gazed down at the candle. It softened her features. Finally, she said, 'You have kept this in you for a long time.'

'I have.'

'And all that time, you thought about destroying.' She allowed that statement to seep into the silence. The candle played across her face. 'Before I can help you, I must also know what you will build.'

He breathed hard, agitated. Finally, he collected himself. 'I had not expected you to speak like this.'

Her eyes brushed his hunched shoulders and his furrowed brow. His scarred hands bunched into fists. She studied the knuckles.

What intensity!

'Perhaps,' she said eventually, 'we should not think of these things now. We should defeat Rome, and when it is done we can talk.'

'Yes.' He nodded vigorously.

She reached out and touched him for the first time in seventeen years.

'Tomorrow you will meet someone. Learn from him.' She stroked his hand and they watched it open. 'Tomorrow, we can speak again.'

Chapter 36

'I DO NOT LIKE TO BE left alone here,' Silius exclaimed guardedly. He glanced at the door of the hut. 'I was told not to let you out of my sight. You have already disappeared once!'

'My mother wanted to speak to me alone.'

'Vala said – '

'Vala is not here.' Arminius towered over the officer. 'As you saw yesterday in the hall, the Roman ultimatum made them angry. You understand enough Suebic to know that.'

Silius glared at him.

'We have to be careful. Our best chance is for my mother to help us.' Arminius asserted

'You should have let them give that hostage to the army.'

'It would have made no difference.'

Silius paused. 'You are plotting something.'

Arminius stared at him icily.

'You are up to something,' Silius said, more nervous this time. He cringed involuntarily as Arminius retorted, 'I am here to save your life, and the lives of hundreds of Romans, and perhaps the entire province!' Arminius stabbed his finger at Silius's heart. 'I am risking *my* life for Rome, and I am not even *Roman*!'

'Vala says – '

'I do not care what Vala says! If you cannot trust me, of all the Germans, then you cannot hope to build a province! I am your best hope, and I am tired of having to prove it!'

Silius watched him storm out, swearing only once Arminius was out of earshot.

* * *

They entered a beech wood. The smooth grey trunks stood massive and straight. Foliage turned the sky emerald green, dashed golden with catkins. The earth was a brown bed of leaves. In the centre of the wood was a barrow mound. Upon the mound waited Maroboduus.

He stood alone, but like a giant, as if the forest were his. He was about forty, with a black beard that cascaded over mail armour. He held a long stave like a shepherd's crook.

'Young Armin!' he exclaimed in Suebic. It was laced with another tongue. A smile wrinkled his face.

'He is my son. Treat him with respect,' Hildreth told him.

'Of course.'

Maroboduus descended from the mound, scattering clumps of earth.

'I received your message, the one you left during the raid,' he told Armin.

'I am glad that you did.'

Maroboduus laughed. 'This son of yours was very impressive. In the middle of winter, he sneaks into my lands, murders a whole village, and then makes it to one of my iron mines. We never thought it possible! You have become a demon to the Marcomanni!'

'Your tribe is careless,' Armin said.

'Tribe? It is a bit more than that.' He made eye contact with Hildreth. 'So, why do you bring him to me?'

'He has a proposition for you,' Hildreth said.

'I want an alliance. I, personally,' Armin told him.

Maroboduus's mask of frivolity dissipated as if it had never been. He stared frostily at Armin. 'Do you?'

Maroboduus was strong of build, and on his bare arms were old scars. He wore a barbarian tunic and loose trousers, and leather boots. Around his neck was a metal torque in the shape of a double-headed serpent with ram's horns. He carried a Roman-style sword, and the mail was Roman.

'You, and that Vala, have been butchering my people.'

'It was necessary. I regret it deeply.'

'You have murdered my people!' Maroboduus spat.

'I had to prove to them that they could trust me,' Armin said.

'Trust you? And now you want me to trust you. Why would I?'

'I shall explain,' Armin said.

'Rome has murdered my men, raped my women, enslaved my children, burned my huts and fields; broken *my* laws protecting *my* people in *my* land! And you have been their servant in this!'

'You have to listen,' Hildreth implored him.

'Why? My entire kingdom lives only to fight Rome! That is who we are.'

'*Listen*,' she repeated.

Marodobuus dismissively gave Armin the opportunity to speak.

'You have done well. Starting the revolt in Pannonia and Illyria was very clever. Smuggling weapons to the Cherusci Bear clan has been risky, but successful. You have also been providing warriors to the Semnones – a major commitment.' He paused. 'All this makes you a great defender of the people. But it is not enough.'

Maroboduus ran his tongue across his teeth.

'It is not enough,' Armin repeated slowly. Maroboduus's eyes flitted to Hildreth. 'In three years, the Romans will have subdued Pannonia. Then, thirteen legions will attack you – ten from the south and three from the west. Your people will die. There will be nothing you can do to stop it.'

'I shall still fight them.'

'You will be destroyed. And the Semnones will be next.'

'I will try.'

'There is a better way.'

Maroboduus sat back against the barrow. 'Making peace with them? Is that what you are here to ask?'

'No.'

Maroboduus did not listen. 'I know these people. I know their methods and their avarice. They will not stop; they will never stop, until we are all slaves, until we are utterly without humanity.'

'I know.'

'He has a plan,' Hildreth said.

Maroboduus looked confused.

Armin began. 'When I was a child, I was taken as a hostage to Rome. At first, I hated them. Then, they taught me their ways, and I learned that I could defeat them.'

'I, also, studied them…'

'I know. That is why I asked my mother to see you. I know that you see things as I see them.'

Maroboduus snorted.

'I guarded their emperor. I was within sword's reach of him a hundred times. Yet I did not kill him. *That* is how certain I am of victory.'

'You should have killed him.'

'No. One emperor can be replaced: we can do much, much worse to them.'

Hildreth noticed a fire in her son's voice she had not heard before.

'I have an *ala* of cavalry here. In winter, I control the border between the Marcomanni and the Cherusci. Whatever weapons you can supply, I can use.'

'For what? I need all the weapons my people have.'

'I can do more with them.'

Maroboduus sneered. 'Do tell me.'

'An uprising in Germania which will simultaneously destroy all Roman forces in the province.'

Maroboduus cackled. 'All of them?'

'*Every single Roman.*'

Maroboduus glanced at Hildreth. His eyes bulged mockingly. 'I *am* impressed. What *have* you brought me?' He regarded Armin. 'And how do you intend to do this?'

'First, I need iron spearheads and swords. If this works, your northern and western flank will be safe, and I shall help defend your people against the legions.'

'That is not the answer to my question.'

'I cannot tell you yet. I shall, in time.'

'And how can I trust you? Why should I arm my enemy?'

'My mother vouches for me.'

Hildreth nodded. 'I stand for my son.'

Maroboduus was amused. 'Oh, they *did* make a mistake with you!'

'Give me the weapons and I shall take all the risks.'

'You still have not told me how you will do it.'

'I said, trust me.'

'I need to know more.'

Armin paused and then said, 'An ambush.'

'Large enough to destroy three legions?'

'Yes.' He looked at his mother. 'If I can get the Romans to trust me, it can be done.'

'And do they trust you that much?'

'Not yet, but they will soon.'

Maroboduus stood up and turned towards the barrow. He stared at it as if he could see its contents. Hildreth and Armin waited for him. Finally, he said, 'Do you know what this is?'

'A grave.'

'Yes, it is a grave. Some people say that there is a warrior inside, a man from long ago. Others say that it contains a worm.' He turned around. 'A dragon. Everybody agrees that it contains treasure. The question is, what will you find when you open it – a mouldy old corpse, or a serpent?' He chuckled. 'This situation reminds me of that.'

'If we fail, you gain a few months. If we succeed, you are free of Rome.'

'But there is a price.'

'Yes.'

* * *

Silius listened as the warlord, whose name was Theowen, spewed out the Semnones' terms. Arminius was translating almost instantaneously. He had been missing for most of the previous morning, but had been cheerful when he returned, and had even apologised for his earlier outburst. Silius was not mollified. That evening, the three Roman emissaries had listened from afar, as a noisy meeting had taken place in the great hall. The barbarians had left them liquor. After initially refusing to drink, Silius had eventually matched Arminius cup for cup.

He had told Arminius how much he despised Hairies. He did not care any more. They could kill him if they wanted to.

Now, the warlord's words amazed him. The burly warrior spoke loudly over the cheering crowd. Behind him was a semicircle of elders. Among them were women, including Arminius's ferocious mother, with her beefy arms and bony face.

They did not want to fight, but they had thousands of warriors ready. All thirty tribes would counter any move against their holy grove. However, if the Romans respected the Semnones's independence, the tribe would guarantee safe access to any barbarian who wished to visit the sacred grove. The Semnones claimed to have accorded other tribes this right from time immemorial, but had curtailed access when the Romans had created a border along the river. To Silius's surprise, in addition to guaranteeing the safety of pilgrims, they now also promised to cease all raids across the Albis.

'And what about the slaves?' Silius asked. He had been urged by the governor to press this point.

Arminius responded with the answer, 'They will resist any further slaving in their lands, but they are willing to sell you their criminals, and to guide you to other tribes.' They would allow the Albis to be used to transport these captives.

'And the Amber Coast?' he enquired, again on behalf of Varus.

'They will provide guides there. We are free to build trading posts and mines there, and to gather slaves among the scum that live there.'

The proceedings ended with raucous cheers, followed by heavy drinking. Silius was barely conscious as he was carried back to the hut. As he lay groaning on his bed, Arminius told him that he had some matters to see to before they rejoined the legions.

'Are you going off again?'

'They are showing me the Sacred Grove. Unfortunately, you cannot attend. You are unclean.'

'You are up their arse.'

'It is best to humour them.'

Silius dismissed him with a wave. Vala was right about Arminius. Fuck him, if he wanted to be a Hairy.

CHAPTER 37

ARMIN STOOD WITH HIS MOTHER before a hill in the late-afternoon gloom. Hildreth wore an undyed woollen smock. She was barefoot. He was naked. He had washed in a nearby pond.

The sacred area lay before them, its border circumscribed by poles, each cut from a great tree trunk. The poles writhed with carved beasts and plants.

He held out his wrists and his mother bound them together with a flax rope – no man could enter the Grove unbound.

'Do not speak unless spoken to. If you are given something to eat or drink, do so. Do not wander away from me. If you stumble and fall, crawl for the rest of the way.'

She produced a handful of leaves from a pouch. 'Chew these. Do not spit them out until I tell you.' He obeyed, feeling a stinging sensation on his tongue as he pulped them.

They entered the wood, following a stone-marked path, and ascended the hill. At the base of every mature tree lay sacrifices – sometimes just bunches of flowers, or dolls from clay and wood, but also fabric – half-buried in the loam.

He began to cough, his throat dry. His breath became shallow. He stopped at one point to touch his pounding heart. His mother told him to keep chewing. When they reached the top of the slope, she allowed him to spit the cud into her palm. He felt light-headed, his vision blurred. He looked unsteadily at a nearby tree. At its base lay spears, their points driven into the earth, their shafts snapped; shields, hacked in pieces and strewn on the ground; swords, bent or broken and thrust into the earth to rust. Some were Roman-style weapons, even shields, their paint faded and peeled. Further on, he saw a helmet in the Valich style, tossed amid the vegetation. Gradually, he made out other domes of iron and bronze, helmets half covered with earth, red with rust. The scale of the site, and the pattern of some of the arms, suggested a place of immense antiquity.

He gazed at his feet, swaying, and realised that he stood on a stone blade.

Movement. Colour. He swung his head, but saw nothing but the forest and the dead things. He turned towards his mother. She had changed. The patterns on her skin stirred. She held out another leaf to him and he took it from her fingers with his lips. He grunted huskily, his throat tight.

'Come,' she said.

They walked along the ridge, passing more weapons: the legacy of ages of war. To their right was a bowl dominated by immense oaks. He looked closer at one. At first, he could not quite judge what he was seeing. Then he realised that the tree was decorated with jawless skulls. The bleached bones, hammered into the trunk, were so dense that one could barely see the bark. Hanging from the branches were jaws, long arm- and leg-bones, shoulder blades and pelvises. Here and there were traces of flesh. He blinked at an adjacent tree, just below the ridge. It was decorated similarly, as was the next oak, and one some fifty feet further on. The skulls and bones of horses and carnivores were interspersed with the human remains. The skulls all looked outwards from the bowl.

He saw a face. It was there but an instant, and when he focused, it drained into dry, eyeless sockets.

He gagged. His mother allowed him to spit. She dug a hole to bury the pulp. His head spun. The earth bucked. He wheezed.

They came upon a particularly large pile of weapons – Roman weapons. By the style of the helmets and their crumbling state, they had to be thirty years old. One object was different from the others.

It was a golden legionary eagle.

'The Sugambrii destroyed a legion,' she told him. Vague recollection surfaced. 'They sacrificed it to the Grove when Rome tried to take it back.'

The tiny eagle represented thousands of lost lives. A legion would fight to ruin to protect its eagle. Rome would conquer the earth to recover one.

'You will give it back to them' – her voice was distant – 'as a sign of our friendship.'

He choked. Phlegm flecked his lips. He turned to her in consternation as he collapsed.

'*Crawl,*' she said, and walked further into the Grove.

He crawled. It became dark, and he slid down the hill, through the mould, among the bones. He crept towards a light. Pungent smoke hung among the oaks. His mother stayed ahead. She sang, but the words were too old for him to understand.

The women waited for him. They were by the light. There was an immense fire pit. They fed the fire from the forest. It burned always. They scattered leaves onto the fire. Smoke rose over the pond, and seeped into the oak copse, and they sang. Armin knelt by the edge of the pit. There was another man there, naked. He was shouting in Latin. Armin's mother cut the man's throat, and smeared his blood on Armin's body. They sang to him in a language older than men.

They sang of death to Rome.

CONTINUED in
The Heaven Tree

GLOSSARY

Aegyptus: Egypt

Africa: Roman province in modern Libya

Ala (Quingenaria): Roman cavalry unit of about five hundred men (see **Cohort**)

Albis: Elbe river

Angrivarii: a minor Suebic tribe, living immediately north of the Cherusci on the north German plain; they pay tribute to the Cherusci proper, in particular to the Bear clan, and are regarded as of low status by the Cherusci

Asia: modern Turkey

Augusta Vindelicorum: Augsburg

Aurochses: wild cattle

Auxiliaries (*Auxilia*): troops other than legionaries in Roman army

Beor: beer, a barbarian drink

Boimia: territory of Boii tribe, a section of the Marcomanni

Bosphoran kingdom: non-Roman territory set in modern Crimea

Bructeri: westernmost Suebic tribe, concentrated on the confluence of the Lippe, Ems and Rhine in the Roman province of Germania

Caldarium: hottest part of a Roman bath

Castra: a fort

Castra Carnuntum: Roman military headquarters in Pannonia, modern Petronell

Castra Drusus: Roman military headquarters in Germania, at the town of Aliso on the Lippe river

Castra Octa: major Roman fort, at the town of Anreppen in the northern reaches of the Ems

Centurion: Roman non-commissioned officer

Chasuarii: a minor Suebic tribe, living north of the Cherusci towards the coast

Chatti: Valich tribe, living south of the Cherusci on the Lupia

Cherusci: a barbarian tribe, part of the Suebic nation; tribe of Armin and Sigimer

Cisalpine Gaul: northern Italy

191

Clan: subdivision of a Suebic tribe, responsible for producing its own battalion for the tribe in wartime, and defending its stretch of the tribal borders against raids; headed by an elected war leader and his advisors

Classis Germanica: Roman fleet on the Rhine

Cohort (*Cohors*): an infantry unit normally between four and eight hundred men strong; (***Cohors Equitata***): units of five hundred soldiers, part cavalry and part infantry

Colonia Agrippina: Cologne

Cultus: the Roman ideal of civilised behaviour

Comitatus: the retinue of a barbarian warlord, composed of soldiers attracted by his fame, prowess and gifts, and free to leave at any time

Cuneus: 'swine's head' – a triangular formation used by shock troops in the Roman army

Decurion: Roman cavalry officer in charge of fifty men (see ***Turma***)

Dulgubinii: a minor Suebic tribe, living just north of the Cherusci

Embla: the first woman in Suebic mythology

Eb: see ***Su Eb***

Ev: see ***Su Ev***

Erz: Harz mountains, modern Czech Republic

Frisii: tribe living in the Rhine delta

Gaul: Roman province equal to modern-day France, Belgium and northern Italy

Gauls: see **Valich**

Germania: a Roman province, equal to modern western Germany and the Benelux countries, bordered in the west by the Rhine

Germans (*Germanni*): Roman name for people speaking the Suebic language

Groma: a Roman surveying tool

Governor: top-ranking civilian in a Roman province, normally of senatorial and noble rank

Hellas: Greece

Hercynian Forest: forest stretching in Roman times from today's Rhine to the Black Sea

Hermunduri: a Suebic tribe, faithful allies of the Romans and mortal enemies of the Marcomanni, living in south-east Germania; the only Germans allowed to trade within Roman territory of Raetia without Roman intermediaries

Hierosolyma: Jerusalem

Hispania: Spain

Hundred: a subdivision of Suebic tribal territory, composed of a number of villages; all adults in a hundred vote on communal issues, and the men fight together as a unit in battle

Iberia: western Spain

Illyria: Roman province along the modern Dalmatian coast

Ister: the River Danube

Istria: modern Croatia

Jossfir: "the World Serpent" – a giant snake lurking on the edge of the earth; the eater of life in Suebic mythology, defeated by the goddess Nerthus and by her child Tuisto; the greatest and most ancient of dragons (see **Mannus, Nerthus, Tuisto**)

Judaea: Roman province – modern Israel and Palestine

Kush: the Upper Nile region; modern Sudan

Legate (*Legatus*): a high-ranking Roman officer; (*Legatus legionis*) a legionary commander

Legion (*Legio*): the basic large military unit of the Roman army, with roughly five thousand infantrymen at full strength, and normally accompanied by several thousand auxiliary troops and five hundred cavalry

Luxor: a city on the Nile, sacred to Egyptians

Lupia: the Lippe, a river flowing west into the Rhine at Wesel

Mannus: the first mortal man created, in Suebic mythology, from Yggdrasil (see **Embla, Nerthus, Yggdrasil, Jossfir, Tuisto**)

Marcomanni: a federation of barbarian tribes based in modern-day Czech Republic and Slovakia

Marser: a relic Valich tribe, specialising in river trade in Germania

Massilia: Marseilles

Moesia: Roman province located around modern Romania

Moguntiacum: Mainz

Narbonensis: Roman province in southern France

Nerthus: Mother Earth; chief deity of the Suebi

Niflhem: the primeval world in Suebic mythology

Numidia: Tunisia and Algeria

Pannonia: a Roman province near modern Croatia

Pax Romana: the "Roman peace" – Roman ideal of law and order within their territories

Prefect (*Praefectus*): a high-ranking officer, normally commanding an auxiliary or allied battalion, or a fort

Pontus Euxinus: the Black Sea

Publicania: site occupied by civilian businessmen and contractors accompanying Roman armies

Publicanii: civilian businessmen who follow Roman armies

Rhenus: the Rhine

Sacred Grove: holiest site in the Suebic religion

Sarmatians: nomadic tribe living outside Roman territory in modern Ukraine; provided heavy, armoured cavalry to the Roman army

Scop: a barbarian poet or storyteller

Scythia: modern-day Ukraine

Selas: a tributary river of the Albis

Semnones: oldest and most senior tribe of the Suebi, living around modern Berlin and guarding the most sacred religious sites of the tribes

Signifer: standard bearer in the Roman army

Strigil: a blade used to scrape oil off the skin during bathing

Stola: a Roman-style long dress

Suebi: a collection of tribes speaking Suebic, and occupying modern-day north-central Europe in Roman times

Suebic: language of the Suebic people; an ancient form of German

Su eb / eb: (Suebic) "son of"

Su ev / ev: (Suebic) "daughter of"

Sugambrii: barbarian tribe, living on the Rhine bank, that destroyed a Roman legion under Marcus Lollius in 16 BCE, and took its eagle

Syria: Roman province, composed of modern western Syria

Tencteri: a tribe with both Valich and Suebic elements, living on the east bank of the Rhine

Tepidarium: lukewarm section of a Roman bathhouse

Tiro: Roman army slang for a raw recruit or inexperienced soldier

Trans-Istria: the territory of the Marcomanni, north of the Ister (the Danube)

Tribune (*Tribunus*): senior officer serving directly under legion commander

Tuisto: the divine son of Nerthus; patron of warriors in Suebic tradition

Turma: a military unit of about fifty mounted men

Valich: Suebic name for the people called Celts by the Greeks and Gauls by the Romans, translated as "foreigners" or "others"; originally dominated Central Europe, but displaced by the Suebi; tribes like the Cherusci absorbed many Valich through enslavement, adoption and alliance, but most Suebi consider the Valich inferior, whereas the Valich consider the

Suebi uncivilised; the name persists today in the names "Walloon" and "Welsh"

Vexillation (*Vexillum*): a detachment of Roman soldiers

Visurgis: Weser river

Wergild: blood money; the value placed on each person's life and limbs by tribal law

Yggdrasil: "Grandmother of the Forest" or "the Heaven Tree"; shape assumed by the earth goddess Nerthus in Suebic mythology, in order to defeat Jossfir

CHRONOLOGY

BCE

58–49	Caesar campaigns in Gaul. Suebi tribes reach the Alps.
52	Cherusci attack Valich on Lupia river.
44	Berinhard defeats the Chatti Valich.
38	Birth of Sigimer.
32	Birth of Maroboduus.
16	Birth of Armin.
13–11	Maroboduus serves in Roman army.
11	Romans under Prince Drusus invade Germania.
9	Drusus defeats Cherusci. Armin and Frimunt taken as hostages to Rome. Province of Germania declared.
7–6	Varus Governor of Africa.
6–4	Varus Governor of Syria.
1	Arminius becomes an adult and a Roman citizen.

CE

1	Marcus Vinicius crushes Cherusci revolt.
3	Arminius joins Prince Tiberius on campaigns in Armenia.
4	Cherusci under Sigimer gain privileged status within Roman Empire.
4	Arminius becomes Roman knight and joins imperial bodyguard.
6	Pannonian revolt erupts.
8	Arminius transferred to Germania.
9	Teutoburgerwald incident.